RYAN REIGN

NEW YORK RUTHLESS: BOOK 4

SADIE KINCAID

RED HOUSE PRESS

Cover Design: Red House Press

Editing/ formatting: Red House Press

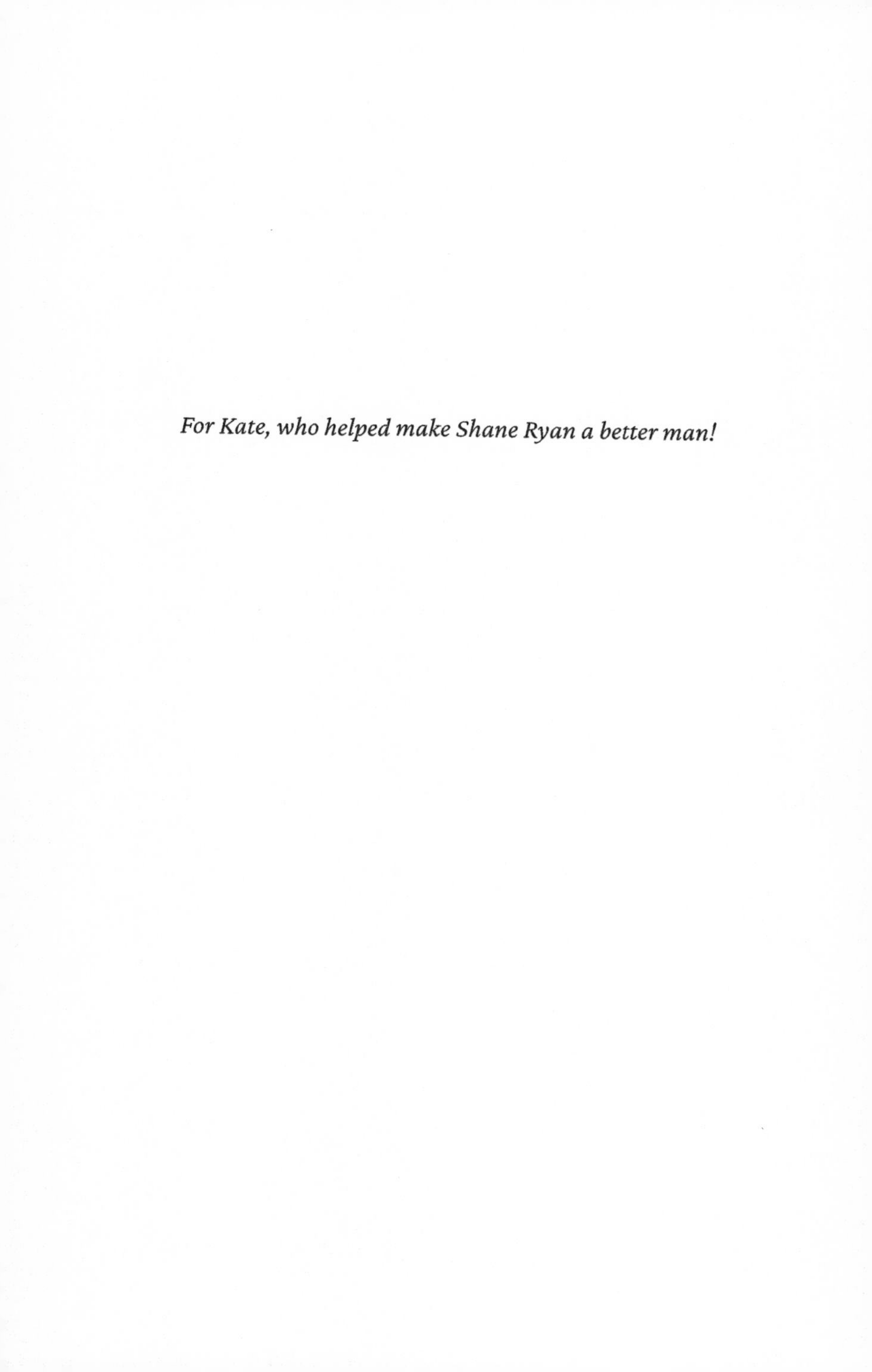

For Kate, who helped make Shane Ryan a better man!

NEW YORK RUTHLESS

Ryan Reign is book 4 in the New York Ruthless series. It is a dark Mafia, reverse harem romance which deals with adult themes which may be triggering for some, including, but not limited to kidnap, reference to sexual assault, as well as scenes of a violent and sexual nature.

If you haven't read books 1, 2 and 3 in the series yet, you can find them on Amazon

Ryan Rule
Ryan Redemption
Ryan Retribution

CHAPTER 1
JESSIE

Adrenaline courses around my body and blood thunders in my ears as I sit at the dining table trying to process the information I've just been given.

The Wolf is back.

Conor rests a reassuring hand on my thigh, while Liam places one on my shoulder as they sit either side of me. We have just finished our 'Thanksgiving in July' dinner, but the celebrations have now come to an abrupt halt.

I'm vaguely aware of the Ryan brothers talking to Vlad, the head of the Bratva, and the man who's just brought my world crashing down around me. Suddenly, their voices seem so far away. The room is spinning and the air has become thick and cloying, making it difficult to swallow. I reach for my throat as I gasp for breath. Something is happening. Has Vlad somehow poisoned me? Is he really working for the Wolf?

"Jessie!" Conor's voice cuts through the fog as he takes my free hand and curls his fingers around it.

I turn to him, my eyes wide as I struggle to breathe. He places his other hand on my cheek while he circles the pad of his thumb over the pulse point on my wrist. I look down at his strong fingers wrapped around my arm.

"Look at me," he commands.

Lifting my head, I look into his deep brown eyes.

"Breathe, Angel," he says softly.

"I can't." I shake my head as I draw in ragged breaths.

"Yes, you can. Breathe with me, okay?"

I nod.

"In." He takes a deep breath and I try to mimic his movements. "Out." He releases. He continues doing that and I try to keep pace with him. The room is silent, as though there is only him and me in it. I don't know how long it takes but eventually my breathing matches his and I no longer feel like I'm about to suffocate.

He smiles at me. "Better?"

"Yes," I whisper, and he lifts my hand to his lips and presses a soft kiss on my wrist.

I turn back to the table to see four pairs of anxious eyes trained on me and heat flushes over my cheeks. I can't believe I just had a panic attack.

Liam reaches for my other hand. He squeezes gently and I offer him a faint smile. When I catch Mikey's eye, he winks at me, but Shane goes back to staring at our visitor.

"So why is it you're so certain he is back, Vlad?" he asks.

Vlad looks directly at me when he responds. "There have been a few hits recently that have had his particular brand."

"The one in Belarus?" Shane says, making me turn my attention to him. He knew about this and he didn't tell me?

"Yes. I see you've been following him yourself?" Vlad asks with one arched eyebrow.

"I've been tracking hits that have had similarities with the Wolf's style, yes," Shane says with a nod as he glances at me before turning his attention back to Vlad. "There have been more?"

"One in Kazakhstan."

Shane frowns. "I didn't hear about that one."

"Hmm." Vlad rubs a hand over his beard and nods softly. "Politics. It was kept very quiet."

"Hang on a minute," I say, finally finding my voice. "You're telling me that the Wolf has been active again? For how long? And why didn't you tell me?" I direct my last question to Shane.

"I only knew about the hit in Belarus. And while it had similarities to the Wolf, I wasn't sure it was him."

"You should have told me."

"Told you what, Jessie?" He frowns at me. "There was nothing to tell."

I swallow the retort that lodges in my throat. "I didn't even know you were looking for him," I say instead.

Conor squeezes my hand as Shane shakes his head in exasperation. "You didn't think I'd be trying to find him? After everything he did to you? When even the mention of his name sends you into a blind panic?"

Tears prick at my eyes as I realize he's been looking out for me all this time. Of course he has. It's what he does. I can't deal with him right now though and I turn back to Vlad. "What makes you so sure it's him?" I pull my hand from Conor's and wipe the tears from my eyes. Leaning forward, I place my arms on the table. This is no time to get overemotional.

"As well as the two I just mentioned, there was a hit in Moscow last night. Same MO and this time my sources tell me the Wolf has taken full credit. He is now back online and offering his services to the highest bidder."

I feel my heart starting to race again but I take a deep breath and remember the sound of Conor's soothing voice. I reach for his hand once more and the warmth of his skin on mine is comforting. "You're sure it's really him, Vlad?" I ask, desperately trying to keep the tremor from my voice.

"Unfortunately I am," he says with a solemn nod of his head. "I suspect Alexei's death has allowed him to slink out of whatever hole it was he crawled into. But he's using the same call sign and accounts that he did in the past, even though such methods are now somewhat outdated."

"Do you have any idea who it could be?"

"None." He shakes his head and looks at Shane again. "You?"

"No," he replies with a deep sigh.

Vlad clears his throat and turns back to me. "If there is anything I can do, Jessica," he says softly.

I smile at him although my insides have turned to jelly, and not in a good way. "Thank you."

He pushes his chair back and stands. "I'll leave you to your dinner."

"Can you show Vlad out, Mikey?" Shane growls as he rubs a hand over his jaw, his eyes narrowed as he appears deep in thought.

"Sure." Mikey gets up and escorts Vlad out of the dining room.

Once Vlad is gone, Shane stands and walks around the table to me, holding out his hand. "We've got a lot to talk about. Let's go sit in the den?"

I stare up at him blankly, still completely blindsided by Vlad's revelation. "Okay," I whisper.

"Con, can you get the good whiskey?" he asks as he pulls me from my chair.

"Will do," Conor replies. He gives me a soft kiss on the cheek before he leaves the room.

. . .

Ten minutes later, I'm sitting on the sofa in the den, sandwiched between the twins with a glass of Midleton Chapter One in my hand, while Shane and Conor sit opposite us.

I take a sip of the expensive whiskey and the warm, rich liquid soothes my throat.

"How are you feeling, Angel?" Conor finally asks.

"I don't know." I shrug. "I mean, I always suspected he was still alive, so I suppose this shouldn't come as a shock. But to find out he's active again..."

"Yeah. It's fucked up, Red," Mikey says as he puts an arm around my shoulder.

"Did you find out anything else about him, Shane?" I ask.

He shakes his head and takes a swig of his whiskey. "Nothing at all. If I had, sweetheart, I would have told you. I wouldn't have kept the Belarus hit from you if I'd known it was him."

I nod, at a loss for what else to say.

"What about your trip to Ireland?" Conor asks.

Shane looks at me and my heart skips a beat. "I still have to go. But I can put it off for a few days if you need me to, Jessie?" he offers.

"No," I shake my head. "We can still go tomorrow. Nothing has changed. We knew the Wolf was still out there."

"*We*?" Conor narrows his eyes at me. "You're not going, Angel."

"Why not?" I frown.

"Are you being serious right now?"

"Yes. I still want to go to Ireland and I don't see why I shouldn't. Hasn't the Wolf already dictated enough of my life?"

"Shane?" Conor turns to his older brother.

"If Jessie wants to come, then it's up to her," he says with a shrug as he downs the last of his drink.

Liam and Mikey stay silent and look down at their glasses. They know better than to get in the middle of their older brothers.

"She's safer here with me and the twins," Conor snarls.

"She'll be just as safe with me," Shane fires back.

"Boys. You must agree with me?" Conor says to the twins.

"It's up to Jessie what she wants to do, Con," Mikey says and I place my hand on his thigh and squeeze. I love that he always has my back.

"Liam?" Conor snaps.

"I don't want her to go either, bro, but..."

"For fuck's sake!" Conor hisses. "I can't believe you're even considering taking her there, Shane!"

"You think I'm not capable of protecting her?" Shane growls at him.

"Not as well as three of us can here," Conor growls back as he glares at his older brother.

"Hey!" I lean forward and slam my now empty glass down on the coffee table. "I'm sitting right here."

The two of them stop glaring at each other and look at me.

"In case you haven't noticed, I am perfectly capable of looking after myself." Conor opens his mouth to speak but I don't allow him the chance to. "And I hate to break it to you, boys, but if the Wolf wants me, he'll find me. He's a patient man. He'll wait until the perfect moment and then he'll strike, whether that's in two days or ten years. And I'm not going to spend the rest of my life hiding in here waiting for that to happen."

"Red!" Mikey snaps as he sits forward, cupping my chin in his hand, he turns my face to his. "You know we would never let him take you. I promise."

I stare at him. I wish I could believe him. But when I see the look of anguish in his eyes, I don't have the heart to tell him that I can't. "I know," I whisper instead.

"So, you're still going to Ireland tomorrow then?" Conor scowls.

Shane looks between me and Conor and sighs. "If the reason the Wolf is back is because Alexei is dead, then there is every chance he knows that Jessie is here too. She's safer in Ireland than she is here."

Conor leans back in his chair and runs a hand over his jaw.

"Shane's right," I say. "Besides, I'm not just going to sit around in this apartment, waiting for the Wolf to come and pick me off. Now that he's active again, I'm sure I'll be able to track him, but let me have one more week of not being completely consumed by him first. Please?"

Conor rolls his eyes but he doesn't speak.

"The Wolf will have no idea I'm in Ireland," I add.

"And I promise I will take care of our girl, boys," Shane offers as he shoots me a look that tells me not to open my mouth and contradict him. Then he stands and places his empty glass on the coffee table. He walks over to me and grips my chin in his strong hand, tilting my head to look at him. "I'm going to pack. I'll meet you by the elevator at ten tomorrow morning."

"Okay," I blink at him. It's only six p.m. so why am I not going to see him until morning?

He turns to his brothers. "You've got sixteen more hours with our girl, boys." Then he walks out of the room and I'm left with his three siblings.

"What do you feel like doing, baby?" Liam says softly as he curls his fingers around mine. "We can watch a movie if you like. We never did get to that pumpkin pie."

"Or pussy," Mikey mumbles beside me.

I turn to him, my mouth open as I feign my indignation, but

the truth is I can't think of a better way to take my mind off the Wolf. And I'm going away from them for at least a week, and despite how much I'm looking forward to my trip with Shane, I'm going to miss these guys like crazy.

"You're really thinking about pussy right now?" I nudge him in the ribs.

"I'm *always* thinking about your pussy, Red," he says with an apologetic shrug.

I push myself up from the sofa. "You can come help me pack if you like," I offer.

Mikey and Liam are beside me before I can even finish the sentence but Conor stays in his chair. He frowns at me. I know he's worried about me but he must see that Shane and I are right.

I hold out my hand to him. "I'm not going to Ireland with you mad at me, Conor Ryan."

"I'm not mad at you, Angel," he says as he stands and walks toward us. He leans down and presses a soft kiss on my temple. "But I have something to do. I'll come find you later."

CHAPTER 2
CONOR

I watch Jessie and my brothers walk to her room before I head off to find Shane. Vlad's announcement has completely floored me. I suppose that Shane has a point about her being safer in Ireland. If the Wolf knows she's here then it's only a matter of time before he comes for her. Despite that, I can't shake the feeling that she would be safer here with me and the twins. Safer with me. I would never let anyone harm a hair on her head, even if it meant never letting her out of my sight for a second. I consider the possibility of going with them, even though I've sworn never to set foot in Ireland again, but I would for her.

Shane is in his room when I find him. I walk inside and sit on the bed while he packs his small suitcase.

"I'll keep her safe, Con," he says, reading my mind. We've always been in sync, he and I, but I don't agree with him on this one.

"I know you will, Shane..."

"But?"

"You'll be distracted there. You won't be able to watch her every second of every day."

He closes his suitcase and shoves his hands into his trouser pockets. "The Wolf is in Moscow. I'm certain if he knows about Alexei then he knows about Jessie too, and it's only a matter of time before he comes here looking for her, Con." He shakes his head and I see the worry etched on his face.

"You really think she'll be safer there with you?"

He nods at me. "Liam still isn't one hundred percent. You'll be running the businesses. Mikey will be run off his feet helping you. There are more distractions here, and you know she won't stand for being locked up in this place."

"And in Ireland?"

"She'll either be with me or she'll be in the suite at the hotel."

I let out a long breath and close my eyes. "I can't believe he's back, Shane. I was starting to believe he was dead. I think she was, too."

"I know. But once we get back, we can focus our energies on finding him. When I've sorted out Patrick's estate and tidied up all of our affairs, there will be nothing tying us to Ireland any longer. Liam will have had another week to recover. We'll be back to full strength and we can focus on what needs to be done."

"I suppose you're right." I look up at him. "You sure you don't need me to come with you?"

He narrows his eyes at me. "You want to come?"

"No!" I shake my head. "But I will if I need to. If you both need me to."

"I need you to take care of business here, Con. Jessie and I will be fine."

"You just want her to yourself for a week," I say, throwing a pair of balled up socks at him.

He shrugs and grins at me. "Yep."

"Lucky fucker."

"I sure am," he winks at me.

"I'll miss you both," I say. The thought of him in Ireland makes me feel something I can't quite put my finger on. Perhaps I'm worried that he'll remember how much he loved the place and never come back home.

"I'll miss you too, Con. We've spent more time apart these past few months than we have in our whole lives. She'll miss you too," he adds, "so you'd better go and give her the send-off she deserves."

"Yep," I say as I stand. "I'll catch you in the morning, bro."

"I love her just as much as you do, you know?" he says as I'm near the door.

I turn to him and frown. "I know."

He nods. "I know it might not always seem like it, that's all. But I would die before I let anyone hurt her."

"Well, yeah. How much you're into Jessie isn't quite the secret that you think it is, bro," I chuckle. "Anyone can see you've got it bad for her."

He picks up the socks I just threw at him and launches them across the room at my head. "Asshole."

CHAPTER 3
LIAM

Jessie zips up her suitcase and rests her hands on the top. "You think I've packed enough?" she asks with a flash of her eyebrows.

"You've packed plenty. If it was me you were going on a week long vacation with, you'd barely need a thing," Mikey chuckles as he slides his arms around her waist. "Because we would never leave the hotel room."

She grins as she turns in his arms. "I'm pretty sure this is not that kind of vacation."

"Every vacation with you is that kind of vacation, Red," he growls as he squeezes her ass and runs his nose along her throat. "You think Shane isn't thinking exactly the same thing as I am right now?"

"I'm sure he's thinking of sorting your family's estate," she purrs.

I put the suitcase on the floor and lie back on the bed as I watch the two of them.

"How many pair of panties do you think you can wear between now and when you leave tomorrow?" Mikey asks as he arches an eyebrow at her.

"Not many. Why?" she laughs.

"Because your clean panties just don't do it for me the same, Red, and I'll need a supply to keep me going while you're away."

She opens her mouth, feigning her horror as she pushes him in the chest. "You and my panties. You're such a deviant, Mikey Ryan!"

"I'm a deviant?" Mikey looks over her shoulder at me and rolls his eyes. "This coming from the woman who needs all four of us to keep her satisfied."

"I do not *need* all four of you to keep me satisfied," she protests.

"Really?" Mikey grins at me.

"Yes, really."

"If that's true, how about we send Liam out then and I'll have you all to myself?" he suggests.

I frown at him. That's not happening and he knows it.

Jessie turns to me and smiles. "No way. I said I don't *need* all four of you, but that doesn't mean I don't *want* all of you."

I smile at her as she chews on her bottom lip. "Come here, baby." I pat the top of my thighs. Mikey releases her from his embrace and she crawls onto the bed and straddles me. I reach up and brush her hair from her face. The dark brown dye she used when she went to Arizona is finally fading and her hair is almost back to her natural shade of red. Packing for her trip seems to have taken her mind off the Wolf at least, but it's also a reminder that this time tomorrow she is going to be thousands of miles away from us.

"I'm going to miss you."

"I'm going to miss you too," she breathes.

I reach for the t-shirt she's wearing, which is one of Conor's, and peel it off over her head. She lifts her arms in compliance and my cock twitches against her pussy. Mikey watches us as I reach forward and unhook her bra before sliding it over her arms and letting her gorgeous tits fall free. When I cup them in my hands she moans softly and I rock my hips against her as my cock hardens further.

"Liam," she pants.

"Come up here," I touch my lips and she looks down at me. She leans forward, about to kiss my lips, but I shake my head. "Not your mouth, baby. I want your pussy. Right here."

I see her swallow as she sits back up but then she moves up the bed until she is hovering over my neck and shoulders.

"Closer, Jessie," I growl. "I want your pussy on my face, baby."

She shifts closer and I wrap one arm around her waist and pull her toward me as I tug her panties to the side with my free hand. "Let's make these panties nice and wet for Mikey," I say as I lick the length of her slick folds before sucking her swollen clit into my mouth. Fuck! She tastes so fucking good. How am I supposed to live without this pussy for the next week, or maybe even longer?

"Liam." She shudders as I flick my tongue over her clit and suck her sweet juices into my mouth. I love making her come this way.

She grinds herself on my face and my balls draw up into my stomach as her soft moans and whimpers vibrate through her body.

I grab her ass before I slide a finger inside and she inches forward, pressing her sweet pussy further against me. As I graze her with my teeth and move my finger in and out of her ass, I feel her teetering on the edge of oblivion. A final flick of my tongue has her tipping over the edge and she comes all over my face, her thighs squeezing me instinctively as she rides the waves of her orgasm and I suck and lick her through it.

When she has stopped trembling, I lift her hips and she looks down at me, those incredible blue eyes of hers dark with desire. I palm my cock through my sweatpants as I think about her lips around it in a few moments time, because our girl sucks cock like she was raised in a bordello.

Sure enough, when she can breathe again she moves down the bed and tugs the waistband of my sweatpants down. I brush her hair back so I can see those beautiful lips sucking every inch of me. Mikey has been quietly watching the show up to now but he climbs on the bed behind her and starts to take off her panties.

“Let’s get these off you, Red. I don’t want any of my own cum spoiling them,” he chuckles as he peels them down over her legs and she helps him by wriggling herself out of them. Then she bends her head low, sticking her beautiful peach of an ass high in the air as she sucks my cock all the way to back of her throat.

“Fuck!” I hiss and watch as Mikey grabs her by the hips and prepares to rail her while she gives me head. When he drives into her a few seconds later, he forces my cock further down her throat and she groans loudly. The sound is muffled because her mouth is so full and her moans vibrate through my whole body. She pulls back, running her tongue the length of my shaft before swirling it over the tip and driving me crazy.

“Liam made your pussy so fucking wet, Red,” Mikey growls as he slams into her from behind. “You’re such a good girl the way you take us both.”

“Fuck, baby!” I hiss as I guide her head back down. I want to fuck every single part of her, and before this night is done, I will.

CHAPTER 4
CONOR

It's been over five hours since I left Jessie and the twins and I figure that will have been plenty of time for them to do what they need to do before I steal her away for the rest of the night. When I walk into her room the three of them are curled up in bed together, with her in the middle. They are kissing but not fucking. They don't stop when they hear me. We are all well used to sharing her now. It's not until I sit on the bed that the three of them take a breath and look at me.

"You all okay?" I ask.

"Hmm," Jessie purrs and stretches like a cat.

"Sure am," Liam says with a grin as he puts his arms behind his head.

"It's almost midnight," I say, looking at the clock on the nightstand.

"So?" Mikey shrugs.

"That means it's my turn." I wink at Jessie and she smiles at me.

"Aw, Con. You can stay in here with us if you like?" Mikey offers as he lifts the duvet, which makes Liam laugh out loud.

"Thanks for the offer, boys, but I think I'll pass." I reach out and take Jessie's hand and pull her up.

Liam sits up and kisses her softly. "We'll see you in the morning, baby."

"Yeah, Red," Mikey agrees as he kisses her neck.

"Goodnight," she whispers to them while she looks at me through her long dark lashes.

"Come on, Angel," I stand, pulling her off the bed and picking her up. She wraps her arms around my neck and presses her face against my chest, her legs swinging in the air as I carry her to my room. Once we're inside I set her on her feet and close the door behind us.

I trail my fingertips over her cheek and she shudders. "What did my little brothers do to you, Angel?"

"Everything," she whispers as her cheeks flush pink.

"Shall we take a shower first then?" I arch one eyebrow at her.

"I think that's probably for the best," she purrs. Then she stands there, chewing on her bottom lip as she watches me pull off my t-shirt and sweatpants and toss them into the hamper.

Taking her hand, I lead her to the bathroom and turn on the shower. I step in first. After the day we've had, the hot water feels good on my face. I pull her in with me and she squeals as the first jets of water hit her body.

She presses herself against me. Her nipples are hard against my chest, making my cock stiffen. Reaching for the soap, I squeeze some into my palm and start to wash her. My soapy hands glide easily over her soft, wet skin and she moans as I wash every part of her body. I am desperate to fuck her, but this will be our last night together for over a week and I want to take my time. Patrick Ryan's funeral date isn't even set yet, so I suspect it will be closer to two weeks that she and Shane will be away.

I'm going to miss her so damn much. I feel like we only just got her back. And now we have the Wolf to worry about too. I sigh heavily and she looks up at me.

"Is everything okay?" she asks.

I slide my hands to her ass and press her body against mine. "Are you okay?"

"Here with you? Yes," she whispers.

"And what about in Ireland with Shane?"

"I'll be okay there too," she says with a smile. "I am not going to hide away any longer, Conor. Besides, *he's* in Russia, not Ireland."

I sweep her wet hair back from her face. "As soon as you're back, we're going to find him. Okay?"

"Okay."

I lean down and kiss her softly as the water runs over us, washing the soap from our bodies. She slides her tongue into my mouth and pulls my hair gently and my cock twitches against her stomach. "Conor," she moans as her hands slide down my back, but I don't want her here.

I break our kiss and shut off the water before handing her a towel and we both dry off. She watches me the whole time and I wonder what is going on in her head. She almost passed out earlier when Vlad told us about the Wolf, but she seems much calmer now.

I narrow my eyes at her. "What are you thinking about?"

"Those beautiful tattoos of yours," she grins at me as she drops her towel onto the floor and steps closer to me.

"Anything else?"

"Yes. Your amazing fingers," she breathes as she threads hers through mine before she pushes herself onto her tiptoes and dusts her lips over mine. "And your hot mouth."

"Is that all?" I growl as I wrap my arms around her and squeeze her ass cheeks, because this is how my girl deals with all the shit that goes on in her life and in her head. And if she wants to use my body to deal with her trauma, then who am I to stop her?

Her hand slides down my chest until she grips my cock in her hand. “And this too,” she whispers, suddenly coy all of a sudden.

“Well, you’re going to get all three, Angel,” I growl as I lift her until she wraps her legs around my waist and I carry her back into the bedroom. I lower us down onto the bed until she is lying on her back and I am nestled between her thighs. I nudge the tip of my cock at her entrance and she winces for a split second before she smiles at me again.

“You want me to take it easy, Angel?”

“You don’t have to,” she whispers.

I narrow my eyes at her. “But that’s not what I asked you.” As much as I love to fuck her hard, tie her up and spank her ass, I love being gentle with her too. I have never fucked a woman the way I do her. I have never wanted to. But she makes me want to savor every single kiss. Every single touch. Every single whimper and moan. “I am happy to fuck you any way you need, Angel. I just want inside you.”

“Then taking it easy would be good,” she whispers.

“Good girl,” I mumble before I start to trail soft kisses over her neck and breasts, squeezing each one gently in my palm as I kiss the other and making her moan my name. Her fingers thread in my hair, urging me to the spot where she wants my mouth, but I take my time. Tasting her skin. Covering every inch of her with soft kisses and tiny bites until she is writhing beneath me.

“Please, Conor?” she groans and I smile against her skin.

“I thought you wanted to take it easy, Angel?”

“I do, but this is torture,” she pants.

“Torture? Really?”

"Delicious torture," she smiles as my hand slides up her leg to the apex of her thighs and she bucks her hips, making me chuckle.

"Soon, Angel. I got you," I murmur as I keep kissing the inside of her thighs until she is whimpering with need. When I finally slide a finger into her hot pussy, she is dripping wet. She moans with relief and my cock twitches at the sound.

"Oh, you're so ready for me, Jessie," I chuckle as I add a second finger and she grinds her hips onto them. As I pull them out again, they are thick with her cream and I can't resist sucking them clean before I ease them back inside her. "You taste so fucking good, Angel," I growl before I press the flat of my tongue against her opening and run it up to her clit. She shudders and bucks and begs me for more, but I keep taking my time. I finger fuck her slowly, drawing them in and out of her as I suck softly on her clit. Each time I push back inside her, she squeezes me, trying to pull me in deeper. Her cum is dripping down my fingers and onto my palm and I keep easing her to the edge of orgasm before bringing her back down.

"Conor, please let me come," she groans and I take pity on her as I curl my fingers deep inside her, pressing down on her abdomen with my free hand before I flick my tongue over her clit as I suck harder.

"Oh, fuck! Conor!" She shouts my name as her orgasm tears through her body and she coats me in her slick juices. The sound of her wetness as I keep finger fucking her through it makes me feel like I'm on the edge myself.

When she finally stops shaking, I crawl up the bed and settle between her thighs. My cock is beyond weeping now as I press it against her. "Wrap your legs around me, Jessie," I whisper and she does as she's told. Completely submissive in my bed, even if she's not when she's out of it.

With my hands fisted in her hair, I seal my mouth over hers, kissing her so deeply that I can feel her moans of pleasure and relief rumble through me as I finally drive my cock inside her. She tries to break away but I keep her there, swallowing every single delicious sound she makes as I fuck her slowly.

This right here is everything I've ever wanted.

CHAPTER 5
JESSIE

Looking up at the private jet as it sits on the runway I feel like I've entered an alternate universe. "This is actually your buddy's plane?" I say to Shane as I stand there open mouthed.

"Yep." He grins at me. "We thought about getting one for ourselves, but we don't fly enough to get the use out of it, and Alejandro lets us use his if it's free."

"Wow! But imagine just being able to jump in your own plane and go anywhere you fancy, like the Bahamas?" I flash my eyebrows at him and he slides an arm around my waist.

"Flying to places where you will spend most of your time in nothing more than a string bikini might just change my mind, sweetheart," he whispers in my ear.

I shiver in anticipation at the thought, but the moment is ruined by Erin walking up behind us. "Shall we board?" she purrs as she sashays past in cream pants and a cashmere cardigan. Even dressed for travelling, she is the picture of elegance, while I'm dressed in skinny jeans, a tank top and a hooded sweatshirt.

Shane rolls his eyes, but he takes my hand and follows her

to the steps of the plane. He looks effortlessly classy too. In dark jeans and a white polo shirt, he looks just as hot as he does in a suit. I wish that Erin wasn't on this flight with us. No matter what Shane says, I can't help feeling inferior whenever I'm around her. And I know that she hates me. Even when I try to be nice to her, she just looks down her perfectly shaped nose at me.

I hold onto Shane's warm hand and remind myself that this is just an eight-hour flight, and after we land in Ireland, I'll get him all to myself, and hopefully we'll have to spend only a minimal amount of time in Erin's company.

As we board the plane, Shane introduces me to the pilot and co-pilot, Theo and Andrew, who give me a quick tour of the cockpit because I have never seen one before. Shane comes with me while Erin rolls her eyes at my lack of culture and goes to take her seat. Theo is young for a pilot, or so he seems to me, given that I've never met one before. He is tall, dark, and handsome, while Andrew is slightly older and has sandy blonde hair. Both of them are charming and cute, but they have nothing on my Irish bodyguard who keeps his hand on my waist or my ass the whole time I'm in there. I can't help but smile to myself because I love his possessive side.

As we walk into the cabin, I nearly bump into the stewardess. She is almost a carbon copy of Erin. Tall, blonde, skinny. "Jessie, this is Wendy," Shane introduces her.

She smiles widely. "It's a pleasure to meet you," she says as she extends her hand.

"You too," I smile back.

"This your first time flying?" she asks.

"No. I've flown coach a few times, but I've never left the States before and I've never been on a plane quite like this," I look around at the spacious cabin which is tastefully decorated in cream leather, walnut and chrome.

"Yeah, this plane is quite something," she giggles softly and I realize she is nothing like Erin. "If you could take your seats and I'll be along to take your drinks order before we take off."

"Thank you, Wendy," Shane says.

"No problem, Mr. Ryan," she purrs and I wonder if he has that effect on all women.

When we're settled in our seats, which are as big as armchairs, Wendy comes back through. "Can I get you anything?" she asks.

"I'll get a large Jameson on the rocks," Shane says.

"Jessie?"

"Umm." I shrug. "A Coke?" I don't drink a lot and I get giddy enough flying without having alcohol too. My stomach grumbles loudly and Shane chuckles. I was too excited to have anything to eat before we left the house.

"Anything else?" Wendy smiles. "We'll be serving a meal in a few hours, but we have snacks?"

"Cheetos?" I arch an eyebrow.

She nods her head. "Perfect."

I sit back in my seat and look out of the window. I could get used to this kind of living. I can hear Wendy taking Erin's order now. "A Dry Martini and some green olives," she purrs and I roll my eyes. Even her order is classy. If that isn't a perfect example of how different she and I are, then I don't know what is.

After Wendy serves our drinks, the plane takes off and I watch out the window like an excited toddler while Shane and Erin talk about some land he wants to sell now that his father is dead. I listen at first, until they start to discuss deeds and property law, and then I switch off and concentrate on the view.

"You okay?" Shane says as he leans forward and places his warm hand on my knee.

I turn to him. "Yeah, just admiring the view."

"Me too," he says quietly and my pulse quickens. Why is everything he does and says so damn hot? "You didn't eat your Cheetos." He nods to the bag on the small table beside me.

He reaches over and picks them up before opening the bag and eating one. He hands them to me and his fingers brush mine when I take them from him, sending sparks of electricity skittering over my skin.

"Those things will turn your insides orange," Erin snipes as she pierces an olive with a cocktail stick before sucking it into her mouth.

"Maybe," I shrug, "but they taste pretty good."

"Hmm," she sniffs as she looks at me.

If only to try and make this entire journey more bearable, I try to make conversation with her. "I've never tried olives," I say as I toss a Cheeto into my mouth and chew, swallowing it before I add, "some guy I once worked with told me they taste like pussy."

Shane was in the unfortunate position of having just taken a mouthful of his whiskey and the sound that he makes as he almost chokes on his drink, while simultaneously laughing and coughing, makes me giggle.

I look over at Erin, who simply rolls her eyes in disgust as Shane tries to stop whiskey from running out of his nose. It is a beautiful sight to see the usually cool, calm and collected alpha I have come to love, so completely undone, and I don't think he has ever looked sexier.

When he finally regains his ability to breathe normally he looks at me. "Fuck, Jessie," he says as he shakes his head.

"Well, do they?" I ask with an arch of one eyebrow.

"Not like any pussy I've ever tasted," he replies as he starts laughing again.

"Well, you would know," Erin says, almost inaudibly. "You've tasted every pussy on this plane."

Shane stops laughing and scowls at her as I blink at him. There are three women on this plane. I think of the beautiful, tall, blonde stewardess who just served us. Damn! He really does have a type.

"Erin!" he snarls.

I blink at him in confusion. "You and Wendy?"

He takes a deep breath and opens his mouth to answer but Erin speaks first. "Oh, yes. You and she had quite the trip to Italy, didn't you?" she says over the rim of her martini glass.

"Italy?"

"It was an extended layover."

"An extended lay," Erin snorts.

"Enough!" Shane barks to her.

I sit back in my seat feeling wounded. I know that Shane has slept with plenty of women before me. It shouldn't be a big deal. But the fact that, once again, Erin has been allowed to blindside me, stings. Not to mention he took her to Italy! Like one of the most romantic places in the world.

He leans forward and places a hand on my knee. "I didn't realize she'd be on this flight, or I would have told you before," he says quietly.

I turn my head to look out of the window and hear him sigh as he leans back in his seat.

Only a few minutes have passed when he stands up. He holds his hand out to me so it is practically in my face and I can't ignore him.

I want to, but then I see Erin watching us from the corner of my eye. I know where Shane wants to take me. There is a bedroom on this plane and isn't that how we always work out our differences? A part of me would like to tell him to take one of his other conquests in there instead, but if only to wipe the smug grin of that woman's face, I take his hand and follow him to the back of the plane.

I step inside the room and he closes the door behind us. He reaches for my hand but I back away from him.

He frowns at me. "I didn't know she was going to be on this flight. I haven't seen her for years."

"You should have told me once you knew that she was," I say as I fold my arms across my chest.

"Really? How would that have gone? Jessie, meet Wendy. We used to fuck back in the day."

"You don't have to be sarcastic," I snap.

"For fuck's sake!" He runs his hands through his hair. "So we fucked? I fucked a lot of women before I met you, Jessie."

"Okay," I say as I take a step towards him. "How would you have felt if Erin had just casually announced that I had sucked every cock on this plane?"

His face darkens as he glares at me. "Then one of us would be learning to fly a plane real quick, sweetheart, because you only just met them today!"

I shake my head. "You know what I mean, Shane. Don't make out like I'm always being unreasonable. You took our stewardess to Italy and fucked each other's brains out, and Erin had to be the one to tell me."

"I didn't take her to Italy. She was working on the plane. We hit it off."

"So you did fuck her brains out then?" I ask, noticing he didn't deny that.

"Jessie!"

Of course he did. This man fucks like it's an Olympic sport.

"It was just sex. Nothing more," he adds softly.

"Well you and I were just about sex once. Remember?"

He bends his head lower, his breath dusting over my cheek. "You and I both know that we have *never* been just about sex, sweetheart. Now, stop being a brat or I will take off my belt and spank your ass so hard that everyone on this plane will hear."

Why the thought of that makes my pussy contract in anticipation is beyond me, but this man does things to my body that I can barely fathom. "I doubt they would hear it over the engines," I whisper as I slide my hands around his neck and curl his hair around my fingertips.

"You willing to bet your ass on that?" he breathes.

"No." I give a small shake of my head. As much as I love his spankings, I really don't want Wendy or Erin to hear that. "But are there any more little secrets that Erin might spring on me?"

"None that I can think of. But we might run into an ex-girlfriend or two when we're in Ireland. You okay with that?" He slides his arms around my waist.

"Yes. But please let me know when I do."

"I will." He bends his head and brushes his lips over mine, taunting me with the promise of a kiss.

"Did you fuck Wendy in this bed?" I whisper and he pushes me back against the wall, sliding one of his hands up my body, he wraps it around my throat, tilting my neck slightly so I am staring up into his incredible green eyes.

"No," he growls. Then his free hand slides to the waistband of my jeans and he tugs open the button before reaching for the zipper.

"What are you doing?" I whisper.

"Getting you naked so I can fuck *you* in it."

"But what if Erin or Wendy hear us?"

He pulls my zipper down and slips his hand inside my panties. "You just said they wouldn't hear because of the sound of the engines. Besides, I don't give a fuck who hears us, Jessie. If I thought you'd be into it, I would take you out there and fuck you right in front of them."

"Shane!" I gasp as he rubs soft circles over my clit.

"I would show them how hard you come for me, sweetheart. Then there would be no doubt that you belong to me and that I am entirely yours."

"You really want to fuck me in front of your ex-girlfriends?" I pant as the warm wetness begins to pool in my core.

"I would fuck you in front of anyone. Anywhere. It takes all of my goddamn restraint not to bury myself in your cunt every time I look at you."

"You have such a filthy mouth," I pant as I press my head back against the wall and suck in a breath while he pulls his hand from my panties and starts to work my jeans down over my legs.

"You love my filthy mouth." He winks at me before he drops to his knees and presses his face between my thighs. "Fuck, Jessie, you smell fucking delicious."

"Shane!" I groan as he pulls off my socks and sneakers before tugging my jeans over my legs. Then his hand slides up my leg, over my calf and up the inside of my thigh. I shiver at his touch and he looks up at me and smiles. He knows exactly what he does to my body. I crave him like a drug.

"You still mad at me, sweetheart?"

"Yes!" I lie.

"What can I do to make you forgive me?" he growls as his fingers trail higher and he tugs my panties to the side. He pushes one finger inside me while he circles my clit with the pad of his thumb.

"You could keep doing that for a start," I groan.

"You like that?"

"Yes," I gasp. As if he needed to ask. He knows my body better than I know it myself.

"You just want my fingers, Jessie?"

"No," I whimper as he adds a second one and my walls clench around him.

"What else do you want, sweetheart? Tell me."

"You know, Shane," I pant as I rock my hips against him.

He chuckles softly before he pulls his fingers out of me and stands up.

I groan in frustration as I blink at him. He trails his fingertips, damp with my arousal, over my cheek and leans his face close to mine, until his hot breath skitters over my neck. "Seeing as you're being so shy in asking for what you want today, shall I tell you what I'm going to do anyway?"

"Yes," I whimper shamelessly.

"I'm going to take off these panties and carry you to the bed. Then I'm going to bury my face in your sweet cunt and eat you so good that you scream my name all over this goddamn plane. And when you think you can't take any more, I'm going to slide my fingers inside you and fuck you just the way you like."

"Shane!" I gasp as the wet heat builds in my core.

"You're going to squirt for me, Jessie. You're going to drench these sheets with your cum."

He lifts his head and I stare into his eyes. They are dark with desire and longing, and they make my breath catch in my throat. "And then what?" I whisper.

"Oh then I'm going to fuck you, sweetheart. I'm going to fuck you so hard you won't be able to tell me what day it is."

With that, he lifts me up and carries me the few steps to the bed before lying me down on it.

"You're a devil," I whisper.

"But I'm your devil," he grins at me.

TWO HOURS LATER, when Shane has delivered on every one of his promises, we walk out of the bedroom together. Erin glares at me. Her eyes burn into my skin with the heat of a thousand suns, but I walk to my seat, willing myself not to blush as I wonder if she just heard any of that. Shane Ryan is a devil, but he also makes me come harder and louder than anyone I have ever known.

I reach my seat, holding my head high and being super proud of myself for maintaining my dignity despite Erin looking at me like she just stepped in me on the pavement. I almost make it, but then Shane slaps my ass just as I'm about to sit down. The sound echoes around the cabin and my cheeks flush with heat. I turn and glare at him but he pulls me into his arms and kisses me so deeply that I no longer give a single damn about Erin and what she might think of me.

CHAPTER 6
JESSIE

With the five hour time difference, it's after midnight by the time we arrive at our hotel in Belfast. Erin is staying at the same one as us, much to my annoyance. I assumed she might have family here she could stay with, but I can't help but feel some sympathy for her when I see the look of sheer anguish on her face as Shane checks us in to the presidential suite under Mr. and Mrs. Ryan.

Jessie Ryan is the name on my false passport, after all, and I can't very well pretend to be his sister, can I?

I know that she comes off as a cold, heartless bitch, but I can imagine how much that must hurt. I glance at her but she avoids my gaze and for the first time ever, I feel like she is the one who may be envious of me. She had this incredible man all to herself. He was going to marry her. I know that the end of their engagement was due to her lying to him, but Shane is as loyal as they come. I bet they would have stayed together forever. It can't be easy to spend so much time with him and be reminded of what she's lost. Especially when I'm tagging along for the ride this time.

. . .

WHEN SHANE UNLOCKS our room with the electronic key, he opens the door and I step inside. The room is palatial, with floor to ceiling windows, a huge living area and a bar.

I kick off my sneakers and flop down onto the huge sofa. "This place is bigger than the house I grew up in." I smile at him as he tips the bellboy before walking over to me. He lifts my feet and sits down beside me before placing them over his lap.

"Bigger than the house I grew up in too." He cocks an eyebrow as he looks around the room.

"I thought your family always had money?"

He nods. "My father always had money, but he squandered most of it on women, fast cars, and anything else that gave him a buzz. It wasn't until I started earning for myself at fifteen that my brothers or I had any real money."

"You started working for your father at fifteen?"

"No." He shakes his head and smiles. "I started getting paid for it at fifteen. And I made much smarter investments than my father ever did."

"How old were you when you made your first million?"

He tilts his head to one side as he considers my question. "Twenty," he finally answers.

"Wow!" I stretch my legs over his and he rubs my feet. "You're pretty amazing, Shane Ryan."

"Well, that means a lot coming from you, Jessie Ryan," he smiles at me and I feel the heat building in my core, but then I'm reminded of when we checked in a few minutes ago and I feel a pang of guilt. "What is it?"

"You think that was a little insensitive before? Checking in as Mr. and Mrs. Ryan?" I bite on my lip.

"Why?" he frowns.

"Because that was almost you and Erin. She looked really hurt, Shane."

He reaches over and brushes his fingertips over my cheek.

"She knows who you are to me. She chose to travel with us. To stay at the same hotel as us. I'm not going to apologize for being with you, Jessie."

I swallow hard. This man makes my entire body tremble with need just talking to me. "Okay," I breathe.

He stands up and holds out his hand to me. "We've got a long day tomorrow. I have to go meet with some of my father's business associates and fake a smile while they pay me condolences for my loss. I want you to come with me."

I take hold of his hand and allow him to pull me up. "Of course. I'd love to meet some of your old friends."

"There won't be any friends of mine there, sweetheart, which is why I want you with me."

"I will be anything and do anything you need me to this week."

He arches one eyebrow at me. "You're going to do as you're told the whole time we're here?"

"Yes."

"No attitude? No acting like a brat?"

"No!" I frown at him. "I am not a brat!"

He slides one arm around my waist and pulls me closer to him, brushing his fingertips over my cheek with his free hand. "That doesn't sound like much fun at all," he grins before he hoists me up onto his shoulder and slaps me on the ass before carrying me to the bedroom, which is almost as big as the living area outside. He throws me onto the huge super king-size bed and I bounce into the middle with a giggle.

My stomach growls loudly as he holds himself over me and I blush. I didn't eat much of my meal on the plane, conscious of Erin watching every move I made.

"We should get some room service," Shane says as he checks his watch.

"Sorry!" I bite my lip and glance down at my stomach. Damn my hunger ruining the mood.

"I'm starving too, sweetheart," he says before pressing a soft kiss on my stomach. "And besides, we've got the whole week together."

"I know," I breathe as I look into his eyes. The thought of an entire week in this beautiful hotel room with him makes me tremble with anticipation.

"I am going to enjoy doing filthy things with you, Mrs. Ryan," he growls.

"I'm pretty sure I'm going to enjoy it even more, Mr. Ryan."

CHAPTER 7
JESSIE

After breakfast in our room the following morning, Shane and I meet up with Erin in the hotel lobby. I could barely hide my disappointment when he told me that she would be joining us today too, but I suppose this is a business thing and that's what she's here for. Shane has hired us a town car with a driver for the week and when the huge, sleek black car pulls up outside the hotel, he opens the door for me and I climb inside and scoot along to the edge of the seat. Erin climbs in next and sits in the middle beside me and I curse under my breath. I hadn't thought that through. Now she'll be sitting beside Shane instead of me.

Shane pokes his head inside the car and he looks at the two of us. "Unless you want to sit on my lap, sweetheart, I'd suggest we rethink this seating situation," he flashes an eyebrow at me.

I look to Erin beside me. "Can you scoot over, please?" I ask, forcing a smile.

She rolls her eyes so hard I think they may have fallen into her brain.

"You really want to sit next to Shane while he's feeling me up on his lap the entire way?" I ask and that seems to do the trick as she slides along the seat with a deep sigh and I scoot into her place.

"Thank you," Shane says as he steps inside and sits beside me.

I lean close to him and he rests his warm hand on my thigh. I fidget and pull at the hem of my dress, not used to wearing them, and Shane takes hold of my hand to stop me. This dress is one of the ones Conor chose for me. Shane packed it in his suit-case, knowing full well that all I would bring would be jeans and tank tops, which I am much more comfortable in. I'm grateful he did though. I would have felt out of place otherwise.

Erin, as usual, is effortlessly chic and stylish. I have to give her that. She is to clothes what peanut butter is to jelly.

I sit back in the seat and we drive to the venue in almost silence. The air is thick with tension and I feel the frustration seeping into Shane the closer we get to our destination. His fingers flex in my hand and his chest is rigid as we drive through the streets of Belfast. From the little he's told me, this event today has been put on just for him. A chance for all of his father's friends and associates to see him after all this time and pay their respects, but mostly to talk business — notably, who is going to take over operations in Ireland now that Patrick is dead.

As soon as we get inside the pub where the gathering is happening, Shane is accosted by a group of men who all offer their condolences and push glasses of whiskey into his hands. They try to usher him into a corner of the room which is full of men in suits drinking and smoking cigars. He looks at me apologetically but I smile at him. "I'll be fine," I mouth.

"I'll look after her," Erin says coolly.

Shane frowns at her as I almost pass out with shock, but I

hide my surprise. "Go," I say to him and he winks at me before disappearing into the crowd.

"Shall we get a drink?" Erin says as she turns to me.

I look behind me to see if she's speaking to somebody else, but there is no one else here. "Umm. Yes, okay," I say and then I follow her to the bar where she orders us each a whiskey. "I don't have any money with me," I whisper as I look around the room for Shane.

She rolls her eyes. "Relax. You don't need any when you're with Shane. He takes care of everything," she says and there is a sadness in her voice. As much as she annoys me, I understand how much it must hurt her to see the two of us together.

The bartender hands us each a whiskey over ice and I raise mine to Erin. "Cheers," I offer.

"Cheers." She actually smiles at me and clinks her glass against mine. "Come on, I'll introduce you to a few people," she says with a nod of her head and I follow her into the crowd wondering for a second who she is and what the hell she's done with the real Erin.

She makes a beeline for a small group of men standing at a table on the other side of the room.

"Sean?" she says as she reaches them and the man with his back to her turns and smiles.

"Erin McGrath?" he grins at her. "How long has it been?"

"Not long enough, Sean," she smiles at him and reaches back for me before pulling me to stand beside her. "This is Jessie. Shane's girlfriend."

"Hi," I say, extending my hand and feeling incredibly awkward all of a sudden.

"It's a pleasure to meet you, Jessie," Sean says as he takes my outstretched hand and kisses my knuckles.

"I have to talk to a few people. Can you look after Jessie for me?" Erin flutters her eyelashes.

Sean nods his head in agreement. "Of course. Anything for Shane." He turns back to me and winks.

"Great. Thanks," she says before she disappears in a waft of Chanel perfume.

"So, Jessie?" Sean says as he looks me over. "You and Shane Ryan?"

"Yes," I stammer.

"Me and Shane go way back," he smiles at me. "I'm glad to see he's dumped that one." He indicates his head toward Erin's retreating back. "She has a stick so far up her arse, it's a wonder she can sit down."

I smile and stifle a laugh.

"And she's a lawyer," he says quietly behind his hand, pretending to hide what he's saying. "Do you know what the difference is between a lawyer and God?"

"No," I frown at him.

"God doesn't think he's a lawyer," he winks at me and I can't help laughing now. It's a terrible joke, but that's what makes it so funny.

I'M WALKING TO THE LADIES' room when a strong arm grabs me by the waist, pulling me into a dark corner and pressing me against the wall. I look up into Shane's fierce glare. He leans down, his breath dancing over my neck and making me shiver. "If you don't stop flirting with Sean O'Connor, I will take off my belt, along with your panties, and spank your ass in the middle of this room," he growls.

"What?" I suck in a breath as I look into his eyes to determine whether he's being serious or not. He glares back at me, his green eyes almost black as they smolder like the embers of a fire. "I wasn't flirting with him." I try to pull back from his grasp but that only makes him hold me tighter.

"You weren't?" He narrows his eyes at me. "Because the two of you looked all kinds of friendly over there."

"Exactly. Friendly. We were just talking. He is friendly," I start to say but he cuts me off.

"So, he was flirting with you?"

"No," I shake my head.

"Because if that's case, I'm more than happy to walk you back over there and fuck you over his table if that's what it takes to show everyone in this room who you belong to."

"You wouldn't," I swallow.

"Watch me, Hacker. And I will take perverse satisfaction in making them watch while you come so hard that you scream my name."

"You're an asshole," I hiss.

He leans closer to me, caging me in with his arms and pressing his groin into mine. "Yeah? But I'm your asshole, sweetheart. And you belong to me. So behave your fucking self."

Despite my annoyance, I feel a familiar fluttering in my abdomen that always comes from being this close to Shane Ryan. But I refuse to accept that I have done anything wrong. "I was just talking," I snap.

"No," he takes my hand and pulls me forward so that we are no longer in the shadows. "That," he points at Erin, who stands demurely with about two feet of space around her entire person, "is just talking."

The tears prick at my eyes and I swallow the emotion that balls in my throat. *Erin*! How fucking dare he! I spin on my heel and glare at him, wishing I could make him feel some of the pain he just caused me. "No! *That* is having the personality of a fucking ice cube. But if she is the woman you'd rather I behaved like, why don't you just go fuck her in front of all these people instead. Because I am going back to the hotel."

"The fuck you are!" he hisses.

"So, you expect me to just stand in this room on my own and not smile or make eye contact with anyone? Is that it?"

"Just fucking behave, Jessie," he snarls, but before I can respond we're approached by an older couple.

"Are you not going to introduce us to your lovely lady, Shane?" the man says loudly while the woman I assume is his wife beams at the two of us.

Shane smiles as he slips an arm around my waist. "Of course, Jacob. This is Jessie," he says with a warning glance and I force my best smile as I greet them.

They ask Shane about his brothers and listening to him talking about them makes me miss them so much, but after a few minutes someone else comes along and demands his attention. He leaves me talking to Jacob and his wife, Ruth, and I assume Shane's twisted logic considers them safe for me to converse with.

I'M STILL TALKING to Jacob and Ruth when I catch Erin staring at me with a smug grin on her face. I excuse myself and make my way over to her.

"Is something about me amusing you this afternoon, Erin?"

She tilts her head as she looks me up and down. "Hmm. Perhaps I should have warned you how much Shane hates Sean O'Connor," she says with a smile before she takes a sip of her champagne.

God, she is a Grade A bitch. But why did I expect any less from her? I can't even be bothered arguing with her about it. "Why does he hate him so much?"

"Because Sean was always his father's right hand man, at least until Shane was old enough to be anyway. He hated that Patrick's son took over and he did everything he could to make his life as difficult as possible. He was especially partial to fucking Shane's girlfriends if he ever got the chance to be alone with them, whether they consented or not," she says with a shudder and suddenly I wonder if she was ever a victim of Sean's advances.

"But why didn't Shane deal with him?" I frown because I can't imagine the man I know allowing any of that to go unpunished.

"Because Patrick Ryan loved Sean. No doubt he saw a lot of himself in the sadistic prick. So he was basically untouchable. If Shane had retaliated, then Mikey and Liam would have borne the brunt of their father's frustrations."

I shake my head. The more I learn about Patrick, the more I wonder how his sons turned out to be the men they are today.

"It was fun watching Shane's face turn purple when he saw you and Sean chatting like old pals." She laughs and it's not a pleasant sound, more of an annoying, high-pitched whinny.

I glare at her, wondering how much of a commotion it would cause if I were to punch her in the face right now. But that would only make her look like the victim and I can think of a much better way to hurt her.

"Yeah, he sure was pissed," I say with a smile. "So, thank you, Erin."

She frowns at me. "What for?"

I look over at Shane. He is talking to a group of people and they are all hanging on his every word. Dressed in his exquisitely tailored suit that hugs his broad shoulders and thick thighs perfectly, he can hold a room like no one I have ever met and he is the sexiest man in here by a long shot. He glances at me, and our eyes meet for a second, making me swallow in anticipation before I turn back to Erin. "You must remember how well that man fucks? And when he's pissed? *Wow*!" I fan myself with my hand. "I doubt either of us will be getting any sleep tonight." I flash my eyebrows at her before walking away and leaving her standing with her mouth open and the shadow of a scowl on her botoxed forehead.

As I walk away from Erin, I look around the room for Jacob and Ruth again but they're talking to Sean O'Connor, and despite the fact that I'm still completely pissed at Shane, I understand now why he wouldn't want me talking to him. I make my way to the bar instead and sit on a stool while I order a glass of soda.

I've only been sitting alone for a few minutes when I feel a warm hand on my back. I turn, expecting and hoping to see Shane, but it's Sean O'Connor's face that smiles back at me. I shrug his hand off me.

"Something wrong?" he grins at me. "You were much more friendly before."

"I don't like to be touched by people I don't know," I say as I scoot back in my seat, looking around the room for Shane but I don't see him.

"But we know each other now, don't we?" He leers at me as he trails two fingers over the bare skin on my arm and I shudder. How did I not notice how creepy he was before?

I'm about to tell him to go to hell when his hand is forcibly removed from my arm and twisted up his back. I hear the cracking of bone as Sean winces and howls in pain before his head is slammed onto the bar in front of us and he stumbles to the ground with blood pouring from his nose. When I look up again Shane is standing right in front of me with a murderous look in his eyes.

"We're going!"

I blink at him.

"Now!" he barks as he reaches for my hand and pulls me from the stool.

I allow him to walk me out of the crowded bar while everyone stares at us. Nobody says anything and I doubt they would dare after what he just did. When we're outside in the afternoon sun, I wrench my hand from his grip.

"What the hell, Shane?" I snap.

He turns to me, full of anger and venom. "I told you to stay the fuck away from him."

"I did!" I protest. "He found me."

"You should never have spoken to him in the first place."

"Erin introduced me to him. Why does she get to do whatever she wants with no reproach?" I scowl at him.

He grabs my chin in one of his strong hands, squeezing as he bends his face close to mine. "Because I don't give a fuck what Erin does," he hisses. "I don't care who she talks to, who she smiles at, who she fucks." He shifts closer to me, pressing his groin into mine until the heat from his body sears against my skin. "But you..." He narrows his eyes at me before dipping his head lower, brushing his lips against my ear and making a shiver skitter along my spine. "I see you talking to another man and I want to rip his tongue out. When you smile at him, I want to gouge his fucking eyes out. And if anyone touches you, like even brushes against you when you're passing by, it makes me feel so fucking angry that I feel like ripping their head off with my bare hands."

"Shane! I didn't..." I start to plead but he turns away from me.

"Get in the car," he snarls and I do as he orders, rolling my eyes once his back is turned. Once inside the car, I scooch over onto the back seat, shrinking into the corner so I can sit as far away from him as possible. But when he climbs in after me, he follows me, sitting on the seat directly beside me. I bristle at his touch but he seems to take that as a signal to pull me up and onto his lap as he settles back into the seat.

"Shane!" I hiss as I wriggle from his grip, but he wraps his powerful arms around me and holds me in place.

"Stay!" he growls, as though I'm a puppy dog and not a person. I am about to tell him to go to hell when I notice Erin climbing into the car too and I press my lips together. The look of anguish on her face at seeing me wrapped in the arms of the man she still so clearly loves is obvious, if only for a fleeting moment, before she disguises it with an eye roll and a look of disgust.

There is no way I will give her the satisfaction of making a scene here in the car, so I reluctantly settle into Shane's lap, leaning against his broad chest. Some of the tension slips from him as he hugs me tighter. He barks an order to the driver and then he sighs softly before he plants a soft kiss on my shoulder. It's such a tender kiss that it almost makes me forget how mad I am at him.

Almost.

CHAPTER 8
JESSIE

As I take off my make-up in the bathroom, I see Shane's reflection in the mirror. He leans against the doorframe with his arms folded over his chest and his legs crossed at the ankles, wearing just his suit pants and looking as hot as hell, which is pretty fitting considering he is the devil's own spawn.

I avoid making eye contact and he just stands there watching me until I'm done. I don't want to leave this bathroom. I don't want to have to walk past him, or ask him to move out of my way, because I am beyond pissed at him. I feel like taking a plane straight back to New York and crawling into bed with one of his brothers for a bear hug. I blink away the tears at the thought of Conor and the twins and how much I miss them, and wonder why the hell I agreed to come here with their asshole big brother.

"You going to speak to me at all tonight?" he snaps.

"No!"

"Because of what I did to some prick you barely know?" he growls.

I spin around. "You think I give a damn about that jackass?"

"Then what the fuck is wrong with you?" he snarls.

I glare at him. The fact that he doesn't even realize why I'm so upset only makes me more annoyed with him. "You told me to be more like Erin!" I spit the words at him before I turn back to the mirror so he doesn't see the tears in my eyes.

"Jessie!"

I don't respond.

"I'm sorry," he says with a heavy sigh, making me turn around.

"I don't care," I reply as I walk towards the door and try to push past him. He doesn't move and I glare up at him.

"This place makes me crazy," he frowns at me.

"No. It makes you cruel and heartless," I snap. "Just like your father."

The shadow falls across his face and I know that's a line I shouldn't have crossed but he crossed one too today. He wraps a hand around my throat, pushing me back into the room until I am pressed against the bathroom counter. "You know nothing about the kind of man my father was."

"Don't I?" I challenge him. "Didn't he like to take people's insecurities and exploit them? Wasn't he cruel and bitter?"

He swallows hard. "You think that's who I am?"

I blink the tears from my eyes. "No. But that's how you made me feel today."

I expect him to argue with me but he kisses me instead as he presses me against the countertop. Planting my hands on his chest, I try to push him away but he is undeterred. His hands slide to my waist before he lifts me onto the counter and wraps my legs around his waist. I bite his lip but it only seems to make him more determined as he kisses me so fiercely that I struggle to breathe.

I push at his chest again but he takes hold of my wrists and pins them behind my back as he keeps on tongue-fucking my mouth. I am completely powerless to resist him. Heat rolls through my core and I feel wetness pooling between my thighs as he grinds his cock against me making me whimper shamelessly.

Damn my treacherous body letting me down like this.

When I stop struggling, he releases my wrists and I wrap my arms around his neck, scratching his skin as I pull him closer to me.

"I need to fuck you," he groans as he unzips his pants and takes out his cock. Then he tugs my panties to the side and slides two fingers deep inside me, making me gasp out loud.

"Shane!" I hiss, reaching between us and squeezing his hard cock. I need him to fuck me too. I need to release some of the anger and frustration that has been building all afternoon.

He curls his fingers inside me, pressing against my G-spot and my legs begin to tremble as I coat him in a rush of slick heat.

"You make me so fucking hard," he grunts as he slides his fingers out and rams his cock into me instead, pushing me back against the mirror before he sinks his teeth into the tender skin on my neck and sucks hard.

"Jesus, Shane," I pant as I rake my nails down his back.

He keeps on sucking my neck as he nails me to the wall and my pussy muscles clench around him, drawing him in deeper as though my body can't get enough of him. He drives at the sweet spot deep inside me over and over until he tips me over the edge and I shout his name. That seems to light a fire under him as he fucks me even harder and faster until he finds his own release a few moments later.

As we catch our breath, Shane presses his forehead against mine. "Damn, I love to fuck you," he pants.

"Is that all you want me for?" I breathe.

"I'm going to pretend you didn't just say that, Jessie," he growls as he pulls out of me, but he keeps his arms around my waist and presses his body flush against mine. "I'm sorry," he whispers as he rubs his nose along my jawline.

"You said you wanted me to be more like Erin," I whisper.

He narrows his eyes at me. "I never said that."

"Not in those exact words, Shane. Do you have any idea how much it hurt to have you compare me to her like that?"

His Adam's apple bobs as he swallows. "Yes," he nods. "Maybe I said it because I knew it would hurt you."

"You wanted to hurt me?" I whisper. "Why?"

"Because I hate Sean O'Connor and I saw him with you and it made me feel like I was sixteen again with all of this rage inside me."

"But—"

"And," he interrupts me. "What if I really am my father's son, Jessie?"

"No. You're not," I say as I run my hands over his handsome face.

"But what if I am?" he whispers.

"You aren't. Because, despite you being a complete jackass today, you are one of the best men I know. You always put your family first. You take care of everyone before yourself. And even though you're a possessive asshole, I love you."

"What did I do to deserve you, Hacker?" he smiles.

I suck on my lip for a few seconds as though I'm deep in thought. "You must have been an absolute saint in another life." I smile at him.

"I must have been," he mumbles before he starts to plant soft kisses along my throat.

"I haven't forgiven you for being a complete asshole yet, you know?" I say with a sigh.

"I know." He lifts his head. "I'll spend the rest of the night making it up to you."

I flash my eyebrows at him. "Really?"

"Really."

"Can we order every dessert on the room service menu?"

He frowns at me. "You do know you can do that anyway, right?"

"I can?" I whisper.

"Jessie. This is your hotel room too, sweetheart. You can order whatever you want, whenever you want it. You can do whatever you want in here."

"Really? Like even invite Sean whatshisface for breakfast or something?" I grin at him.

He glares at me and I press my lips together to stop myself from laughing. "Too soon?"

"Much too soon," he growls before he seals my mouth with one of his incredible kisses.

After he fucked me for a second time, Shane actually did order all eight desserts from the room service menu, and now we are sitting on the bed surrounded by plates of half-eaten cakes, profiteroles and macaroons.

"Oh, God, I am so full," I groan and he laughs as he wraps an arm around me. I rest my head on his shoulder and sigh contentedly as he twirls a strand of my hair between his fingers.

"Would you really like me to be more like Erin?" I whisper.

"No! Not even a little bit. And I could happily kick my own ass for giving you the slightest indication that I would." He rolls on top of me, brushing my hair back from my face as he stares down at me, his face full of emotion. "I love you, sweetheart. But if you ever go near Sean O'Connor again, I will give you the spanking of your life and I will make you watch while I slit his throat."

I chew on my lip, because his possessiveness is so freaking hot. I love that I belong to him. But the irony of what he just said seems completely lost on him. "You have some pretty stark double standards, you know that?"

"And why is that?" he frowns.

"I can't even talk to a guy you don't like, yet Erin is allowed to fawn all over you whenever she wants, and when I bring it up you accuse me of acting like a child," I challenge him.

"That's completely different," he snarls.

"Oh really?" I flash my eyebrows at him. "And why is that?"

"Because you are envious and I am possessive. They are two entirely different things."

I shake my head in frustration. "You're going to have to explain that one to me, because they seem like the same thing from where I'm standing."

He laughs, but not his nice one that turns my insides to jelly. "You think I'm jealous of Sean O'Connor?"

I press my lips together.

"I am not jealous of him, sweetheart. I have no fucking worries that he's going to sweep you off your feet and you're going to run off into the sunset with him. It doesn't even cross my mind that you might want to kiss him, or even fuck him."

"You're an arrogant asshole," I snap.

He tilts his head to one side as he stares at me. "I'm arrogant because I know that you love me?"

"I never said that," I protest. He's twisting my words. I hate the way he does that.

"But you are saying that. I don't worry about you with other men, because I trust you."

I swallow hard. Damn him and his twisted logic. "So why did you just break Sean O'Connor's arm and face today then?"

"Because he touched you," he growled. "And you belong to me. Nobody touches what is mine. Nobody touches you but me or my brothers. I am not envious of any man, sweetheart, but I told you how seeing you with another man makes me feel. You would be wise to remember that in future."

I chew on my lip as he glares at me and the fire starts to build between my thighs.

"But the reason you don't like being around Erin is because you're jealous of her," he goes on.

I open my mouth to respond but I realize that he's right, even though I won't admit it yet. "You think that she's somehow better than you, or that she has something you don't."

I stare up at him, not responding because I have no comeback.

"But she isn't, and she doesn't. If the only reason you didn't like me being around her was because you wanted to scratch her eyes out for looking at me, I wouldn't give a damn. But you hate her being around me because you think I'm going to fall for her or fuck her."

"I don't," I whisper.

"No?" he frowns at me.

I roll my lips together. Damn his insightfulness. "I worry that you're going to realize she is right for you, and I'm not," I admit.

"Fuck, Jessie!" he snaps and I feel like we might be on the verge of another epic fight. But then he looks into my eyes and I see them blazing with fire. "Maybe I don't tell you this often enough, so listen to what I'm about to say and believe that I mean it with every single fiber of my being. I love you. I would die for you. There is not one single fucking thing I would change about you and I am fucking honored to call you mine. But when you bring this shit up about her, you question my loyalty to you.

Don't you get that? She could lie next to me naked all night long and I wouldn't fucking touch her."

"Now I *would* scratch her eyes out if she did that." I arch one eyebrow at him and he smiles. "But, I'm sorry, Shane. I never thought of it that way. I do trust you."

"I should fucking hope so," he growls before he kisses me and I forget what we were even talking about.

CHAPTER 9
JESSIE

The following morning, Conor and I are chatting on the laptop when Shane walks out of the bathroom with a white towel wrapped around his waist, sitting right below his perfectly chiseled abs.

"Jessie was telling me about last night," Conor says with a chuckle as Shane walks over to the bed.

Shane chuckles too. "You've gone to the wrong brother looking for sympathy from Conor, sweetheart. He hates Sean O'Connor even more than I do."

"What?" Conor growls. "Sean O'Connor was the guy you were flirting with?"

"I wasn't flirting," I protest.

"She was, Con," Shane says as he crawls onto the bed, holding himself over me and pressing a kiss between my shoulder blades. "She smiled at him."

"You smiled at Sean O'Connor?" Con asks me, his eyes narrowed as he leans closer to the screen.

"He told me a funny joke about lawyers."

Shane continues kissing my back, making me squirm as heat sears between my thighs. "It wasn't her regular smile, Con.

It was that one that makes her eyes twinkle. You know the one?"

"Our smile?" Connor shakes his head and I open my mouth to protest but for a few seconds, I am completely lost for words. "Why do I feel like you two have some kind of secret code or language that I don't understand?" I eventually ask.

"Because we do," Shane mumbles against my skin.

"So why is her ass not raw?" Conor grumbles.

"Because I was an asshole," Shane replies. "I had some making up of my own to do."

"Yes. He was an asshole," I say with a vigorous nod of my head. "That's what we were talking about, not me smiling at some random dude who I have zero interest in."

"But Shane is always an asshole, Angel. I am far more interested in you smiling at that cunt, O'Connor."

"I didn't know how much you hated him," I whisper as Shane's warm hand slides beneath my tank top and I shiver at his touch.

"Well you will know as soon as you get home, Angel. Because your beautiful ass is going to get the spanking of its life. You'll be sleeping on your front for a week."

"I was just being polite." I offer in a feeble protest because wet heat surges between my thighs at the thought.

"Shane will have to punish you for now, until you get back here."

"You can't punish me now and then when I get home for the same thing. That's not fair!"

"Did our girl just tell us we couldn't do something?" Conor looks behind me and at Shane who stops kissing my back and looks up at his brother on the screen.

"I think she did," he chuckles. "But I gotta say I love our girl talking about getting home and knowing that's with us."

"Hmm," Conor nods.

"But you're right, Con, she needs to be punished." His fingers trail down my back, making me shiver in anticipation and excitement. "What are you thinking?"

I glance at Shane behind me and he licks his lips, but the wicked glint in his eyes makes my entire body tremble.

"For starters, that ass needs to be turned a pretty shade of pink," Conor says, running a hand over his beard.

"What?" I shake my head.

"Hands? Belt? Something else?" Shane asks, ignoring my question as he starts to take off my top.

"So we're really doing this?" I ask as Shane continues peeling my tank over my head before pulling my arms through. I wriggle beneath him but he is straddling me now and he is too heavy for me to shift.

Shane tosses my top onto the floor. "Yes," he growls as he leans down and cups my chin in his hand, tilting my head before he kisses me softly.

"Hands will do fine," Conor replies.

"Hmm," Shane mumbles as he rubs one over my ass.

"And then some good old fashioned edging should do the trick. Until I can get my hands on her."

"What's edging?" I ask, my mouth hanging open as I look between the two of them.

"Oh, Angel," Conor growls.

"Orgasm denial," Shane whispers in my ear before he pushes himself up and hooks his fingers into the band of my underwear and begins to pull them off me. "Let's get you naked, sweetheart."

I look up at Conor on the screen as Shane tosses my panties onto the floor.

"Which way do you want her, Con?" Shane asks.

"Facing the head of the bed. Ass in the air," he orders.

"You heard him. Up," Shane commands as he taps me on

the ass and I push myself onto all fours and maneuver myself into position as he grabs two pillows and slides them beneath my stomach. Once he's done he takes my hands and lays them flat on the bed, my arms outstretched above my head and my face pressed against the duvet so I can see Conor on the laptop screen. He licks his lips in anticipation as he watches his brother work.

My thighs tremble as I wait for whatever Shane is about to do to me. I do love his punishments, but I don't know how serious the two of them are about this flirting thing – which I definitely wasn't doing.

"That okay, bro?" Shane asks as I lie there in position. Waiting.

"Perfect!" Conor growls.

"Let's see how red we can turn this ass then," Shane chuckles to himself before he kneels on the bed behind me.

A few seconds later, I feel the sting of his first slap as it echoes around the hotel bedroom. Then another. And another. Over and over as Conor encourages him from the screen. His spanking is hard but I've certainly had worse from him and the burning sensation on my ass is making the burning need in my pussy grow stronger with each passing second. I squirm on the pillows and Shane chuckles behind me, knowing exactly what he is doing to me. Fiend!

"How wet is she, bro?" Conor growls.

Shane slides two of this thick fingers deep into my pussy and I bite my lip to stifle the groan.

"Soaking," he says as he pulls them out of me again. "See?"

I realize he must be holding them up for his brother to see as Conor groans in appreciation, then the sound of Shane sucking his fingers clean makes my cheeks flush with heat. "So fucking sweet," he growls.

"I know. She's always sweeter after a spanking too," Conor chuckles.

"Hmm," Shane agrees as he smacks my ass again before sliding his fingers back inside me. Then he finger fucks me while he spanks me at the same time and I feel like I'm about to lose control, but he won't let me. He keeps me teetering on the edge of oblivion.

"Shane?" I plead with him to take pity on me.

He leans over me until I feel his cock pressing against the seam of my ass. "It's Conor's show, sweetheart."

"No way, Angel," Conor says in response and I groan in frustration as Shane pulls his fingers out of me and slaps my wet pussy making me cry out in pleasure. *Devil*!

"This ass is fucking beautiful, Con," he says as he circles his finger over my asshole. "It think we should buy our girl some nice jeweled plugs for it, don't you?"

My pussy clenches at the thought.

"Hmm. If she can learn to behave herself, maybe?" Conor replies.

"Imagine taking her out knowing she was wearing one? Fuck!" Shane hisses as he slides one wet finger inside my ass, right up to his knuckle, making me whimper as he slowly finger fucks me there now. His other hand slides between my folds and he begins rubbing gently on my clit, bringing me to the verge of orgasm again.

"Fuck, you look good getting punished, Jessie," Conor growls.

I look at the screen to see him stroking his rock hard cock while he watches his brother and me and the sight of him causes a rush of wet heat that makes me shudder. Sensing I am about to fall off the edge, Shane sits back on his heels, stopping his delicious torment and making me groan in frustration.

He rubs his hands over my ass instead.

"Am I fucking her cunt or her ass for you?" he asks his brother.

"Both," Conor replies and I gasp for breath. I don't know how much more of this I can take. Shane obliges by grabbing hold of my hips, keeping me in place as he drives his cock into my pussy. My walls clench around him and I can't stop the yelp of pleasure escaping from my throat. Then he slides his thumb into my ass at the same time and I whimper shamelessly.

He fucks me slowly as Conor keeps on urging him on from his office in New York.

I am on the verge of passing out if he doesn't give me some relief soon. I reach down and slide my hands between my thighs but Shane grabs hold of it and plants it back on the bed beside me. "You touch yourself again, sweetheart, and you won't come at all," he warns.

"You're a devil," I groan as he goes back to his punishing steady rhythm.

"Fuck her harder, Shane," Conor groans.

"If I fuck her any harder, she's going to come. So it's up to you, Con. You wanna see our girl come hard all over my cock, or do you want me to keep torturing her for you?"

"Fuck!" Conor groans in frustration as though this is a really difficult decision and it's him being tortured and not me.

"Please, Conor?" I beg as I gasp for breath.

"Oh, Angel. I love the way you beg," he sighs. "But fortunately for you, I love hearing you come even more."

With permission finally given, Shane pulls the pillow from beneath me and presses me flat to the bed with the weight of his body. "Spread those legs wide for me, sweetheart," he growls in my ear and I do as he tells me. Then he rolls his hips, pressing deeper and further into me, hitting that sweet spot that makes stars flicker behind my eyelids. As I think I can't take any more he pulls out and drives back in ever harder than the last time and I come with a rush of wet heat that soaks the duvet beneath us.

"Fuck!" Shane hisses.

"Did you just make her squirt?" Conor groans as his brother keeps on fucking me through my orgasm and the wet sound of him pounding me echoes around the room. With a final thrust, Shane finds his own release too and after he has emptied himself inside me, he lies down on top of me, panting for breath. As I glance at the screen, I see Conor cleaning himself with paper towels and realize all three of us have now had our happy ending.

Shane presses a kiss against my temple. "Good girl," he whispers and my pussy contracts. Why the hell do I love him saying that to me?

"You two are devils," I groan and they both laugh softly.

"Will you ever flirt with another man again though, Angel?" Conor says.

"Hmm?" I chew on my lip, because that was epic.

Shane pushes himself up and smacks my ass. Hard.

"No! I won't," I yelp.

"Good," they both say in unison.

"As much as I'd love to hang around chatting with you two, I need to get some sleep," Conor says with a yawn.

"And I've got plenty of shit to do," Shane glances at his watch and then jumps off the bed and walks to the laptop. "Catch you later, Con."

"Later, bro. Love you, Angel."

"Love you, too," I say with a smile and then he winks at me before ending the call.

I roll onto my back and Shane sits beside me and brushes my hair back from my face. "You going to be okay here on your own today?"

I sigh dramatically. "I'm sure I'll survive for one day. I'm going to watch some trashy TV, I think."

"Don't leave the suite. Okay?"

"Okay," I bite on my bottom lip and look up at his handsome face.

"What is it?" he frowns at me.

"Nothing."

"Jessie!" he snaps.

"Do you not want me to come with you because of what happened yesterday?" I whisper. The thought that I somehow embarrassed him has been eating away at me all morning.

I see his Adam's apple bob as he swallows and tears prick at my eyes. I bet Erin would never show him up like that. "Hey," he cups my chin in his hand. "I'm meeting with some people today. It's delicate. That's all."

"And you don't want me to embarrass you." I sniff. "I understand."

"No, sweetheart. You couldn't embarrass me if you tried, but you do distract me and I need to focus today."

"If I'm such a distraction why did you bring me here?"

He narrows his eyes at me. "Jessie, don't."

"Don't what?"

"Don't pick a fight with me when I have to leave, sweetheart."

"I'm not trying to," I whisper, but somehow we always seem to be on the verge of a fight. Is that the way things will always be between us?

"Sean O'Connor is a cunt. What happened yesterday was because he acted like one. But regardless of that, I wasn't planning on taking you with me today anyway. I told you before we left you'd have to spend some time here on your own."

I place my hand over his. "I know," I whisper.

"So don't ever accuse me of being ashamed of you, Jessie

Ryan. I would wear your naked ass like a coat if it wouldn't get us arrested for indecency," he winks at me and I stifle a giggle.

"Now, I gotta take another shower because I'm covered in your cum," he says before leaning down and giving me a quick kiss.

CHAPTER 10
SHANE

I open the door to our suite and walk inside to see her lying on the sofa, her legs draped over the end and a cushion under her head as she flips through a magazine. She hasn't heard me come in and she jumps with fright when I lift her legs so I can sit beside her.

"Shane!" she shrieks. "You almost gave me a heart attack!"

"Sorry, sweetheart," I chuckle as I take a seat. "You were lost in your own little world."

"I was reading about this man who married his truck." She arches one eyebrow at me. "His truck! Like he has sex with it and everything."

"With a truck?"

"A truck!" She places the magazine on the floor beside her. "Those things are addictive," she giggles and it makes me smile. She's never had the chance to switch off and relax before and it is fucking beautiful to see her doing it, and especially with me.

"Why are you back so early, anyway?" she asks as she slides her bare foot onto my groin and rubs my cock. I take hold of it, keeping it in place.

"Not to fuck you, as much as I would love to, but we don't have time right now."

"Why?"

"I'm taking you to meet someone." I smile at her and tap her legs. "Put some shoes on. We need to leave."

She sits up and reaches for her socks and sneakers beside the sofa. "Who?"

"It's a surprise."

She rolls her eyes at me. "Is it business stuff?"

I shake my head.

"Can I have a hint?"

"No."

AN HOUR LATER, we pull up outside the cottage in the countryside and Jessie peers out of the window. There are wind chimes hanging all around the outside as well as overgrown bushes that hide the house largely from view. It hasn't changed much since I was a kid. I love this place.

"Come on," I say as I climb out of the car and Jessie follows suit.

"Whose place is this?" she asks, wide eyed as she looks around at the flowers in huge colorful flowerpots. There is a giant sundial on the middle of the lawn and a fountain a few meters behind it. "I love it," she breathes.

I take her hand and walk her up the path. I don't even have a chance to knock on the door before my Aunt Em opens it. She has barely changed either, except her hair is slightly grayer, but she still wears it loose and wavy. She still wears long flowing skirts and dozens of bracelets and I only just realized how much I have missed her.

"Shane!" she says as she steps out and pulls me into a hug. The smell of patchouli and jasmine takes me back to the summers we would spend at this cottage when we were kids. It was my grandmother's back then. Em inherited it when she died, given that she was the only surviving daughter.

When she releases me, she doesn't even let me introduce Jessie before she wraps her in her arms too. "And this must be Jessie. Shane has told me so much about you."

"This is my Aunt Em," I say as Jessie looks at me over Em's shoulder with a huge smile on her face.

"Come in," Em says when she finally lets Jessie go. "Aoife is here too."

"Who's Aoife?" Jessie mouths to me as we go inside.

I slide my hand around her waist and press my lips close to her ear. "My cousin."

We follow Em into her sitting room and are immediately greeted by a tall, dark haired woman in her mid twenties, with a huge pregnant bump, whose smile is even wider than my aunt's.

"Shane!" she says excitedly. "You haven't changed at all. From your pictures, I mean."

"Well, you certainly have. I think you were about one the last time I saw you?"

"Yes," Em replies. "It was about a year after your mum's funeral." She wipes a tear from her eyes. "It was the last time I saw any of you."

"I know," I say as I wrap an arm around her shoulder and kiss the top of her head.

"Come on, tough guy," she sniffs and straightens up. "You can help me make the tea."

I FOLLOW Em into the kitchen and she fills the kettle and places it on her stove. I recognize it immediately. It's an old fashioned kind that whistles when the water is boiled and it belonged to my grandmother too. She turns to face me, her hands resting on the countertop either side of her.

"Your Uncle Paul came to see me," she says, searching my face for a reaction.

"Oh? I didn't realize he was back yet?"

"It was late last night," she replies with a slight bob of her head.

I don't speak. I stand in her kitchen, listening to the sound of the water boiling while neither of us mentions the thing that is most obviously on both of our minds.

"I told him that I know," she finally says before letting out a long, slow breath that it seemed like she'd been bottling up for a while. "I told him that you know too."

"Fuck, Em!" I shake my head in exasperation.

"What else could I do, Shane? He was standing right here, asking me questions about you and the boys."

"What did he say? Did he confirm it?"

She nods her head.

"Fuck!"

"You haven't told them yet then?"

"No. There just hasn't seemed like the right time to do it. Every time I tried to, I just froze, you know? I mean how do you tell someone something like that?"

"I'm sorry that I burdened you with it, Shane." She wipes a stray tear from her eye. I step closer to her and put my arms around her and she leans against me.

"Don't be. Someone has to tell them, and it's better that it comes from me. And now that Paul knows we know," I sigh, "I need to tell them as soon as possible, but I want to speak to him first."

The whistling of the kettle pierces the air and she rushes to take it from the heat.

“That makes sense. And what about Jessie? Does she know?” Em asks as she pours water into her old yellow teapot.

“No. It’s not fair to ask her to keep a secret like that.”

“Of course not,” she purses her lips and then looks up as the kitchen door opens and Aoife walks in.

“Do you have any of those ginger biscuits, Mammy?”

“Of course, petal,” Em turns and opens a cupboard. “You feeling queasy again?”

“No. I told Jessie how amazing they are,” she laughs. “So I said we should have some with our tea.”

I roll my eyes. My girl has such a sweet tooth.

“I’ll bring some through,” Em says with a smile and Aoife walks out of the kitchen, leaving us alone again.

“Did Paul leave a contact number, or tell you where he’s staying?” I ask.

“No,” she replies with a shake of her head. “As elusive as he ever was. Does he still have that old place out in Antrim?”

“Not as far as I know. My lawyer told me it was sold off years ago. Did he say what his plans were?”

“Not really. He did say he intended to catch up with you soon, so I expect you’ll be seeing him shortly.”

“Did he tell you why, Em?” I ask, conscious that Aoife or Jessie could walk into the room at any moment.

She looks up at me with tears in her eyes. “He said that he loved her,” she replies with a shrug. “Isn’t that the reason any of us do anything, Shane?”

CHAPTER 11
JESSIE

After we've finished our tea and eaten some of Em's homemade ginger biscuits, Aoife and I go into the garden. It is a truly beautiful place. Em has so many wildflowers growing. The wild jasmine smells incredible and she has promised to make me some soaps with it and send them out to New York. Seeing her and Shane together has been so lovely. I see a completely different side of him with her. He is sweet and helpful and gracious, and he rarely curses in front of her.

"How long have you known Shane?" Aoife asks.

"Umm. About nine months now."

"How did you meet?" she asks with a smile.

Hmm. He blew up my old boss's house and then threatened to kill me too, but I persuaded him and his brothers to kidnap me instead. "Through work," I say.

"Oh. Have you always lived in New York?"

"Umm. No. I've moved around a lot."

"Really? I've never left Ireland. Your life sounds so exciting."

Too exciting.

"It just sounds wonderful," she says with a soft sigh.

"Yet your life seems so wonderful to me," I smile at her.

I hadn't heard Shane walking up behind us and he startles me as he slips a hand around my waist. "We should get going soon, sweetheart."

"Oh, let me get you that recipe for Irish stew before you go," Aoife says. "My mammy makes the best, I swear."

"Thank you," I say with a smile as I watch her disappear back into the house.

"Did you mean that?" Shane asks when we are alone.

"What?" I frown in confusion.

"That Aoife's life seems wonderful?"

"Well, yes. Imagine living here and never having to worry about some psychopath trying to murder you. She's in love with Noel. They're getting married. They have a lovely baby on the way. Of course it seems wonderful. For someone else, anyway," I sigh and tears unexpectedly prick my eyes.

Shane slides his other arm around my waist and pulls me closer to him. "I can see you living in a house like this. With a huge garden and six kids running around your feet."

"You can?" I smile at him.

"Yes." He brushes a strand of hair from my face. "In another life, maybe I could have been standing right beside you."

"But not this life?" I ask as my heart feels like it's about to break. I had never realized how good a normal life could be, and now that I've had a glimpse of it, I wonder if it will always make me wonder what if. He knows it too and I sense something shifting between us.

"If this is the life you want, Jessie, I would give that to you," he swallows.

I blink at him. "You would?"

"If you wanted marriage and babies, you could have that," he breathes. "With Conor."

"With Conor?" I frown at him. What the hell is he on about?

"I told you I'll never get married or have kids."

"What about the twins?"

"They would never leave each other. They would get over it eventually, if they knew you were happy."

"And what about Conor? Does he get any say in you marrying us off and becoming a dad to six kids?"

"Are you kidding?" he laughs softly. "He would fucking love it."

"Are you being serious, Shane? You really think that's what I want?"

"I'm just saying that you don't have to give up on that life if that's what you really want."

"You think I don't want to be with you?" I blink a tear away because he is breaking my heart here. "Don't you want this any more?"

"Of course I do. I love you, sweetheart. More than anything in the world, and that's why I would never stand in the way of your happiness. I want you to at least think about it."

"There's nothing to think about, Shane!" I snap at him but then Aoife and Em are walking over to us and the conversation is over, at least for now.

CHAPTER 12
JESSIE

We spent an incredible evening with Em and Aoife yesterday. They are both so lovely and kind. Em told me so many stories of Shane and Conor when they were young that my sides hurt from laughing so much. She never really got to know the twins after their mom died; Patrick kept her away from his boys and I could see how sad that made her. But I have made them both promise that they will visit us in New York once Aoife's baby is born.

Aoife is marrying her fiancé, Noel, in a few weeks' time and I realized after we got back to the hotel last night that he was the guy who Shane had me look into all those months ago when I first met him. I love that even halfway across the world, he was still looking out for his family.

Shane has gone out to do more business today and I have been alone in the hotel suite all day.

I'm lying in the huge jacuzzi tub when I see the message from him pop up on my cell phone.

I'm sending you a gift. I'll pick you up at 6 x

I grin at the screen. A gift? I wonder what it could be? And we're going out! Shane has been so busy, I've hardly seen anything of Ireland since I got here. Full of excitement, I jump out of the tub, grab a warm fluffy towel from the rail and wrap it around myself. I open the closet, trying to think of what I'm going to wear, until I realize I have no idea where we are going.

I'm about to grab my cell and ask him what I should dress for when there is a knock at the door to the suite. I actually squeal with excitement, like a teenage girl.

Is this my gift?

Peering through the spyhole, I see a woman with black curly hair and bright red lipstick standing outside our room, holding three boxes.

I open the door and she smiles at me. "Mrs. Ryan?"

"Yes," I breathe, still not used to being called that.

"Mr. Ryan asked that I had these personally delivered to you," she says in an accent that I could listen to all day. I think she's French. I stare at her open-mouthed and she laughs softly as she hands over the boxes.

"Thank you," I whisper.

"I hope you enjoy them," she purrs. "I picked them out myself, although he gave me very specific instructions."

"Oh." I blush to the roots of my hair. Just what the hell has that hot devil had her pick out for me?

I wonder if I should tip her, but then realize I have no cash on me. Damn! "I'm sorry. I don't..." I start to say but she holds up her hand to stop me.

"Mr. Ryan has taken care of everything. Have a good evening," she says and then she walks away elegantly in a cloud of sweet perfume. I watch her strut to the elevator in her heels and smile. She's one of the most beautiful women I have ever seen.

I carry the boxes inside. They are pastel shades of pink, lilac and mint green, and have a discreet label embossed in the corner. 'Lady Mademoiselle.'

I place them on the bed and resist the urge to tear open the pretty boxes. I open the first one carefully and find a pair of black patent Louboutin pumps with a six inch heel. They are stunning but I have no idea how I'm going to walk in them.

I open the second box and pull out a black mini-dress. It has long sleeves and a high neckline, but it is obscenely short. The material is beautiful though. It has a soft, almost velvety feel, yet it looks like leather. I brush it over my cheek and sigh softly. It feels like it cost a fortune. I leave the pink box until last. It is the smallest and I already have an idea of what I'm going to find in here. My stomach flutters in anticipation anyway. I open it and unfold the pink tissue that it is so exquisitely wrapped in.

I smile as I see the flimsy black material. He is so predictable. I pull out the bra first and check the size, which of course is right. It's all black lace and is so beautiful I almost want to wear it as outerwear. Next, I take out the matching panties. They are gorgeous too. It's only when I hold them up that I notice they are not ordinary panties. They are crotchless.

My cheeks flush with heat as I think about wearing these out in public, and beneath that tiny dress. But my stomach dances with excitement too, as the prospect of being out in public with Shane Ryan when he has such easy access to my pussy makes the warmth pool in my core.

Checking the time on the clock on the nightstand, I see it's a little after four, which means I have just under two hours to get ready. I put the expensive underwear back in the box and lie on the bed, wondering what other surprises Shane has in store this evening.

. . .

At one minute before six, Shane walks into the hotel suite. I am standing waiting for him and he smiles when he sees me in the clothes that he sent.

"Thank you for the outfit," I flutter my eyelashes at him, trying to appear like the confident sex kitten he's had me dress as.

"You're welcome, sweetheart. You look good enough to eat," he growls as he walks towards me. When he reaches me, he drops to one knee, pulling a velvet box out of his pocket. It's clearly far too big to be a ring though, so I know I'm not about to receive a marriage proposal. Still, I can't resist teasing him.

I look down at him and flutter my eyelashes. "Are you proposing to me, Shane Ryan?"

"I'm proposing something, sweetheart," he says with a wink as he snaps the box open with one hand as his other hand snakes up the inside of my thigh and beneath my dress. I shiver at his touch as I look down at the two rose-gold metallic orbs inside.

"They are beautiful," I say with a sigh. "But my ears aren't pierced." I lick my lips as his fingers trail over my skin.

"They're not for your ears," he growls.

"Oh, I know what they are," I purr. "And *you* are a deviant."

"Hmm," he agrees, reaching down to take them from the box. He holds them up and they click together, the small weights inside rolling around.

They are very pretty for a sex toy, and even the silicone retrieval cord has a beautiful rose-gold heart attached to the end. He puts the box on the floor and taps my ankle, indicating that I should lift my foot. I do as he commands and he takes hold of it, planting it on his shoulder before running his warm hand from my ankle and along my calf, causing goosebumps to prickle over my skin. His every movement is so considered and controlled.

I press the heel of my shoe lightly into the spot just beneath his shoulder blade and he narrows his eyes at me in warning as his hand slides beneath my dress again and all the way up between my thighs.

"Ordinarily, these would require some lube," he says as he pops one into his mouth for a few seconds and sucks. My pussy throbs at the sight of him and my legs tremble.

He looks into my eyes, sucking on the ball as his fingers slide through my pussy and he pushes one into my wet heat, making me shudder and groan at the same time. When he pulls the ball from his mouth and licks his lips, I feel an intense rush of wetness. "But not with you, sweetheart," he growls as he pushes a second finger inside me and I bear down, grinding onto them. "Why are you already so wet, Hacker? Have you been playing with yourself all day?"

"No," I protest. "I've just spent the last half an hour getting ready for you take me out, and these panties made me think of..."

He grins at me. "Of what?"

"Of all the things you might do to me," I whisper as a blush creeps over my neck and cheeks.

"Jessie!" he groans loudly as he slides his fingers out of me. He presses one of the Ben Wa balls against my opening. It is warm from his mouth and I groan loudly as he pushes it easily inside. I feel the weight of it instantly and when he pushes the second one inside me a moment later, I have to reach down and hold onto him to steady myself as my legs almost buckle.

"They feel good?" he asks with a soft chuckle.

"Yes," I pant. "Are these why you chose the crotchless panties?"

"They're *one* of the reasons, sweetheart," he growls, planting a soft kiss on my ankle before setting my foot down on the floor.

He holds onto my hand as my legs are still shaky. "How do they feel?"

"Heavy," I groan. "Like deliciously heavy. But what if they fall out?" I chew on my lip as Shane jumps to his feet with a grin on his face.

"They won't," he assures me.

"How do you know that?" I whisper. "We could be walking through the restaurant and they'll fall out and roll beneath someone's table. What if that happens? I would die!"

He slides his hand onto my ass and bends his head close to me, brushing his lips over my ear. "Then make sure they don't, sweetheart," he growls before he slaps my ass and straightens up. "Besides," he reaches for my hand and we head for the door. "I've been inside you enough to know that your tight cunt could hold those balls even if they were made of solid granite."

I nudge him in the arm and he laughs loudly, and I'm not sure if it's his laugh, or these damn balls that make my entire body thrum with anticipation.

As we walk along the hallway to the elevator, the balls move inside me, massaging my walls as they jiggle. I squeeze to try and stop them jiggling so much but it doesn't help, in fact it only seems to make it worse. The weights inside are constantly moving, rolling around and sending waves of pleasure pulsing through my body and the weight of them, just sitting there inside me, is making my pussy throb. Shane brushes the pad of his thumb over my knuckles and I whimper.

"I can feel these things moving," I whisper.

"That's kind of the idea, Jessie," he chuckles.

"I can't do this. I can't go a whole evening with these inside me," I chew on my lip. "I can barely think straight."

He lifts my hand to his lips and brushes them over my knuckles and I squirm even more. "It's because you're walking, sweetheart. They won't be so obvious when you're sitting down. We'll be in the car soon."

"Okay," I swallow and take a deep breath. I am going to be nothing more than a puddle on the floor by the time we get to the restaurant.

SHANE KEEPS my hand firmly clasped in his as we walk out of the hotel. "We're over here," he says as we walk towards the valet, who is standing in front of the sexiest car I have ever seen in my life. A Lamborghini Sian. The valet hands the keys to us as we reach him.

"Good evening, Mr. Ryan."

"Did you look after her, Stu?" Shane asks.

"I certainly did, Sir. She's a beauty."

Shane looks at me, his eyes roaming over my body. "She sure is." He licks his lips and I realize he's not talking about the car. The valet coughs awkwardly and excuses himself.

"Wow!" I say as I step towards the car. "This is beautiful. Is it yours?"

"No. I borrowed it." He shakes his head as he leans down to open the door for me. "But we can get one for home if you like?"

"Yes!" I squeal. "And are you letting me drive?"

"No," he says before he kisses me softly. "We drive on the other side of the road over here, sweetheart." He laughs and I look down and realize it's the passenger door he just opened and not the driver's one.

SHANE DRIVES the Lamborghini like he stole it, gunning the engine as hard as he can down the country roads as we head to the restaurant. He was right about the balls. They are less obvious when I'm sitting down. But this car is like one huge tease. Its engine roars so beautifully that it vibrates through my body and whenever Shane's hand is not on the wheel, it is on my thighs, sliding between them and squeezing as if to remind me he is there. As if I could forget.

By the time we reach the restaurant, I am a trembling mess.

Shane gets out of the car first and walks around to open my door. I take his outstretched hand and step out, pulling down the hem of my incredibly short dress.

"You look beautiful," he growls as he slides a hand onto my ass and closes the door behind us.

The damn balls start their incessant rolling again when I take a step and I am overwhelmed by a rush of wet heat between my thighs.

"Shane!" I gasp quietly, holding onto his arm with my free hand.

He turns and looks at me, his face full of concern as his eyes roam over my face. But then his concern turns into something else as he realizes why I'm struggling to even breathe.

"Aw, sweetheart, do you need some relief?" he soothes, his voice as smooth as chocolate and a wicked glint in his eyes.

"Yes," I pant with a nod of my head. "Like, now."

He bends his head down, dusting his lips over the delicate skin on my neck. "Soon, Jessie," he murmurs against me and I whimper.

When we reach the restaurant, Shane is greeted by the owner and one of the waiters. He introduces me, and I force a smile as they make polite small talk with us, while my pussy throbs like a Harley Davidson engine.

When we are finally seated, I am pleased to see we're situated in a booth in a quiet part of the restaurant. Shane slides onto the bench next to me until our thighs are pressed together.

"How're you doing, Hacker?" he chuckles.

"This isn't funny, Shane. I need to get these things out of me."

"Not yet," he says as he slides his hand between my thighs.

"What are you doing?" I clamp my thighs together. "We're in the middle of a restaurant."

"Open," he narrows his eyes at me.

"But someone might see," I gasp as tiny waves of pleasure keep rolling over my body.

"Do not make me ask a second time, Jessie!" he warns.

Like the obedient, dripping mess that I am, I spread my thighs apart slightly, allowing him access to my pussy. He takes hold of the silicone cord.

"What are you doing?" I ask again. Surely he's not going to pull them out here at the table? I was planning on going to the ladies' room.

"Just a little adjustment," he flashes his eyebrows at me as he pushes the balls deeper inside, while twisting them slightly and the jolt of pleasure rockets through my pussy, releasing a rush of wet heat.

"Shane!" I hiss as I hold onto his forearm, digging my nails into his suit jacket. "You're not helping."

"Breathe, Jessie," he soothes in my ear. "You'll be okay now we're sitting down."

I take a deep breath and close my eyes and he pulls his hand from beneath my dress. "Hey," he says and I blink and look at him. "Better now?"

"Yes. A little," I nod my head as the heat starts to subside.

"Dammit, Hacker," he laughs and shakes his head.

"What's so funny?"

"If I had known those things would have you all worked up like this, I'd have used them on you long before now."

I'm just about to reprimand him when the waiter comes

over to take our drinks order. I press my lips and my thighs together as Shane discusses the wine menu and focus on my breathing. By the time the waiter walks away, I feel much more in control.

CHAPTER 13
SHANE

I finish the last bite of my steak and lean back against the bench while Jessie finishes her pasta. Seeing her almost ready to come at the table earlier made me as hard as fucking stone, but it was so much fun watching her squirm. I picked up those balls as an afterthought, thinking they'd be an added element of fun for our evening. I'd had no idea they'd turn her into a trembling mess. I swear I could have kissed that spot on her neck earlier and she'd have come apart at the table. I had considered it too, but making her come would have meant I'd have had to take her out of here and fuck her, and I was hungry. Besides, I had promised her dinner and I always deliver on my promises.

She seemed to have calmed down while we were eating and I figure she's getting used to the sensation of those things rolling around in her pussy. Now that we have almost finished dinner, they won't be staying in there much longer, because I can't wait to get inside her sweet little cunt myself. My cock is twitching in my pants at the thought.

Jessie puts her silverware onto the table and pushes her

plate away. "I'm done. If I eat any more I won't be able to move," she declares.

"You want dessert?" I ask.

"Nope," she shakes her head. "Not in this dress," she laughs as she rubs a hand over her stomach. "You?"

"No. Nothing from this menu, anyway."

"Oh?' she purrs as she turns to me brushing her hand over my thigh. "And where is your dessert menu then, Mr. Ryan?"

I lean closer to her, brushing my lips over her ear. Damn! She smells so fucking good. Sweeter than any dessert I've ever tasted. "You already know that my dessert is in your panties, sweetheart. So, if you don't want me to eat it at this table, I suggest you behave yourself."

"I am behaving." She bites her lip and my cock throbs.

"Come here." I reach for her hand.

"I am here," she whispers.

"Here!" I look down at my lap.

"You want me to sit on your lap here in the restaurant?"

"It's dark back here. The staff know not to disturb us," I pull her towards me and she shuffles her body until she is sitting with her legs draped over mine, her feet resting on the bench and her back to the room.

"How is my dessert doing?" I whisper in her ear as I slide my hand between her thighs.

"It's kind of..." she tilts her head as she considers her reply, "creamy?"

"Damn! Jessie. I'm going to fuck you so hard when we get out of here, sweetheart. My cock is busting to get inside you."

"So shall we leave?" she arches one eyebrow at me.

"You want to?" I ask as my fingers slide between her folds and I tug gently on the balls.

"Shane!" she groans and shudders on my lap.

"Or you want me to make you come first, sweetheart?" I tug

again as I brush the pad of my thumb over her clit, and she wraps her arms around me, pressing her face into my neck. "Your choice?" I growl as I hook my finger into the small heart loop at the end of the retrieval cord and move them in and out of her while I keep toying with her clit.

"God!" she pants. "Make me come, Shane. Please."

"Good girl."

I work the balls in and out of her pussy and her juices run out of her, soaking my fingers. I can smell her sweet cum and it makes me desperate to taste her, and while I would happily eat her out in front of these diners, I know she would rather I didn't.

"Shane!" she whimpers, so close to the edge I feel her muscles trembling. My girl has been on the edge of this all night, and I'll be fucked if I'm going to let some metallic balls have the pleasure of feeling her come. I pull them out of her and she groans into my neck in frustration as I stuff them into my jacket pocket.

"It's okay, I've got you," I whisper in her ear, pulling her tighter to me as I slide two fingers inside her hot cunt. My own balls draw up into my stomach when I do because she feels fucking incredible. "Damn, Jessie. You're fucking soaking, sweetheart," I groan as her cum runs down my fingers and onto my wrist. "You really liked those balls inside you, huh?"

"Yes," she groans as she rocks her hips against my hand. "But not as much as your fingers."

I curl the tips of them inside her, pressing against that spot that makes her shudder and she clings onto me even tighter. I don't even see the waiter approaching our table as I work her and my cock weeps as my girl keeps on whimpering in my ear. "Would you like to see the dessert menu, Sir?" he asks.

Jessie gasps at the sound of his voice but I keep going, and I scowl at him. "I'm kind of fucking busy here."

"I'm sorry, Mr. Ryan," he stammers.

"You will be. Don't ever fucking interrupt me again." He nods before he skulks away and I press my lips against Jessie's ear. "It's okay, he's gone."

"I don't care," she groans as she rakes her nails over my chest and back. Her cunt squeezes around my fingers and I push harder. With my free hand, I push her face against my neck because she is about to come. Hard.

"Shane!" she groans loudly and her entire body shudders on my lap as her pussy draws my fingers deeper and her juices coat my whole hand.

"Fuck, sweetheart!" I growl as I brush her hair back from her face. "I am desperate to taste you." I slide my fingers out of her and suck them into my mouth, cleaning her juices from them while she clings onto me, letting the last of her orgasm roll through her.

"That was..." she pants into my neck, "incredible."

"I know. Damn, you taste so fucking sweet, I need to get you out of here because I'm about half a minute away from nailing you right here in this booth."

"Okay," she nods and I straighten her dress before she climbs off my lap. My suit pants are stained with her cum but I have never been more desperate to get inside a woman as I am right now for her. I want to eat her alive and then I want to fuck her until neither of us can stand. I consider taking her into the restroom but I need to spread her open somewhere and bury my face in her pussy.

CHAPTER 14
JESSIE

We leave the restaurant in a hurry and Shane practically runs us to the car.

"I wish I'd chosen a car with a bigger fucking interior now," he growls when we're inside and he looks around the tiny two seater.

"Me too," I giggle.

"Fuck, sweetheart. I'm gonna die if I don't fuck you soon," he growls as he starts the ignition and the engine roars to life. "Let's get the hell out of here."

We've been driving for a few minutes when Shane turns down a tiny country lane. I assume he knows a short cut to the hotel but when then he pulls over and turns off the engine. Before I can even ask what's going on, he has unclipped his seatbelt and jumped out of the car. He runs around to the passenger side and opens the door.

"Come on," he holds out a hand to me.

"What are you doing?" I say as I grab his hand and a thrill of excitement shoots through me.

"If I can't fuck you in this three million dollar car, sweetheart, then I'm sure as hell gonna fuck you on it."

I step out into the road. It's dark and the only light is from the interior of the car and the moon. "What if someone sees us?" I gasp as he pulls me toward the front of the car and pushes me back against the hood.

"I'm beyond caring, Jessie," he growls as he pulls my dress up until it's bunched around my waist before he pushes me all the way back. The metal of the car is warm from the engine but goosebumps skitter over my skin.

"Shane! We can't..." I begin to protest but then he drops to his knees and plants my feet on his shoulders before he wraps his arms around the back of my thighs. My pussy throbs in anticipation as he presses his face against it and inhales deeply. The animalistic grunts he makes vibrate through my body.

"These panties are soaking, Jessie," he groans. "You're dripping with cum, sweetheart."

"Oh God," I gasp loudly as another release of wet heat flushes between my thighs and Shane begins sucking at my opening as he rubs his nose over my clit and I feel the waves of another orgasm already building. When he runs his tongue the length of my folds, I shudder. But when he sucks my clit into his mouth and pushes a finger inside me at the same time, my hips almost shoot off the car, but he presses on my lower abdomen, holding me in place.

It starts to rain and tiny droplets of water start to pepper my skin but he is undeterred. He increases the pressure and pace until my orgasm tears through my body like he has ignited a keg of gunpowder.

My legs tremble as he licks and sucks every last tremor from me and I moan his name. When he stands, his hands go straight to his belt and zipper and I look up at him. His eyes blaze with fire and he licks his lips which are glistening with my arousal. The rain is falling heavier now, but neither of us care as he pulls his beautiful cock free and edges closer to me.

Lifting my legs, I wrap them around his waist as he presses the tip against my opening. "I have never wanted to fuck anyone as much as I do you right now, Jessie."

"Please, Shane?" I pant as I reach for him, tugging at the lapels of his suit jacket until he folds over me, pressing his lips against mine as he drives his cock into me. His tongue slides into my mouth as he nails me to the hood of this beautiful car. The rain gets heavier and heavier, until it is dripping from his hair onto my face and the back of his jacket is saturated, but all we're focused on is the primal need to take as much of each other as we possibly can.

I run my fingers through his hair, pulling at the wet strands as I squeeze my legs tighter around his waist while his hands fist in my hair and he rails into me like we might never get the chance to do this again.

"Your pussy is a magnet for my cock, sweetheart," he groans into my mouth. "I can't keep the fuck out of you."

As he keeps on fucking me relentlessly, I tip over the edge again, shouting his name into the darkness as he grinds out his own release.

CHAPTER 15
JESSIE

Shane is sitting up in bed with his hands behind his head when I walk out of the bathroom. We were both soaked through by the time we got back to the hotel an hour ago, and even more so after when we ended up in the shower together fully clothed. Not that our clothes stayed on for long.

I take off my towel, grab one of his t-shirts from the drawer and pull it on before I walk to the bed.

He watches me with a wicked grin on his face. "There are no clothes allowed in bed. You should know that, Jessie. It's the law here in Ireland."

"Oh really?" I smile back. "And whose law is that? Ryan's law?"

"Well, that's the only one you need to concern yourself with, sweetheart. Now take it off."

"But I'm cold."

"That's what duvets and hot chocolate are for."

I glance over and see the two mugs of hot chocolate on the nightstand, each with tiny marshmallows floating on top.

"You made hot chocolate?"

"Relax, Hacker. I only poured water onto some powder," he says with a roll of his eyes. "Now take off the damn t-shirt."

Knowing this is an argument I'm not going to win, not that I particularly want to, I peel it off over my head and jump into bed. He wraps an arm around me and pulls the duvet over us both before he hands me a mug.

I wrap my hands around it and take a sip of the hot, frothy liquid. It has quite a kick. "You add your own special ingredient too?" I ask with a sigh as the chocolate and liquor warm my throat.

"Hmm. I might have," he chuckles.

"Are you trying to get me drunk, Shane Ryan?"

He hugs me tighter to him. "Now why would I want to do that, sweetheart, when I only have to kiss your neck to make you wet?"

I nudge him lightly in the ribs and he chuckles. "You're an arrogant asshole. Have I ever told you that?"

"Many, many times," he says before he plants a kiss on the top of my head. "Doesn't mean I don't speak the truth though."

I snuggle into him, sipping my chocolate. He does speak the truth. In fact, he doesn't even have to kiss my neck. Just the way he looks at me has me a hot trembling mess.

"No sassy comeback?"

"No," I say with a contended sigh. "Now what are we watching?"

He picks up the remote with his free hand and turns on the TV and *Mamma Mia* is on. "I love this film," I shriek.

"Fuck no!" he snaps as he lifts the remote to switch over.

"Aw please, Shane. I don't usually like rom-coms, but this one just does it for me. Please can we watch it?"

He groans loudly. "For fuck's sake!" He tosses the remote onto the bed, but then he leans back, wrapping his arm tighter around me and resting his cheek on my head. “You owe me big time for this, Hacker.”

“I’ll do anything you want, Sir,” I purr as I snuggle against his chest.

“Behave!” he growls. “Or you won’t get a chance to watch the movie or finish that hot chocolate.”

“And why is that?” I whisper.

“Because your mouth will be otherwise engaged.”

THE FOLLOWING MORNING, I lie in bed, still in an orgasm induced haze as I watch Shane dressing. He is going out for the day and I am once again confined to the hotel room. Not that I haven’t enjoyed a few days of relaxing, but I am easily bored.

“Maybe I’ll go down to the pool today,” I say as I chew on my lip.

“You know I’d rather you didn’t leave the suite,” he frowns at me.

“I know you said that, but I get bored.”

“Call Conor or the twins. I’m sure they’ll keep you busy,” he winks at me.

“Oh, I know. But what about the rest of the time?” I sigh dramatically. “And I have a beautiful pink string bikini that I’ve still not worn.”

Shane glares at me. He is aware I have such a bikini, because he bought it for me. It is indecent bordering on the obscene, and I have no intention of wearing it anywhere other than at the rooftop pool back home in New York.

“You brought that here?” he asks with a frown.

“Hmm?” I screw my face up as though I’m deep in thought. “Actually, I don’t think I packed it.”

He arches one eyebrow at me as he fixes his cufflink. “Do you try and grind my gears on purpose?”

"You know that I do," I grin at him.

He sits on the bed beside me and grabs my chin in his strong hand, his eyes narrowed as he stares at me. "You looking for another spanking sweetheart?"

"Well the one you gave me the other day was pretty tame. For you anyway."

"Oh really?"

"Really," I purr. "You know I can take much more than that."

"Hmm." He leans down and gives me a soft kiss on the lips that makes my insides melt like warm butter.

I snake my arms around his neck. "Stay with me today."

"I would love to, but I can't, sweetheart," he replies with a frown as he brushes my hair back from my face. "I've still got plenty to do before we go home."

"Anything I can help with?"

He shakes his head. "Not really. But I appreciate the offer." He sucks in a breath. "Please stay in the room today. And then tonight, I am all yours. And if you want that pretty ass of yours spanked hard, I am very up for that."

Heat surges between my thighs at the thought. "With your belt?"

"With anything you want, Hacker," he growls as he kisses me again.

"Can we go out too? I know you're going to let me drive that car some time, right?" I bite on my lip, trying to appear as seductive as possible.

"We'll see," he growls. "My uncle is in town. I'm hoping to catch up with him today. I'd like for you to meet him. Maybe later?"

"Is he as lovely as your Aunt?"

That makes him laugh out loud. "Lovely is not how I'd describe him, but he is certainly interesting."

"I like interesting."

"I'm sure you'll like him," he winks at me. "But I've got to go." He untangles himself from me and stands up. Grabbing his suit jacket from the chair, he shrugs it on. "Behave yourself and I'll be back as soon as I can."

"I'll miss you," I flutter my eyelashes at him.

He glares at me for a few seconds, those incredible green eyes of his ablaze with fire, then he stalks toward the bed in two strides and pushes me back, lying on top of me with the full weight of his body. He threads his fingers though mine and pins my hands either side of my head before he presses his lips over mine and kisses me so fiercely that my head spins. Our tongues swirl together and I spread my thighs wider so he drops between them. I feel his cock hardening through the duvet. I whimper into his mouth and it sends him into a fervor as he deepens our kiss.

When he finally lets me up for air he stares into my eyes. "I love you," he whispers.

I blink away a tear. "I love you, too," I breathe.

"I'll see you tonight." Then he kisses my nose and pushes himself off the bed and I watch his fine ass as he heads for the door and walks out without looking back again.

CHAPTER 16
SHANE

I walk through the parking lot of The Peacock Club and look around at the cars parked up outside. From the shiny BMWs to the Audis, it seems like most of Sean O'Connor's men have turned up for this meeting today, as well as the arrogant prick himself. My brothers and I have just bought a chain of these clubs. They are a little different to what we usually deal in, but when I heard they were for sale, my interest was piqued. They cater to a very particular clientele. Sex clubs, I think most people would call them, but from my research I have discovered they are so much more than that. And now my brothers and I own six of them across the world. I can't deny that Jessie influenced my decision, not that she knows about them yet, but I can't wait to take her to one of them some day.

The club is closed during the day, so it's the perfect spot to do a little business while I'm here. The manager opened up for me half an hour ago and has now left to allow me the run of the place undisturbed.

I open the double doors and walk down the hallway. I don't know what I'd expected the place to look like, but it wasn't this. It is tasteful and elegant, with muted colors and chrome and glass. I suppose I'd been expecting leather and red paint. There are huge mirrored doors at the end of the hallway which I assume lead into the main club area. Someone leans against the wall just in front of them. I haven't seen him for twenty-five years and he has a long beard now, but I would still recognize him anywhere. He grins at me as I approach and I smile back. "What the fuck are you doing here?"

He holds out his arms. "It's good to see you, kid."

I walk into his embrace. "It's good to see you too, Pol."

We hug for a few seconds and I realize how much I've missed him. After my mom, my Uncle Paul was my favorite grown up when I was a kid. He taught me how to shoot and how to skin a rabbit. The former skill I have been grateful of, and have perfected over the years. The latter, not so much. "How the fuck did you know I'd be here?" I ask as I step back from him.

"What?" he arches an eyebrow at me. "O'Connor has been telling every fucker who will listen he's meeting you here today."

"He never could keep his mouth shut."

Paul arches an eyebrow at me. "I hear he's got a busted face and a broken arm."

"Yeah? Well, he touched what didn't belong to him."

"A girl?" Paul chuckles softly.

"My girl."

Paul nods his head. "She something special, is she?"

"Like you wouldn't believe."

"Oh, I can believe it," he says with a nod and a faraway look in his eyes that makes me wonder who he's thinking of.

"Where the fuck have you been Pol? I thought you were dead?"

"Here. There. Everywhere." He shakes his head as though he's annoyed with himself about something.

"You married? Got any kids?"

"No and no."

"But there is someone, right?" I ask, thinking of his reaction a few seconds earlier.

"Hmm. There was."

"Was?"

"Is," he snaps and I wonder what the story is there because I have definitely pushed some kind of button. "Look, we gonna stand here reminiscing or are we gonna get in there and fuck up Sean O'Connor's day?"

"And what makes you think I'm going to do that?" I frown at him.

"Well, you're not handing operations over to him, are you?" he asks, a little more of his Irish accent creeping into his voice the more he talks to me.

"Not a chance in hell."

"After you then, kid," he says as he indicates the door.

I pull it open and walk inside the room with my uncle close behind me. There are a dozen men in the room. Sean O'Connor sits in the middle of them, the ringmaster of this particular circus. His face is a mess and his arm is in a sling and I can't help but smile as I approach him.

"You're late," he snarls.

"What can I say? My girl wouldn't let me get out of bed."

"I bet," he snarls. "She looked like a slut."

I don't have to act because Paul does it for me, walking straight over to O'Connor and grabbing him by the throat. "Apologize!" he snarls as O'Connor's men look on. Although, I suppose they are no longer O'Connor's men. They are mine.

O'Connor's face is turning blue. He fumbles at his jacket but Paul only squeezes tighter and Sean looks like he's about to pass out. "Sorry!" he eventually wheezes and Paul releases him.

"Thank you for coming here this morning, gentlemen," I say

as I shove my hands in my pockets and finger the brass knuckles I have in there. I'll be happily using them on Sean O'Connor's face if he utters one more word about Jessie. "I won't keep you long, but I wanted to tell you how things are going to be now that my father is dead."

Sean snorts and shakes his head.

"You got something to say first?" I snarl.

"Yes." He pulls a gun out of his jacket and points it at me. "*We* are going to tell *you* how things are going to work around here. Now that your father is dead, the reign of the Ryan family is officially over."

I narrow my eyes at him. "You think so?"

"I know so," he spits.

I look beside him at his second-in-command, Cormac Macaulay, who rolls his eyes.

"Can someone kindly escort this piece of shit out of here?" I ask as I look around the room for a willing volunteer. Five men stand up.

"I can, Boss," one of them says.

Sean stares at them with an open mouth and waves his gun at me again. Cormac stands up and no doubt thinking his right-hand man is leaping to his defense, Sean stands with him.

"I think it's only right that I do it," Cormac says.

"What the fuck?" Sean snarls but Cormac has disarmed him and has his arm up his back before he can even finish the sentence.

"Didn't you know Cormac and I are old friends, Sean?" I frown at him. "I would have thought a man of your intelligence would have figured that out by now."

"Snake!" Sean spits. "Macaulay, you ungrateful cunt!"

"Yeah, okay," Cormac chuckles. "Your time is up, Sean, but I'm willing to at least let you walk out of here with a little dignity."

Sean shrugs Cormac off him and straightens his coat. "Cheeky fucking cunts! Every one of you!" He points at the men seated around the room. "You'll all fucking regret this!" he hisses and then he storms out of the room.

Once he is gone, I turn back to the assembled men. "As I was saying, here is how things are going to work from now on. I'm going back to New York as soon as my father's funeral is over. I don't have time to be back and forth to Ireland every five minutes to check on what you are up to. I trust Cormac, so as far as you're concerned, he speaks for me. I trust that all of you will just keep doing what you're doing. There is no need for anyone to be negatively affected by my father's death. Things will continue as they were, but with Cormac at the helm. Understood?"

"Yes," they all nod their heads and voice their agreement.

"Good. Now clear off," I say and they all stand to leave. "Not you," I say to Cormac and he nods his head and takes a seat again.

"Nicely done," Paul says when there are only the three of us left in the room. "Now how about you fix all of us a nice whiskey from that well stocked bar there?" He nods his head toward it.

"What am I? Your fucking bartender?" I frown at him.

He laughs and shakes his head. "I don't see my nephew for twenty-five years and this is how he treats me." He slides off his suit jacket and hangs it over the back of his chair. "Shall I fetch us a drink then?" He coughs and rubs his chest.

"Sit down, old man," I say with a sigh. "I'll get us a fucking drink."

"Take off your coat if you're staying, lad," Paul says to Cormac. "Makes me uneasy when people wear coats indoors. Like they're hiding something. We're all friends, aren't we?"

Cormac looks at me and I nod my head and take off my

jacket too before I walk behind the bar and pour us all a large measure of fine Irish whiskey.

WHEN WE EACH HAVE A DRINK, Paul, Cormac and I raise our glasses in a toast. "To the most evil cunt to have ever walked this earth," Paul says before he downs his. Both Cormac and I nod our agreement but I have never seen such obvious, undisguised hatred for my father from Paul before. I mean I knew that he always hated him, but his venom now is only matched by my own, and I had plenty more reasons to hate my father than our uncle did. Or so I always thought. Now I know differently and my conversation from two days ago with my Aunt reminds me that I need to speak to him, but it's a conversation we need to have in private.

Cormac and I down our whiskey too and the three of us slam our glasses down onto the table. Paul wipes his mouth with the back of his hand. "I need to go."

I frown at him. "Now?"

"Yeah. Something I have to do." He stands up and puts his jacket back on.

"I need to talk to you about something, Pol."

"Yeah, I know," he nods his head. "Later, though. I want to meet this girl of yours too."

"Then at least leave me your number?" I frown at him.

"Okay," he nods his head and takes his cell out of his pocket before pressing some buttons. My own cell phone vibrates in my pocket.

"Now you got it," he says, still clearly distracted by something.

"Dinner tonight?" I suggest.

"Tonight," he agrees but he is a million miles away.

"Good to meet you Paul," Cormac says as my uncle starts to walk away.

"Yeah. You too, kid. See you later, Shane." He winks at me and then he walks out.

"Seems like he had to be somewhere real fast," Cormac says with a smile.

"Yeah," I frown as I watch him leave. "Slippery fucker. Did he say anything while I was getting drinks?"

"He only asked how long I'd known you, but then I had to take a piss, so we didn't talk long."

I nod my head absent mindedly and then I remember the real reason I am here today. I have known Cormac since we were teenagers, ever since we both started working for my father. He has always hated Sean O'Connor as much as I have, and he was never my father's biggest fan either. I lost touch with him when we moved to New York, but once I found out Patrick was dying, I reached out to Cormac and he soon proved himself to be the perfect choice to take over here.

"I appreciate you giving me this opportunity, Shane," Cormac adds. "I won't let you down."

"I know."

I SPENT another two hours with Cormac discussing the next steps for our businesses here in Ireland, and I am even more sure now that I have made the right choice in appointing him as the new head of our operations. He is a good businessman, rational and fair, but ruthless when he needs to be. I'm happy to be able to leave this behind and focus on our business in New York.

CHAPTER 17
JESSIE

I sip my tea and stare out the window at the beautiful view. I had a hot video call with the twins earlier and it was so much fun I had to shower after, but now I'm bored. I should have insisted on going with Shane today. I hate being in my own company for too long.

I wonder if his Aunt Em is busy? She said we should visit as soon as we could and I bet she wouldn't mind if I went alone. I could ask Shane if his driver could take me and then he could meet me there later. She and I got along so well. Maybe going without Shane would be a better idea anyway, because she could give me all of the stories from his childhood that he'd probably rather she didn't.

I smile to myself at that thought and look around the room for my cell and frown when I don't see it. I must have left it in the bathroom.

As I stand up, I hear the sound of the door handle and look toward it. The door opens and my heart skips a beat. "You're back early," I shout as I make my way to the bathroom.

He doesn't reply and I turn to look at him.

"Hello Jessica."

It's not Shane.

My feet seem to grow roots, anchoring me to the carpet. My blood turns to ice as it trickles through my veins and my heart stops beating in my chest. Time stands still. I want to run but my body won't let me move.

"How?" I stutter as I stare at the face that has haunted my dreams for ten long years.

He holds up the electronic keycard. "Shane gave me this."

"He wouldn't," I stammer.

"No?" he smiles at me. It is cruel and twisted. It mocks me. He stalks toward me but I still stand frozen to the spot. My bladder suddenly feels like it's about to burst and I close my eyes, willing my body not to betray me. "You have no idea who Shane Ryan is, Jessica," he hisses as he steps closer. "He told you he wanted you to meet his Uncle Paul, didn't he?"

My eyes snap open. "No." I shake my head. "You're not him."

"Oh, I am, little bird," he hisses as he finally reaches me. He towers over me. His beard is longer and bushier now, no doubt to hide the scars on his neck from when I almost killed him, but those cold, gray eyes are exactly as I remember. He runs a fingertip over my cheek and I shudder at his touch. I want to shrink back from him. I want to kick him in the balls and run, but I am frozen in fear.

"My nephews have been keeping you warm for me until it was safe for me to claim you again."

I try to swallow but my throat is raw and tight. "No." I shake my head again as tears start to run down my cheeks. This can't be happening. This can't be true. I must have fallen asleep on that huge king-size bed, the one that Shane and I made love on just a few hours ago. The one I was lying on when Mikey and Liam told me how much they loved me.

"Yes, little bird," he croons as he leans closer to me. The

smell of cigarettes clings to his clothes and a wave of nausea almost overwhelms me. "Shane handed me this key himself and told me you'd be ready for me. He's a good boy, my nephew. All of them are."

"You're lying," I hiss, finally able to move I take a step back from him. There's a gun here somewhere. I have to find it. Where the hell did Shane put it?

"I would never lie to you, my love."

At last, adrenaline finally kicks in and it surges through my veins. I lunge for him. "I am not your love!" I screech as I aim for his eyes. But he is still quick. He dodges out of my way and I scratch his neck instead.

"Still my feisty little bird," he mocks me as he grabs hold of my hands and squeezes my wrists painfully. "I taught you so well."

"I hate you," I kick out at him but he steps back. He has a foot and one hundred pounds on me and experience reminds me I am no match for him. Perhaps if I had been prepared? Perhaps if I hadn't been completely blindsided by his revelations.

"You and I have so much to catch up on," he chuckles as he twists me around, holding both of my wrists in one hand now, until my back is pressed against his chest and his hot breath is at my ear. "So much."

I wriggle as I feel him reaching into his pocket.

"You're all mine now," he whispers and that is the last thing I hear. I feel a sharp scratch on my neck, and then there is nothing.

CHAPTER 18
SHANE

I check all of my pockets for my keycard but it's not in there. I'm sure I picked it up this morning. I knock on the door instead and wait for Jessie to answer. She doesn't open and I knock louder before I shout.

"Jessie! It's me."

Still nothing. I take my cell out of my pocket. She must be in the shower. Before I can dial her number, one of the hotel maids steps out of the elevator. She smiles at me. "Good evening, Mr. Ryan."

Everyone in this place seems to know my name. "Evening. Could you let me in here?" I nod toward the door. "I forgot my key."

"Of course, Sir," she says as she walks over and swipes her card.

"Thank you." I smile at her and she giggles before I step inside the room.

"Jessie!" I shout again as I look around the suite and head to the bedroom. I walk inside and she's not there either. The bathroom door is open and I don't hear her in there, but I go in and check anyway. Where the fuck is she? My heart starts to race a little but I tell myself that there's a reasonable explanation. She has gone to the spa downstairs. To the pool, like she said she would. Or maybe to the restaurant or the store.

My cell is still in my hand so I dial her number. A second later, her current ringtone, *Like I Can,* plays loudly in the bathroom and my racing pulse starts to thunder. She would never have gone out without her cell.

I run back into the bathroom and see her phone sitting there, flashing and vibrating while Sam Smith sings at the top of their voice. I end the call and put my cell back into my pocket before picking hers up. She has a missed call from me and one from Conor half an hour ago. I grip it tightly in my hand and walk back out into the suite.

"Jessie!" I shout louder now. I mean, she's so small she could have fallen asleep under a table or something, right?

"Jessie. Where the fuck are you, sweetheart?" I shout again as I search every inch of the room even though I already know she's not here. So many emotions flood my senses that I don't know which one to deal with. Suddenly, I am reminded of that day in New York when we came home to find she'd gone, leaving only a brief note to explain her absence.

I scan the room again, ashamed for even thinking it, but there is no note. My heart sinks as I realize that's worse. Because if she didn't leave of her own accord, then someone fucking took her.

Using the phone in the room, I call down to the front desk.

"Good evening, Mr. Ryan," the desk clerk answers.

"Have you seen Mrs. Ryan today?" I ask, not bothering with formalities as I don't have the time.

"No, Sir," she says, "but I've only been on shift for a few hours."

"Can you check the spa for me? Or the restaurant? Basically, every single place in this hotel. I need to know if she's here," I snap, unable to contain my anxiety.

"Of course. Hold on for one moment."

I sit on the sofa with the phone against my ear and my head in my hand, waiting for her to get back to me and tell me that Jessie is down there somewhere. Because that's still a possibility, right?

The wait feels like forever until she finally comes back to me. "I'm sorry, Mr. Ryan, but Mrs. Ryan isn't in the hotel."

"You're sure?"

"As you're one of our exclusive guests, I contacted security and they have checked everywhere. She isn't here. I also checked with my colleague on the desk who's been on shift all day and he hasn't seen her leave."

"You have CCTV though?"

"Of course."

"Tell your security manager I want to see him at my suite right now," I snap.

"Of course, Sir."

I put the phone down and take out my cell again. I dial Conor's number as I keep searching the room for clues that will lead me to some plausible explanation for her absence. There's a half empty cup of tea on the table near the window next to the easy chair. Jessie never leaves a cup of tea. She says it's rude to not finish a drink someone has gone to so much effort to make, even if the effort was only hers. I feel the side of the cup. It's cold.

"Hey, bro?" Conor answers.

"Hey. Have you spoken to Jessie today?" I ask as I try to keep my voice as calm as possible.

"No. I called her before but she didn't answer, so I assumed you two were busy." He chuckles softly and when I don't laugh too, he stops. "Something wrong?"

"Have the twins spoken to her?"

"Yeah, why?"

"Are they there, Con?"

"Yeah." I hear an edge creeping into his voice. "I'll put you on speaker."

"What's up?" Mikey asks and the hope and happiness in his voice almost crushes me as I realize I am about to bring their world crashing down around them all.

"When did you speak to Jessie?"

"About three hours ago."

"How was she?"

Mikey starts to laugh and Liam answers instead. "She was good, bro."

"She was more than good by the time we were done with her," Mikey adds.

I swallow the ball of emotion that is lodged in my throat. "Did she say anything about what she had planned for the rest of the day?"

"She said she was going to have a shower then hang about the room waiting for you to come back. She was pumped about her plan to convince you to let her drive the Sian," Liam says but the tone of his voice has changed now.

"Why, Shane?" Conor interrupts. "What's going on? Why aren't you asking Jessie this?"

I close my eyes, screwing them tightly shut as I try to find the words. But there is only one way to tell them and to break their hearts. "I came back to the room and she's not here."

"Maybe she just went out for something?" Mikey says but I hear the panic in his voice.

"Her cell is here. Her purse is here," I say as I notice it on the floor. Not that Jessie ever takes her purse anywhere. "Everything is here. Her coat. Her things." I swallow.

"Fuck!" Mikey hisses.

"You know she didn't walk out on us though, right?" Conor asks.

"Yeah."

"The Wolf?" Liam says and I hear the panic in his voice.

"Maybe," I finally admit my greatest fear out loud.

"Fuck, Shane!" Conor snaps and I feel the guilt weighing heavily on me. He was right. She would have been safer with them. He doesn't push it any further though.

"We'll be on the next flight," Mikey says.

"Yeah," Liam adds.

I let out a long breath. They have all sworn they would never set foot in Ireland again, but I can't do this without them. I am more grateful for them now than I have ever been.

"We'll see you in the morning, bro," Conor says. "But keep us updated, yeah?"

"I will. I'm meeting with the head of security in a few minutes. We'll go through the security feeds. See if there's anything."

"You got anyone else there who can help you out?" Conor asks.

"Pol is here," I say as I'm suddenly grateful for my uncle too. "I'll ask him to help. I don't trust anyone else right now."

"It might be that cunt O'Connor who's taken her?" Conor suggests.

"I'll be looking into him, don't worry," I snarl. He was one of the first people who came to my mind too.

"We've got some flights to organize," Liam chips in. "We'll see you soon, bro."

"I'll make sure there is a car with everything you need waiting at the airport. See you tomorrow," I say and end the call just as there is a knock at the door of the hotel room.

CHAPTER 19
SHANE

I open the door to a tall man with dark hair, a goatee and an anxious expression on his face.

"Mr. Ryan, my name is Marvin George. I'm the director of security here at the hotel."

"Come on in," I say to him as I hold the door open.

I note the laptop he is carrying under his arm and he opens it up as soon as he sits down. "I had one of my security guards check the floor as soon as you reported Mrs. Ryan missing," he says and his Adam's apple bobs in his throat.

"And?" I snap.

"If you look at the time stamps," he taps a few keys on the keyboard and an image of the empty hallway outside fills the screen, "there has been an hour of footage wiped from our systems. From every single camera."

"What?" I frown at him. "I chose this hotel because it was a safe place for my wife to stay, and you're telling me someone hacked into your security feed and erased it?" I shout at him, even though I know no matter how good your security is, there will always be someone who can hack it. Someone like Jessie.

"I'm sorry, Sir. We are doing everything we can to discover how this happened, but..."

"But nothing!" I snarl at him. "Do you have anything at all that might help me find her?"

"Not yet, but I can assure you I have all of my staff making enquiries."

"Enquiries?" I run my hands through my hair. "I'm going to need more than fucking enquiries, Marvin!"

"I will do everything in my power to assist you, Sir," he says as he stands and picks up his laptop.

I nod at him. "See if anyone saw or heard anything suspicious today. No matter how small or insignificant it may seem, I want to know about it."

"Of course," he says with a nod. "I'll leave you to it."

I watch him walk out of the door and pick up my cell again and dial Paul's number. It takes him a while to answer and when he does he is out of breath.

"Hey, kid," he answers.

"Paul, I need your help."

"Why?"

"My girl. Jessie. She's disappeared. Someone's taken her."

"You sure she didn't just go out shopping or something? You know what women are like."

"No, Paul. She is gone. Now are you going to help me find her or not?"

He takes a few moments to answer me. "Of course. You think it was that prick O'Connor?"

"Maybe," I say, hoping that it is him, because I know where to find him. But if she has been taken by the Wolf, I am worried we might never get her back. "Can you meet me at my hotel?"

"Sure. I'll be there as soon as I can."

. . .

My heart is in my throat as I close the door to our suite. What if she comes back and I'm not here? I shake my head and walk to the elevator. I'm going to speak to the desk clerk again while I wait for Paul. Someone must have seen her leaving here today. Maybe Erin even saw something? It's a long shot but I am already clutching at straws here.

A few moments later, I stand outside Erin's room and wait for her to open the door. I doubt she will have any useful information but then right now I don't know what's useful.

The door opens a few seconds later. "Shane?" She looks at me in surprise as she fastens her earring. "I was just getting ready for dinner. Come on in."

I follow her inside and close the door.

"You fancy a drink?" she asks with a smile.

"No," I shake my head. "Have you see Jessie today?"

"No. I've been working all day. Should I have?"

"No, but she's gone missing," I say the words and even though I know they're true, they don't seem real.

Erin stares at me and I swear I see a smirk flicker over her lips.

"Did you just fucking grin at me?" I snarl.

She sighs dramatically. "Oh come on, Shane, it's not like she hasn't walked out on you before."

I cross the room to her in one stride. I have never laid a finger on this woman in anger. Not even when I found out she had been lying to me for years. Not even when she accused my brothers of ruining our engagement. I grab her throat and she blinks up at me in shock as I push her back against the wall.

"She did not *walk out*," I hiss as I squeeze her throat harder. "Somebody fucking took her."

"Shane! You're hurting me," she whimpers.

"Hurting you?" I narrow my eyes at her. "You're lucky I don't snap your fucking neck. I know you don't like her, but she is fucking everything to me. *Everything*! And you fucking smile when I tell you she's missing." I release her from my grip, afraid that I might go too far if I don't let her go now.

Erin rubs at her throat and gasps for breath but I don't have an ounce of sympathy for her. She has made her dislike for Jessie clear from the outset.

"I'm sorry," she mumbles.

"Have you seen anything suspicious at all?".

"No," she says with a shake of her head.

I glare at her and then I walk out of her room, but she shouts to me before I reach the door. "Everything? Really?" she sniffs.

I turn on my heel and look at her. "And then some."

CHAPTER 20
CONOR

I close the safe in Shane's office and walk down the hallway to my brothers' room to find them frantically packing. As soon as we got off the call with Shane, I started to look for flights while they made arrangements for the club and the businesses for the next few days. It was good we all had something practical to focus on because it prevented us from spinning out worrying about what the hell has happened to Jessie. Walking inside Liam and Mikey's bedroom, I toss their passports onto the bed.

"Alejandro's plane is at LAX and it will take at least six hours to get here and refuel."

Liam frowns at me. "That's too long."

"I know, so I got us on a flight that leaves in two hours. Better get your asses moving. The car will be downstairs in fifteen."

"Thanks," they reply in unison. I turn to go to my own room and throw a few things in a bag when Mikey's voice stops me.

"We'll find her, won't we, Con?"

I swallow hard and keep heading for the door because I can't look at them and lie. "Of course we fucking will."

I slam the door behind me and take a deep breath as I press my forehead against the wall. My heart is hammering so hard in my ears that I can barely hear myself think. I feel so helpless being thousands of miles away from Jessie and Shane and powerlessness is a feeling I am unused to and one I do not fucking like. It brings up far too many bad memories for me. What if we don't get her back? What if the Wolf has already taken her somewhere we can never find her? What if someone else has her and she's already dead? What if she is out there in pain somewhere, wondering where we are?

Breathe in.

Out.

Don't lose it now, Conor. Not when everyone needs you so much.

The door opens and I snap my head up.

"You okay, bro?" Liam looks at me, his eyes narrowed in concern.

"Just taking a breath, kid," I reply.

He puts a hand on my shoulder. "We'll be there in a few hours and then we'll get her back. I know we will."

I nod in agreement even though I don't share his confidence. I will do everything I can to bring her back to us, but what if it's already too late?

CHAPTER 21
JESSIE

My head throbs as I blink in the dim room.

My vision is blurred.

I'm naked.

I shiver from the cold and instinctively pull my arms to my chest to warm myself, but I can't move. Cold metal cuffs bite into the skin on my wrists.

I pull harder but all I hear is the dull clinking of chains.

Where am I?

The Wolf!

He took me. I look around the room but my head is swimming and the fog in my brain is making it hard to think.

He walked into the hotel suite.

He had a key.

Shane gave it to him. That's what he said.

Bile rises in my throat.

Where is he now? The Wolf? Shane?

I close my eyes and try to shift the fog.

It's helping. I seem to be able to think more clearly with my eyes shut. The Wolf was in our hotel suite. He grabbed me and then I woke up here.

No. I woke earlier too. He was talking to me. Telling me how much he loved me. Talking to me about how his nephews had defiled me. He was disgusted in me. The dull ache in my abdomen reminds me what he did afterwards, though I think I passed out halfway through. He used a condom. I remember that. He said that I was unclean. Disgusting, evil prick! Like he needed protection from me!

I feel a wet sticky substance between my thighs and my cheeks burn with shame. He must have made me climax. Bile surges up again and this time I can't stop it. I retch, managing to turn my head to the side so I at least manage to puke on the bed and not myself.

Icy fingers trail along my calf. Am I imagining this now?

I open my eyes and see his face staring down at me.

He shakes his head. "Well, don't you look a sight," he sneers at me.

"Please!" I croak the word but no sound comes out of my mouth.

"Time to go back to sleep, little bird," he croons as he brushes my hair from my face. I turn my head away from him and then I feel his fingers grip my arm. I buck my whole body, trying to get away from him, but he holds my arm firm in his grasp, his fingertips digging into my soft flesh.

I feel a sharp scratch on my arm.

Then nothing.

CHAPTER 22
SHANE

Paul picked me up outside my hotel eight hours ago and since that time we have been scouring the streets of Belfast looking for Sean O'Connor. We have finally found him at one of his many girlfriends' houses.

It is Paul who goes inside and pulls him out of bed. He drags him naked into the street and throws him at my feet. I look down at him. He was fast asleep in bed with a woman. He crawled away like an injured animal to lick his wounds after our meeting yesterday morning. He didn't take Jessie.

Paul kicks him in the stomach and Sean retches onto the pavement.

"Enough." I put my hand on his arm and he scowls at me. I hate Sean O'Connor as much as anyone, but he won't be able to talk if he's too busy puking.

I crouch down on the floor and glare at him. "Have you seen Jessie?"

"Who?" he blinks at me in what appears to be genuine confusion.

"Jessie. My girl?" I snarl. "The one you couldn't keep your filthy hands off the other day."

"Of course I haven't," he spits.

I grab his head by his hair and tip it back so I can look into his eyes. "Are you fucking lying to me?"

"What would I want with your whore?" he hisses.

I take his head and smash it onto the pavement and he cries out in pain. When I look up, Paul has pulled out a gun and has it aimed at Sean's head.

"What the fuck are you doing, Pol?" I frown at him. "We're in the middle of the fucking street. Kids live around here."

"He took your girl," he snarls at me, "and then he called her a whore."

I put my hand on his forearm, forcing it down so he lowers his weapon. "He didn't take her."

"Then who did?"

"It's a long story. Come on. Let's go."

I walk toward the car and he follows me. The sun is coming up and I feel completely lost and hopeless. My brothers' plane will be landing soon and I only hope that their arrival will spark something in me that gives us a new lead to chase.

The hotel's security has been entirely useless and nobody seems to have seen or heard anything. How a grown woman can just disappear from a hotel suite without a trace is beyond me.

"We will find your Jessica," Paul says as he falls into step beside me.

The name slices through me like ice, sending a shiver down my spine. For once in my life I am grateful to my cold hearted bastard of a father, whose cruelty taught me nerves of steel. Despite my insides churning and my heart racing, I don't miss a beat.

"Yeah."

We stop next to the car and Paul pulls at his collar as he steps closer to me. It's then that I see the scratch on his neck.

I've been so distracted looking for Sean, I forgot to look for the Wolf. "You been fighting with some cats, Pol?" I grind the words out with a smile while my insides boil with rage.

He runs his finger over it and the hint of a smile plays on his lips. "Not exactly," he murmurs.

My fists clench at my sides as my heart races in my chest. My cell phone vibrating in my pocket is a welcome interruption. Glancing at the screen, I see it's Conor calling.

"I have to take this," I say to Paul as I step away from the car and speak to my brother.

CHAPTER 23
CONOR

By the time we land at Belfast airport almost eleven hours later it's the early hours of the morning, local time. I turn on my cell as soon as we land and call Shane who takes longer than expected to answer.

"Hey," he breathes.

"You found her yet?"

"No," he says and my heart sinks in my chest. I shake my head at Liam and Mikey who sit watching my face for clues. "It's a shame Liam couldn't make it, but he needs his rest, and I suppose someone needs to look after things back home."

I frown as I turn to Liam sitting beside me. He's right here and Shane knows that he boarded this plane with me. What the fuck is going on?

I press a finger to my lips indicating he should stay quiet before I answer. "Yeah, a damn shame."

"I'm heading back to the hotel with Paul. Can you and Mikey come straight there and we can plan our next move?"

"Of course we will. See you in an hour, bro."

I end the call and put my cell back into my pocket.

"What was that about?" Liam asks.

"For some reason, Shane wanted whoever he was with to think that you stayed back home," I say to Liam.

"Why?" he frowns at me.

"Because then you're our secret weapon," Mikey suggests. "If nobody knows you're here then..." he shrugs. He doesn't need to finish the sentence for us to know what he means. An invisible man is an asset.

"You know who he was with?" Liam asks.

"No. Except for Paul, I think."

"Uncle Paul?" Mikey asks.

"Yeah. Shane said he was going to ask him to help. But I wonder who else was with them?"

"I'm sure we'll find out soon," Liam says. "So, what I shall I do? Stay in the car?"

I nod. "In the car and out of sight. I'll fill you in on the plan as soon as I know what it is."

"Maybe he knows something that he couldn't say?" Liam offers, his face full of hope and I feel a flicker of it too.

"I certainly fucking hope so."

CHAPTER 24
SHANE

I slip my cell into my pocket and turn back to Paul who is hovering close by. I wonder how much of my conversation with Conor he just heard. It's taking every ounce of willpower I have not to tie that fucker up right now and torture the truth from him. But he never caved under torture when he was in the army or after he left, and I can't risk him dying before I find out the truth. Besides, I have a plan now, and thankfully Conor knows me so well he responded exactly how I'd hoped he would.

"Now that your brothers are here, I'm going to head back to my hotel and get some sleep," Paul says with a fake yawn.

"What? You haven't seen them for twenty-five years. You don't want to even say hello? Not even to Mikey?" I balk at the thought of him and Mikey meeting again, but I swallow it down and look him in the eye.

"I'm not as young as I used to be, kid. I need some sleep. I'll see them later."

"Sleep? Come on, Paul. This is my world we're talking about here, and we don't have a hope of finding her without you." I try flattery instead and the roll of his eyes tells me it is working more efficiently than tugging on his heartstrings – because of course, he doesn't have one.

"Just a few more hours? Help me fill my brothers in on what we've done so far and then you can get some sleep. We can all get some and start again tonight," I lie.

"Fine," he says with a sigh.

"Two hours and then I'm gone."

"That's all I'm asking for."

I HAVE JUST HANDED Paul a mug of coffee when the door to my hotel suite opens and Mikey and Conor rush inside. They both run to me and despite the fact they must be both as pissed as hell that I lost our girl, they wrap their huge arms around me.

"You got any leads at all?" Conor asks as he takes a step back and looks at me full of anxiety and concern.

"No," I look over at Paul and my brothers turn to him, too.

"Hello, boys," he says with a half smile as he makes his way over to us.

"Paul?" Conor holds out his hand to shake it. He remembers our uncle but Mikey won't. He was still a baby when Paul moved away.

Paul shakes Conor's outstretched hand. "It's good to see you, kid," he says but his eyes are on Mikey who frowns at this man he doesn't know, but whose history is so very tied to his own. "And to see you again, Michael. It's a shame your brother couldn't make it."

Mikey frowns at him and I silently urge him not to give the game away.

"He wasn't up to the journey," he answers without pause and I could hug him. "This family reunion is all well and good but where the fuck is our girl?" He turns back to me.

"We haven't found her yet." I rub my hand over my jaw.

"I'm fucking exhausted, boys. I can't even think straight." I sigh and shake my head.

"Then tell us what you do know," Conor snaps.

"Look, Shane," Paul downs his coffee and places the mug on the table. "You should probably get some sleep and we can pick this up again later. I'll leave you to fill your brothers in, but I really need to get back to my hotel."

I nod at him. "Yeah. Thanks for your help, Paul." The words stick in my throat.

"I'll call you later and see if there's anything else I can do. Okay?" he offers.

"Yeah," I nod and then he says his goodbyes to Conor and Mikey before walking out of the room.

My brothers and I watch him leave and as soon as the door is closed I take a deep breath. "Where is Liam?"

"In the car outside. What's going on?" Conor asks.

"I'll tell you as soon as I've spoken to him," I say as I take my cell out of my pocket and dial Liam's number.

"Hey, bro?" he answers.

"Hey, kid. You see that grey Range Rover across the street?"

"Yeah?"

"In about two minutes our Uncle Paul is going to get into it. You can't miss him. He's six four and has a beard. I need you to follow him."

"Okay. Is this about Jessie?"

"Yes. Don't let him see you. Follow him and call us when he stops. Okay?"

"Okay. Fuck! He's on his way outside."

"Call me as soon as you have anything, Liam. We'll be right behind you as soon as you give us the nod. Okay?"

"Yeah," he says and then ends the call.

"Why is Liam following Paul?" Mikey asks me but Conor

stares at me with a look of horror on his face that makes me think he has already figured out the reason why.

I can't even believe these words are about to come from my mouth because it is too fucking crazy to be true, but it also makes perfect sense. "Because Paul is the Wolf."

CHAPTER 25
MIKEY

"What the *fuck*?" I ask as I stare at my oldest brother with my mouth hanging open, because I'm pretty sure I must have misheard him.

"It's him," Shane says, shaking his head as though he doesn't even believe what he's saying himself.

"No way. He can't be," I insist. I mean I don't remember him from when I was a kid, but Conor and Shane always speak fondly of him. He left Ireland shortly after our mom died, but before that, he was our uncle. He taught Shane and Conor how to shoot. He was an expert marksman in the army.

"Fuck! How do you know?" Conor asks, seemingly more ready to believe this than I am.

"He has a scratch on his neck that wasn't there when I saw him yesterday afternoon."

"A scratch?" I interrupt him.

He glares at me and I stop talking.

"He got it in the space of a couple of hours. The same couple of hours during which Jessie was taken."

"Still, Shane..." Conor frowns at him.

"And he called her Jessica," he says and I blink at him as realization dawns on me. Our own fucking uncle? The Wolf?

"Fuck!" Conor hisses. "You never mentioned that's her real name?"

"No. Why would I? Jessica is like a different person to me. I only know Jessie."

"But it's short for Jessica. Maybe he assumed?" I say even though I know I'm clutching at straws. He fits the bill in every other way. A hired assassin, able to disappear without a trace and hide in the shadows.

"And my key card was missing when I got back here yesterday."

"What?" Conor frowns.

"I thought I must have left it behind, but there's only one here and I assume Jessie didn't take hers with her. He was the only person who got close enough to me to take it."

"Why did you just let him walk out of here then?" I ask, suddenly the thought that we just let the Wolf leave here and go back to do who the fuck knows what to our girl, hits me.

"Because he's the fucking Wolf, Mikey," Shane snaps. "You think he would give her up if he thought we were onto him? He would die rather than let us find her. Did you not listen to anything Jessie told you about him?"

"Yes!" I snap as I walk toward him. "Did *you*? Because you knew she was terrified of him and you still left her here on her own. You let him walk into this room and fucking take her. And now our girl is out there somewhere living her worst fucking nightmare and who knows if we will ever fucking get her back!" All the anger and frustration I've been holding onto for the past fourteen hours comes tumbling out of me as I advance on Shane.

It's Conor who stops me in my tracks. "Hey!" he snaps. "We need to focus on finding Jessie right now."

I glare at Shane who hangs his head as though he can't even bear to look at me and now I just feel like shit because how the fuck was he supposed to know our own uncle was such a fucking monster?

"So what do we do when Liam calls?" I ask instead.

"Shane?" Conor says when he doesn't reply. "I need you on your fucking A game here, so get your head out of your ass and tell me what the fuck our next step is?"

Shane looks up at us both and I'm relieved to see his usual look of certainty and control back on his face. "We wait and see where Paul goes and if he stays there or leaves again. It depends on what Liam tells us."

"So we just wait?" I ask.

"For now."

So we all sit down and wait for news from Liam, each of us wrestling with our own emotions alone, because to start talking about our fears and our anger would make it all that more real and for now we have to stay focused on finding Jessie. If I think too much about what she might be going through right now, I won't be able to function, let alone outsmart the Wolf.

CHAPTER 26
LIAM

I follow the beat up Range Rover for about eight miles before it stops outside an old farmhouse in Antrim. I park up a few hundred yards down the road as he walks inside the house. Lights go on in the downstairs windows and my heart races as I wonder if Jessie is in there.

I dial Shane's number and a few seconds later, his voice fills the car.

"Liam?" is all he says.

"I followed him to an old house in Antrim."

"What? He still has that place? Erin told me he sold it years ago."

"Well, he's just walked in there now. Shall I go in after him?"

"No. Just wait and see what he does next."

"But she could be in there, Shane."

"I know, but she might not be, and if you go in then you completely blow our cover and we might never find her."

"I hate sitting here thinking that she could just be a few yards away. Wondering what he might be doing to her, Shane," I say as emotion wells up in my throat. I am so fucking angry I could tear Paul's head clean off his shoulders with my bare hands, but I am also terrified. I haven't been this scared of losing someone since the Russians took Conor two years ago.

"I know, kid. We'll drive out there now, and then at least one of us can follow him if he leaves. And you can check the house."

As I'm talking to Shane the light goes off again and I freeze. I watch as the front door opens a few seconds later. "Hang on. He's leaving."

"Already?"

"Yeah. He's got a gas bottle with him."

"A gas bottle?"

"Yeah. Like the kind we use for a barbecue."

"Fuck!"

"Do I follow him or do I go inside the house?" I ask as my heart starts racing in my chest.

"Fuck! What does your gut say, kid?" he asks me.

"I think she's in there, Shane."

"Wait for him to leave then and go check. If he's taking a gas bottle to be filled he'll come back."

"Okay," I breathe.

"Be careful," he warns.

"I will."

"And be prepared for anything," he adds.

"I will," I swallow hard. I have no idea what state Jessie is going to be in when I go in there and I have no idea how I'll deal with my emotions when I see her, because the thought of anyone touching her, of anyone hurting her, makes my insides burn with fury and guilt that I wasn't able to protect her. But I know in my gut that she's inside that house, and I'm not leaving without her.

My car is parked out of view beneath some trees down the

road. I shrink down in my seat as Paul walks to his car and I wait until I hear him drive off before I look up again.

As soon as his taillights disappear out of view, I drive a little up the road and turn into his driveway. This car was dropped off at the airport by an associate of Shane's and it has a Glock in the glove compartment as well as a small knife. I tuck both of them into my jeans before I jump out of the car.

The lock is easy enough for me to pick and I'm inside the house within two minutes. I walk along the hallway. It's cold and dark and I have to stop myself from calling her name just in case there is anyone else here too. I check each room as I pass but there is no sign of Jessie or anyone else.

The whole place is dusty, like it hasn't been lived in for years, however there are signs of recent occupancy in the kitchen. As I walk into the room, I see two doors. One leading into the yard out back and another I assume is a basement. It has a huge steel bolt on it and my heart lurches in my chest when I see it, because why the fuck would you need to lock your basement door on the inside? Taking out my cell, I turn on my phone's flashlight as I draw back the huge bolt. It screeches like old steel does and I wince as I look behind me to see if anyone has come running, but I'm still alone.

The light from my phone is the only thing illuminating the room as I step onto the dark basement steps. "Jessie!" I whisper.

There is no response. I shine the light down, sweeping it across the room. It is a small concrete room with no furniture except for one single bed in the middle. My phone almost drops from my hand as the light sweeps over it and she is lying there. Naked and alone and chained to the bed.

Blood thunders in my ears as I take the stairs two at a time, trying to get to her as quickly as possible. "Jessie! I'm here baby," I call but she doesn't move.

There is no flicker of life from her. I place my hand on her arm and she is cold to the touch and for one heart stopping moment I think she's gone and that sick cunt has killed her. I move the metal cuff up her wrist as I feel for her pulse and I almost sink to the floor with relief when I feel one. He's only drugged her. I glance over her body, looking for any signs of injury. Her thighs are peppered with fingertip bruises and she has a cut on her mouth. I brush my fingertips over the dried blood on her lips and my heart aches like there is a gaping wound in the middle of my chest. The rage that I've been feeling since I found out she'd been taken threatens to overwhelm me and I have to take deep breaths, sucking in lungfuls of air to so that I can calm my racing pulse and focus on what I need to do. I can't let myself think about what that sick fuck has been doing to her because it will break me and I need to be stronger for her than I ever have right now.

I lift her hand and the clinking of a chain tells me that the metal bracelet on her wrist is chained to the bed. Her feet are chained too. Fuck! I need to move fast.

The ones on her feet are a simple lock and pin mechanism and I remove them quickly, but her hands are a different matter. My heart races as I look around the room for something to help me. I can hardly think straight. What if he comes back here? What if I can't get her out of here before he does?

The car. There are bolt cutters in the car. I saw them when I put our luggage in.

"I'll be right back," I tell her even though she can't hear me. I run to the car faster than I have ever run anywhere in my life. I almost trip over my own feet coming back down the stairs. Resting my phone on the bed to shine its light where I need it, I cut the chains on her wrists, freeing her but leaving the metal bracelets in place for now. I can remove them when I get her to safety.

Shrugging off my jacket, I wrap her in it before I lift her into my arms. As I lean over her, I see the used condom on the floor beside the bed and bile burns the back of my throat. Sick fucking cunt! I will make him feel pain like he has never known when I finally get my hands on him.

She's like a rag doll when I lift her. Completely limp and almost weightless and I don't remember her being this light. "Hang on, Jessie. I'll get you home soon, baby." I choke back the tears as I whisper in her ear, then run up the steps and out of the house. Placing her in the passenger seat of the car, I jump in the other side and lock the doors before I start the engine and get us the hell out of here.

We're half a mile along the road when I see Paul's car approaching from the opposite direction. For a split second, I contemplate running him off the road and putting a bullet in his head, but it would be too merciful for him, and more importantly, I need to get Jessie back to safety as quickly as possible. With that in mind, I dial Shane's number.

"Liam?" he snaps when he answers. "Have you got her?"

"Yes," I reply and I hear the collective sigh of relief from my three brothers and realize I'm on speaker phone.

"How is she?" Conor asks.

"She's unconscious. The bastard drugged her," I say, trying to keep my emotions in check as I glance at her in the seat beside me.

"Fuck!" Mikey hisses.

"Get her back here as soon as you can."

"I know you have friends at that hotel, Shane, but I think if I walk through the lobby with her in the state she's in, the cops will be called on us within five seconds."

"What do you mean the state she's in?"

"Well, she's unconscious. She's naked. And she has bruises on her thighs and face." I swallow hard and focus on the road ahead. Please don't make me think about what that evil cunt has done to her.

"You remember the house in Carrickfergus?" he asks.

"Yeah?" I frown. I thought he'd sold that place. He had it built a few years before we left Ireland. He always intended to live in the countryside one day.

"Take her there. We'll meet you."

"You still have that place?"

"Yeah," he clears his throat. "We'll see you there, Liam."

"I'll be there as soon as I can."

CHAPTER 27
SHANE

Conor, Mikey and I stand on the driveway of the house in Carrickfergus waiting for Liam to bring our girl home. I could have dropped to my knees with relief when he told me that he had her, but then he told me about the state she was in and the rush of rage and the guilt I felt almost floored me for real. I was hoping that Paul hadn't had time to hurt her, but I was fooling myself thinking it wouldn't be the first thing that sick fuck would do. Knowing that it's my fault she's had to go through that makes me feel physically sick. I've never wanted to hurt anyone so much as I want to hurt Paul right now. I know some pretty sick and twisted ways of causing people pain, but all of them would be too merciful for him.

I look over at my brothers and anger and worry is etched onto their faces too. I never told them my suspicion about what Paul has done to her, only the state Liam found her in, and I'm sure like me they have come to the same conclusion. If I don't say it aloud – that our own uncle raped her – then maybe it won't be true.

We all look at each other with relief when Liam's car turns

into the driveway. Conor pulls the passenger door open as soon as the car rolls to a stop and takes Jessie into his arms. She's still unconscious and he cradles her limp body to his chest and carries her straight into the house.

I don't get a good look at her, but I do notice her lip is bleeding and she is only covered by Liam's coat. I shove my hands into my pockets to stop myself from pummeling the gravel driveway to relieve some of the rage that is thundering around my body.

Liam jumps out of the car and jogs toward me. "She's still out," he says as he watches Conor carrying her into the house with Mikey on his heels.

"I know. We'll check her over and see if we need to call a doctor. You did good, kid."

He nods and his eyes brim with tears. "That cunt raped her, Shane."

"I know," I swallow before I wrap my arms around him. It hurts so fucking much to think about. But Liam has said it and now I know it's true. I will make Paul Ryan pay for this if it takes every second of the rest of my life to do it. "But she's safe now, and we'll make him pay. I promise you."

He looks up at me, his eyes red and full of a trust in me that I don't deserve. I push down all of the emotion that is desperate to spill out of me. Now is not the time. "Come on. Let's go make sure she's okay," I say, and then we follow our brothers into the house.

We have prepared the largest bedroom with the en suite for her and Conor has laid Jessie down on the bed. Her hair is stark against the white cotton sheets. He's pulled Liam's coat over her to cover her. I can hardly bring myself to look at her when I think about how badly I have let her down. I feel so much anger and guilt and pain and I don't know which one to process first.

"You think we should call a doctor?" Conor asks.

I walk to the bed and sit beside her. Lifting her hand in mine, her skin is warm to the touch after the heat of Liam's car and her pulse is strong. The cut on her lip has stopped bleeding. I open Liam's jacket and see the bruises on the tops of her thighs and rage threatens to spill out of me, but I swallow it down. There will be time for that soon enough.

"I think she's just knocked out. Let's give her a few hours to wake up and see how she is. You all okay with that?" I look around the room at the three grief-stricken faces of my brothers.

They all nod their agreement.

"You think we should dress her?" Mikey asks, his voice cracking with emotion.

"No," Conor snaps. "She's unconscious. He already violated her. We should let her come round first. Who knows how she's going to react when she wakes up? We have no idea what he's done or what he's told her."

That he might have filled her head with lies about our role in this is eating away at me too. What if she thinks that I led him to her? I can't even begin to deal with the guilt and the anger of it, so I focus on what I can do. "Okay," I nod. I'd prefer to put a t-shirt on her so that she is at least dressed in something familiar when she wakes up, but it's clearly something Conor feels strongly about and I let it go.

"Let's get those cuffs off her at least. Then we can leave Liam's coat around her and pull the covers over her," I suggest. "We're going to need some supplies for when she wakes up. There's no food or anything in this place."

"I'm not leaving her," Conor snaps.

"Nor me," Mikey adds and Liam nods his agreement.

I look around the room at the three of them. None of us wants to leave her. I have always tried to be selfless when it came to my brothers, but I can't now. I need this. "I can't not be here when she wakes up. I need her to know that I didn't hand her over to him," I say, the words sticking in my throat so hard I almost choke on them. I feel like I'm going to break down if they make me argue with them about this.

Silence fills the room as they all stare at me. I know that each of my brothers is in as much turmoil as I am. Each of us is battling to keep a lid on our emotions because she needs us to be clear-headed right now. They all want to be by her side and make sure she is okay. They want vengeance as much as I do, but none of them have the guilt of being the one who allowed the Wolf to take her from right under his nose.

"Okay," Liam says eventually as he taps Mikey on the arm. "We'll go. Come on. We can be there and back in an hour."

Mikey stares at me and there must be something on my face that makes him agree too, because he stands up and walks out of the room with his twin.

"What if she thinks that I handed her to him, Con? What if she thinks I knew all along who the Wolf was?" I choke on my words because the thought that she might have been lying in that cold room all alone, or even worse when that twisted fuck was raping her, thinking that I had let it happen, makes me feel like I can't breathe. If I never get the chance to do anything else in my life ever again, I need her to know that I would die to protect her.

"She won't," he says with a frown.

"He had my fucking room key!"

"She won't think that, Shane. She knows you wouldn't do that to her."

I pull up a chair and sit beside her bed while he removes the cuffs from her wrists with the bolt cutters. I wish that I could believe him.

. . .

Conor and I sit watching her for almost an hour before she finally starts to stir. I edge forward in my seat and my heart hammers in my chest as I wait for her to wake up.

Her eyelids flicker open and the first thing I see in them is sheer terror. She turns her head and looks directly at me. The fear that still lingers in them breaks me.

"Jessie," Conor says softly. "You're safe, Angel."

"Where is he?" she says, her voice hoarse as she looks around the room like a frightened rabbit trapped in the paws of a lion.

"He's not here," he reaches forward and takes her hand but she pulls it from him.

"It's just me and Shane," he adds.

"Shane?" she looks back to me. The confusion and the fear in her eyes almost rips out my heart. Then the tears start running down her face and I bow my head because this is all my fucking fault.

Conor is up off his chair and sitting on the bed beside her. He takes her hand again and this time she lets him.

"He came for me," she whispers. "He said he's your uncle."

"He is our uncle, Jessie. But we had no idea he was the Wolf," Conor says.

"Did you know?" she directs her question to me and that she would even ask hurts more than I can stand.

"No."

She stares at me and I can't tell whether she believes me or not. I figure she's still feeling the effects of whatever drugs Paul gave her because her expression is almost blank now and completely unreadable. "What happened? How did you find me?"

"Shane realized who the Wolf was after he took you. He had Liam follow him and he found you at that farmhouse and brought you back."

"Liam is here?" the light flickers in her eyes at the mention of his name.

"Yes. And Mikey. They've just gone out for some supplies. They'll be back soon," Conor replies.

"And you're here," she frowns as she reaches out and touches his face. "Or am I dreaming?"

"No. I'm here, Angel," he whispers. "I'm never leaving your side again."

She smiles at him. I watch the two of them together. I am relieved that she is safe and that she seems okay, at least physically, but I am hurt that it's Conor she still turns to, and that it was the thought of the twins that made her come back from whatever hell she was just in.

CHAPTER 28
CONOR

Jessie lifts the covers and looks down at herself. She is still wearing Liam's coat and nothing else. I couldn't bear to have one of us dress her earlier. Even though any of us would have treated her with nothing but love and respect, it just didn't feel right to be touching her while she was unconscious. Not after what he did to her.

My heart is breaking as I think about what she has been through in the past twenty-four hours. The next time I see my uncle, I will burn his cock off with a blow torch before I crush every bone in his body, and I will let my girl watch while I do it.

"I need to shower," she croaks, snapping me from my murderous thoughts. I swear if it wasn't for the fact that she needed us to be strong for her now, me and my brothers would have fucking lost it.

"Of course, Angel. I'll help you." I'm not sure if she'll want to be touched but she allows me to lift her from the bed and carry her to the bathroom. Setting her down on her feet, I keep my hands on her waist as she wobbles unsteadily on her feet. She holds onto my forearms as she steadies herself. "I'm fine now," she whispers and I leave her for a second to turn on the shower.

"Hotter," she instructs me and I turn the dial to increase the temperature until steam fills the room.

She walks in, still shaky on her feet and I follow close behind her. The heat from the shower is fierce even though I'm in my shirt and jeans. She turns to me, as though she hadn't expected me to still be here, but there's not a chance in hell I'm leaving her side. She looks up at me and I see the moment she breaks. Her eyelids flicker and she falls forward, straight into my arms. I wrap them around her as she presses her face against my chest and starts to sob like I've never seen her before. Her entire body shudders with the strength of her tears and I feel completely powerless to help her as we stand beneath the scalding water.

I rest my chin on her head and squeeze her tight to me as sobs convulse her body. Her fingers rake down my back, catching on the soaking material of my shirt as she sags against me. I kiss her head and brush the wet hair from her face and just hold her until my clothes are drenched.

When she finally looks up at me, her beautiful blue eyes lock on mine. "Thank you," she whispers.

"Any time, Angel," I say as I reach behind her and take the bottle of soap from the shelf. Keeping my arms around her, I squeeze some into my hands and create a lather before I start to work it over her back. She squirms as my hands slide over her waist and the faintest hint of a smile plays on her lips. She is so ticklish.

"Your clothes are soaking," she whispers as she takes a small step back from me.

"So?" I reply with a shrug as my hands slide over her hips and onto her stomach and she looks down at them as they skim her lower abdomen.

"Is this okay?" I ask, suddenly aware that she might prefer to do this herself. She might not want my hands on her after what my cunt of an uncle has done.

"Yes," she replies with a nod of her head and my soapy hand slides between her thighs as I clean her there. She holds onto me, one hand on my shoulder and one on my forearm as her fingernails dig into my skin through my clothes.

"You sure?" I breathe against her hair.

"Yes. I need you to wash him off me, Conor," she gasps as she looks up into my eyes.

"I will, Angel," I say as my other hand continues washing the rest of her body.

"Not like that," she sucks in a shaky breath. "I need you to take it away. From everywhere." She sobs loudly and I realize what she's asking me to do.

"Jessie!"

"Please, Conor? I can't let him be the last one to..." She blinks at me, unable to finish her sentence. I push back her wet hair. If any of my brothers walk in here and catch me fucking her after what she just went through, they might just lose their shit. And how can I do that after what she just went through?

"Can't you do that now? After what he did?" she asks and my heart breaks in two.

"It's not that, Angel."

"Then what is it?" She blinks at me, her huge blue eyes pleading with me.

I look down at the bruises on her thighs and the rage inside me feels like it might burst out of my chest. The thought of him touching her, of him putting his hands on any part of her, makes me want to rip out his throat with my bare hands. Knowing that he hurt her there makes me feel an anger like I have never experienced before, but none of that changes a damn thing about the way I feel about her. "I don't want to hurt you."

"You won't, Conor. You couldn't."

I stare at her and despite what she's been through, having her naked, soapy body pressed against me makes my cock stiffen. I pull back a few inches. It would kill me if she thought that's all I'm here for.

"It's okay if you don't want to," she whispers.

"Of course I do, Angel," I frown at her. "My cock is already hard just from touching you, but are you sure that's what you want?"

"I need this, Conor," she pleads with me. "Please?"

"I'll always give you whatever you need, you know that, but you're hurt, Angel."

"I'm not. I'm okay. And this is the only way to get rid of him." She looks down at the floor and I cup her chin and lift her head back up so I can look in her eyes.

"Are you sure this is what you need?"

She snakes her hands around my neck and pulls me closer in response. My lips brush hers softly at first until she parts them and I slide my tongue inside. I push her back against the tiled walls and her hands fumble with my belt and zipper until she's able to reach inside and squeeze my stiff cock in her palm.

"Jessie!" I groan into her mouth as my hand slides over her breast and stomach until I reach the apex of her thighs. She parts them slightly, giving me all the permission I need. Sliding my fingers between her folds makes her whimper into my mouth as I deepen our kiss. But then I hesitate and my hand stills. I have no idea how she wants this.

"Conor," she groans as she tugs on my hair and I realize I need to stop overthinking this. She is my girl and she is the same one who left from New York a few days earlier. I know exactly how she likes to be fucked.

I circle two fingers over her clit and she grinds her mound against my palm. When I slide a finger inside her a moment later, she wrenches her mouth from mine and gasps loudly.

"Open wide for me," I growl and she obeys without hesitation, allowing me to slide a second inside her.

"Conor!" she hisses, pulling me towards her until our foreheads are pressed together.

"You like that, Angel?"

"Uh-huh," she nods as she clings to my neck. "But I need more."

"Fuck, Jessie!" I hiss as I work fingers faster inside her and brush her clit with my thumb knuckle. Her walls squeeze me, drawing me in tighter as I bring her to the edge quickly. Just before she tips over, I pull my fingers out of her and she groans.

"I want you on my cock, Angel," I growl, sliding my hands to her ass and lifting her until she can wrap her legs around my waist.

She shivers as I edge the tip inside her. "This what you want?"

"Yes." She bites her lip and I drive myself inside her and she grips me so hard it feels like she'll never let me go.

"Damn, Jessie, you feel so fucking good, Angel," I hiss as I rail into her, nailing her to the wall with each thrust. "I can't get far enough inside you."

"Harder!" she hisses.

"Yeah?" I growl before I suck on the tender skin on her neck.

"Yes!" she whimpers.

I go harder and she shudders in my arms. "Conor!" she moans and the sound of my name on her lips makes my balls tighten. I am so close to losing it inside her, but she teeters on the edge. I roll my hips, trying to get deeper inside her and hit that sweet spot that makes her thighs tremble, but something's holding her back.

I wrap one hand around her throat, pressing her head back against the wall as I stare into her eyes. "You gonna come for me, Angel?" I growl.

"I want to," she breathes.

"So tell me what I need to do to get you there."

"You're being too gentle. I'm not made of glass."

"Fuck, Jessie. I can't..." I shake my head. I'm nailing this girl into oblivion here.

"You're holding back," she breathes. "I can feel it."

"You think?" I grunt, trying to stop myself from coming as her sweet pussy squeezes me for dear life.

"I know."

I release my grip on her throat and plant my hands either side of her head on the wall. "You'd better hold on," I growl and she wraps her legs tighter around me. "You ready?"

"Yes," she pants.

"Are you sure?"

"Yes."

I pull out of her almost all the way before I drive back into her with everything I have.

"Conor," she groans so loudly I'm sure my brothers must have heard in the next room, but I'm past caring. I rail into her again and she drags her fingernails down my back.

"Your pussy loves my cock, Angel," I grunt. "You're squeezing me so hard. You're going to come for me. Now," I order her and she nods her head as she bites down on her lip. I thrust into her again and she shifts a few inches up the wall as she clenches around me and finally lets go, shouting my name when she comes. A few more thrusts has me finding my own release and I spurt hot and heavy inside her.

When she stops trembling, I lower her legs to the floor. She looks up at me. "I love you," she whispers.

"I love you, too, Angel."

. . .

WHEN I WALK BACK into the bedroom ten minutes later, Shane is there. His eyes are burning into me. There is no way he didn't just hear our girl coming for me.

"You two okay?" he asks with an arch of one eyebrow.

I clear my throat. Why do I feel like such a fucking deviant? "Yeah." I nod.

"Don't look so fucking worried, Con," he says with a shake of his head. "You gave her what she needed."

"I know." I run my hands through my hair. So, why the fuck does he look so disappointed in me?

"I'm going to check on the boys," he says before he shoves his hands in his pockets and walks out of the room and it's then that I realize it's not me he's disappointed in but himself. I shake my head and watch him leave. I should never have been so hard on him when Jessie was taken. He beats himself up enough without me adding to his worries.

Jessie walks out of the bathroom a few seconds later and wraps her arms around my waist. "Thank you," she says as she lays her head against my chest.

"You never have to thank me for that, Angel." I rub my hands over her back and she snuggles into me.

CHAPTER 29
JESSIE

After my shower with Conor, I put on some fresh clothes and go into the den where all of the brothers are waiting. Liam and Mikey rush over to hug me as soon as they see me and I hold onto them both for so long, I get cramp in my arm. When I finally let go, Conor hands me a mug of hot, sweet tea and I sit on the sofa.

"You ready to talk about what happened, baby?" Liam asks softly as he takes a seat beside me and takes hold of my free hand. Mikey sits on the other side of me while Shane and Conor sit in the armchairs opposite.

"I was in the hotel suite waiting for Shane to come back and he just walked in. The Wolf. He told me that he was your Uncle Paul. He had Shane's key. He said that you had given it to him." I look at Shane and his face is full of guilt and anger and I wish I could take it away for him.

"You know that I didn't though, Jessie?" he frowns at me.

"Of course I do."

He nods and leans back in his chair and I continue telling them what happened. It's so hazy that I'm still piecing it together for myself. "I saw him and I just froze. I wanted to run.

I wanted to find the gun but my legs wouldn't work." A tear runs down my cheek. "I've waited so long to confront him and when he was standing right there in front of me, I was paralyzed."

"That's completely understandable, Red," Mikey brushes the tear from my cheek with his fingertips.

"I just couldn't believe he was standing there, you know? And when he told me he was your uncle, I couldn't even process what was happening."

The four of them keep watching me and I wonder if they are waiting for me to have some sort of breakdown, but that's not about to happen. What happened in the past twenty-four hours is nothing to what the Wolf has put me through before, and if that didn't break me, then this won't either.

"What happened after that? How did he get you out of there without anyone noticing?" Conor asks.

"I don't know," I shake my head. "There was a struggle and then the last thing I remember from the hotel room is that everything went black. He must have drugged me."

"Yeah," Liam nods his agreement.

"And then I don't remember much at all. I woke up a couple of times in that basement. It was dark and I was cold but I was so out of it. I remember words or things he said but they're not always in order. I remember parts of what he did, but I think I was out for most of it," I shudder and Liam squeezes my hand. I don't need to say out loud what he did. They saw the bruises on my thighs. I was naked for Christ's sake. I would hate if it made them see me differently though. I am not a victim. I am a survivor.

"Tell me about him," I say as I take a sip of my tea. I feel like knowing more about him will help me to defeat him. He is not a wolf, he is a man. And I refuse to call him the Wolf any longer. "Tell me about Paul Ryan."

The three brothers look to Shane who rubs a hand over his jaw. "He left Ireland when I was thirteen, not long after our mum died."

"And before that?"

"He was in the army. Special Forces. We never saw much of him as kids, but..." he swallows.

"But what?"

"When we did, he was... he was our uncle. He taught me and Conor to shoot a rifle and how to skin an animal. He was damaged, yeah, but he was..." He shakes his head. "I can't fathom how he went from that man I knew to the one who did that to you."

"Why did he leave?"

Shane's face pales but it is Conor who answers. "Patrick Ryan drove everyone away eventually. He and Paul had a love-hate relationship – but mostly it was just hate."

"And you never heard from him again?" I ask with a frown.

"Not until a few months ago," Shane replies. "He was a hired gun and we knew he'd worked for some of the most dangerous people all over the world. We assumed he was dead."

"But he got in touch recently?"

"Yeah. I thought it was because his brother was dying, but now I wonder if it was because he'd found out where you were," Shane replies.

"Is there anything else I should know about him?"

"I don't even remember him," Mikey says with a shake of his head.

"Evil cunt!" Liam spits. "Just like his brother." He looks at me and squeezes my hand again. "He's our uncle, Jessie. How the fuck?"

"I don't know. It's so hard to fathom," I admit.

"Can you ever see us the same way, Red?" Mikey asks.

“What?” I blink at him. Here I was worried that they would see me differently and not even considering the repercussions for them of discovering who their uncle is. “I see you exactly the same as I always have.” I put my mug on the coffee table and take hold of his hand. “You are nothing like your uncle.”

“I love you,” Mikey whispers and lifts my hands to his face, brushing his lips over my knuckles.

“I love you, too.”

CHAPTER 30
JESSIE

I lie on the sofa, with my head on Liam's lap and my legs over Mikey's. It is late now and these boys have looked after me all day long. Bringing me my favorite snacks. Watching my favorite movies with me. Conor even read me some Tolstoy earlier. They are all so sweet. But Mikey's hand has been on my leg for the past half hour and he has been rubbing it up and down my calf. I have never known him to touch me for so long without it leading to something more. I watch his strong fingers gliding over my skin and I am willing him to slide them higher, but he hasn't even ventured past my knee. Our relationships are about so much more than sex, but that is a huge part of it. I need to know that nothing has changed between us. This is what I need to feel like me again.

I shift my hips slightly, so that Mikey's hand slides up to my knee. He looks at me and arches one eyebrow, as though he's been waiting for permission to go further. His hand slides up my thigh and his fingertips trail softly over my bruises.

"You okay there, baby?" Liam asks as he notices me fidgeting.

I reach up and curl a strand of his hair between my fingertips. "No," I breathe.

He narrows his eyes at me. "You need something?"

"Yes. You right here," I touch my lips with my fingertips, the same way he did when he was recovering back in New York a few weeks ago and he was desperate for us to be intimate again.

He leans down and seals his lips over mine, slipping his tongue inside my mouth until I feel a familiar fluttering in my abdomen. I let my legs fall open as he kisses me and Mikey responds by sliding his hand further up the inside of my thigh. When he reaches the top, he traces a fingertip along my panties and I moan into Liam's mouth.

"You sure you want this, Red?" he asks.

"Yes," I mumble as I reach for his hand and pull him closer.

He tugs my panties to one side and slowly slides one finger inside me, making me groan into Liam's mouth.

"Such a beautiful pussy, Red," he growls as he gently pumps his finger in and out of me. The wet sound of my arousal is loud in the quiet room. "Always ready for us, too. You're such a good girl."

Liam chuckles softly as he lifts his lips from mine. "You wet for us, baby?" He arches one eyebrow at me.

"Why don't you find out?" I offer.

"Fuck," he hisses as his hand slides down my body. He pulls my panties further to the side as he slides a finger in me too, along with his brother's.

"Oh, she feels so fucking good," Mikey hisses.

"She sure does," Liam agrees and I lift my hips to meet their synchronized finger fucking. Having both of them inside me at the same time is so damn hot and I moan softly as they work in perfect unison.

But then Mikey stops. "I want to eat you out, Red," he

groans. "Right here in front of all my brothers. You okay with that?"

Okay with it? There is nothing I want more right now. "Yes," I pant as I look up at him.

He hooks his fingers into the band of my panties and starts to peel them down my legs while Liam keeps on dipping his finger in and out of my wet opening.

Mikey takes off my panties and tosses them onto the floor before he lies down on the long sofa. He clamps his hands around the backs of my thighs, pulling me closer to him until my pussy is inches from his face. Liam takes that as his cue to withdraw his finger and he begins circling my clit instead while Mikey presses his tongue against me and starts to suck at my juices. Waves of pleasure roll through my body as they work me so expertly.

"You remember the first night we fucked you, baby? Just like this?" Liam asks as he dusts his lips over my cheek.

"Yes," I groan as a rush of wet heat sears between my thighs. How could I forget it? It was almost exactly like this, except that it was Liam with his tongue on me while Mikey worked his magic fingers.

"Conor and Shane watched us that night too," Liam chuckles.

"Shane didn't," I gasp as I look over at the two of them who are sitting watching us intently. Conor is clearly enjoying the show and he rubs his cock through his sweatpants, but Shane glares at us, his jaw working. He has been quiet all day and he has avoided being alone with me at all. I know that could be about so many things, but I need to know that he still sees me the same way, too. This past week with him, before the Wolf turned up at least, has been incredible with him and if we've lost any of that, it will break my heart.

"He'll watch tonight, too, won't you, bro?" Liam asks and Shane sucks in a deep breath, but he doesn't leave.

Liam tilts my head toward him, sealing my mouth with a kiss as he presses harder on my clit and Mikey keeps on sucking and nibbling at my tender flesh.

"You taste so fucking sweet, Red," he groans. "I could come just from eating your pussy."

I wrench my lips from Liam's as my orgasm hits me unexpectedly and I moan both of their names as they coax me through to the other side.

As soon as my legs stop trembling, Mikey pulls me up and lifts me into his arms. "Time for bed, Red," he says with a nod to Liam who stands too.

"Boys!" Shane warns and I feel a rush of love for him. I know the twins would never push me for anything I wasn't one hundred percent okay with, but I love that he's so protective of me.

"We know, bro," Liam says.

"All we want to do is get naked with you and kiss every inch of you, Red. No fucking. Okay?"

"Okay," I smile as I wrap my arms around his neck and he carries me to bed, with Liam close behind us.

CHAPTER 31
SHANE

I sit outside on one of the lounge chairs on the decking and sip my whiskey. The house is in darkness and the only light is from the full moon. I look out into the black night, wondering if he's watching. Thinking about him and what he did to her makes me feel so much rage it's like I can't breathe. All this time the man who was haunting her nightmares was our own uncle. How fucked up is that?

My mum was always a spiritual woman. She was born and raised a Catholic, but she believed in a different kind of God and heaven than the one the priest used to lecture us about every Sunday. She believed in reincarnation and souls being bound together for eternities. I used to listen to her stories about witchcraft and fate, but I never believed in them. But maybe she was right. For some reason, Jessie was bound to us long before we even met her. Maybe it was always meant to be that she would be ours. Maybe Paul and Patrick Ryan were truly put on this earth to test us all, and to bring us all together?

I glance down at my empty glass and shake my head. Surely I've had far too much to drink if I'm entertaining such ridiculous notions. There is something about a full moon that brings out my mother's side of the family in me. Our Aunt Em is a card-carrying Pagan and has always been a believer in all things mystical too.

My thoughts drift to Jessie again. I heard her and Conor in the shower earlier, and for the first time in my life I was jealous of my little brother. Knowing that he was the only one who could give her what she needed sliced through my heart like a blade. She has been polite to me since we got her back, but she can barely stand to look at me. I watched Mikey and Liam with her earlier and it made me as hard as iron. They are so relaxed with her. Their relationship is easy in a way that mine and hers will never be. I thought our time here in Ireland would make us stronger, but I fucked it up completely, and now I wonder if she will ever look at me the same way again.

The sound of the sliding door behind me makes my head snap around. I am on high alert having taken my eye off the ball once already and I will never let it happen again. She must have turned on a light and it illuminates her silhouette as she walks toward me with a blanket wrapped around her shoulders.

"What are you doing out here?" she asks with a frown as she reaches me.

"Drinking." I hold up my now empty glass as proof.

"You should never drink alone, Shane Ryan," she says with a tilt of her head. "So scooch up."

"What?"

"It's so chilly out here. I don't want to sit on one of those cold ass chairs. So scoot."

These lounge chairs aren't built for two, but I shuffle over as much as I can and she squeezes in beside me. Lying on her side with her leg draped over mine, she wraps an arm and half the blanket around me and presses her head against my chest. I look down at her and frown because this doesn't seem like she's pissed at me, but if she's not, then she fucking should be.

"That moon is beautiful," she says with a soft sigh that I feel in my groin.

"Sure is."

"It reminds me of that night by the lake. Do you remember?"

How could I forget it. It was the night I finally admitted my feelings for her. It was the night she promised she would never leave us. I suppose we've both made promises that we couldn't keep. I promised her she would be safe with me. I swore that I would never let him hurt her, yet I handed her straight to him. "Of course I do. It seems like a lifetime ago."

"I think about it all the time."

"Really?"

"Yes. I think you should build that place out on the lake as soon as we get back."

"You do?" I look down at her.

"Hmm. So we can have a place just like this when we need to get away from the city."

I wrap my arms around her and we sit in silence for a while.

"Why have you been avoiding me?" she whispers.

"I haven't been avoiding you," I lie.

"Well it certainly feels like it. Does what he did bother you?"

I look down at her with a scowl on my face. "Of course it fucking bothers me, Jessie. I hate what that evil fucker did to you."

"I don't mean like that," she stammers. "I mean...when I was with your brothers earlier, I was hoping you might..."

Fuck! She thinks that I don't want her. I don't even know what to say in response to that but she fills the silence with another question.

"Why were you drinking out here alone?"

"I just wanted some time to think."

"About?"

"About everything."

"Are you okay?" She looks up at me with those beautiful blue eyes and my heart almost bursts out of my chest. After everything she's been through, everything I let happen to her, she asks if I'm okay.

"No," I say. The whiskey must be some kind of truth serum because I should tell her everything is fine and send her back to bed.

"Shane," she says with a sigh as she rests her warm hand on my cheek. "Please don't blame yourself for what happened."

"I should never have let him anywhere near you. He got to you because of me and that's a fact, Jessie. There is no escaping that."

"No!" She shifts her position so she can look into my eyes. "He got to me because that is what he does. You didn't even know who he was. How could you have predicted that?"

"I made you a promise that he would never hurt you again!" I snarl at her although the only person I am angry with right now is myself.

"And I love that you made that promise, Shane, but don't you see it's one that you can never keep." She shakes her head. "Nobody can."

"I can! I should have."

"No matter how much we love someone, we can never stop them being hurt. We can't protect people from hurt and pain, as much as we want to. You have to accept that or you're going to drive yourself crazy trying to keep everyone safe when it's an impossible task."

"Don't, Jessie! I *can* keep you all safe. I *will*." I feel the wave of emotion crashing over me and I suck in a deep breath. The cool night air fills my lungs but it does little to calm my racing heart. This isn't just about Jessie anymore. This is about every single time Patrick or Paul Ryan hurt someone I love. I sit up and she sits with me, awkwardly perched on my lap now.

"It's not your job to keep everyone safe, Shane," she whispers as she takes my hand in hers. "You are not responsible for your father or your uncle."

"I should have saved her, Jessie. My mother. I tried to..." I shake my head and stare out into the night as I recall the night my father murdered our mother. I heard him beating her. I heard her crying for help. Liam and Mikey were only one year old when he came home drunker than usual and spoiling to cause some real pain. I'd protected them first, taking them and Conor to a neighbor's house before going back to our own. My mom could usually talk him round after a while, once he had beaten her black and blue first, but this night he just kept on going. I banged on that door so hard my knuckles were bleeding as I listened to her begging for mercy. Now I know why he never stopped that night, although it's a secret I wish I'd never learned. When she finally fell silent, my heart broke into a million pieces and it never truly healed, although it had started to with Jessie's help. And now I have let her down too.

"You did everything you could, Shane. I know what it's like to watch the people you love in pain and not be able to do anything about it," she sniffs as a tear rolls down her cheek.

I brush it away with the pad of my thumb. I forget sometimes how much she has endured. She watched her entire family slaughtered in front of her eyes by my evil cunt of an uncle, but she is still so full of compassion and kindness. She is damaged just like my brothers and me, but she's still the best person I have ever met. Perhaps my mother was right. Some stories are truly written in the stars.

"I'm sorry for everything he did to you," I say.

"I know, but it is not your apology to make. If you let anything your father or your uncle did close you off from happiness and love, then they have won. You're capable of such incredible things, Shane. Your love is an amazing gift. Please don't let them take it from you, or me."

"You think I could ever stop loving you, Jessie Ryan?" I frown at her as I cup her cheek in my hand.

"I hope not," she smiles at me. "Because I am completely head over heels for you."

"Head over heels?" I arch an eyebrow at her.

"Yes. I told you, I love you more than candy."

"Yes you did," I smile as I lie back, pulling her with me so that she is lying on top of me now and I have my arms wrapped tightly around her.

We lie in silence for a while and I listen to the sound of her soft breathing. "How are you really holding up, sweetheart?"

"I'm okay," she whispers.

"Okay isn't really an answer," I frown.

"Isn't it?"

"Well it's neither a feeling or a state of being, so it tells me nothing really, does it?"

She sighs softly and presses her cheek against my chest. "Isn't 'okay' a catchall for when you don't really know the answer? I feel so many things, Shane."

"So break it down for me."

She is quiet for a few seconds before she responds. "Right here, I feel happy and safe. Protected," she whispers.

"Right here in the house?"

"Right here in your arms," she breathes.

I have to close my eyes and take a deep breath because this girl just straight up put her hand inside my chest and punched me in the fucking heart. If I had any last line of defense against her then she just tore right through it. She has defeated me. Right here in the grounds of this beautiful house in Carrickfergus, I gave her the very last sliver of my soul.

I kiss her head and breathe in the scent of her hair. If I speak right now, if I try to tell her how much I love her, then she'll know that she has completely fucking broken me.

"But I also feel scared, Shane. Terrified in fact. Not that he will come for me now, but that he'll do it in two, four or even twelve years' time, when I let myself feel happy or relaxed. When I've stopped thinking about him every minute of every day. I might be walking to the grocery store to pick up something for dinner, or be in a restaurant with you and your brothers and go to the restroom alone, or I might just be walking down the street, and he'll take me. And then I'll be gone," she whispers and her entire body shudders.

I want to tell her that I will never let that happen, but we just spoke about making promises we can't deliver on.

"I would tear the world apart to find you, sweetheart," I tell her instead because that is a promise I can keep.

"I know," she whispers. "Now, are we sleeping out here under the stars tonight then, or are you going to take me to bed?"

My cock twitches at the way she says that and I'm grateful for the distraction. But she yawns as she nestles her head against my chest and I remember it's the middle of the night and she has been through so much in the past thirty-six hours.

"We'll stay here a little longer." I dust my lips over her hair and she sighs contentedly.

"Okay, but I might fall asleep right here."

"Then I'll carry you to bed if you do, sweetheart. And to address your earlier question, seeing you with my brothers still makes me as hard as iron and I still want to fuck you as much as I always have." I kiss her again and pull the blanket all the way over her as I wrap my arms tighter around her body.

"Devil," she chuckles softly and the sound makes me smile.

. . .

Half an hour later she is fast asleep in my arms as I carry her to my bed. Crawling in beside her, I pull her to me and she mumbles my name.

"It's okay, sweetheart. Go back to sleep," I whisper in her ear and she smiles sleepily as she wraps an arm around my neck.

We lie in the darkness. I listen to her soft, steady breathing as her heart beats against my own and I have never felt more at peace in my entire life. I only wish that it could last. But my uncle is still out there and I know there will be no lasting peace for any of us until he takes his last breath.

CHAPTER 32
JESSIE

I watch my four handsome men eating their breakfasts and my heart flutters in my chest. How is it that one person gets to be lucky enough to deserve the four of them? I swear one day I'm going to wake up and this will all be a dream that I've concocted in order to survive my time with the Wolf. Perhaps one day I'll wake up and still be in his fortress in the hills.

Thoughts of Paul Ryan make my heart flutter for an entirely different reason and I know it's only a matter of time before he makes his move. I have no idea when or where, but the one thing I am sure about is that we need to act first.

"When is the funeral?" Mikey asks, snapping me from my own thoughts and reminding me why Shane and I came to Ireland in the first place.

"Wednesday," Shane replies before taking a gulp of his coffee.

"So only four more days before we can go home?" Liam adds.

"Yep," Shane nods his head.

"Home?" I interrupt them.

"Yes," Conor frowns at me.

"But we can't go back to New York while Paul is still here."

"We've got more resources in New York," Shane says as he places his mug on the table.

"Yeah. We're kind of sitting ducks here," Mikey says, earning him a withering glance from Conor and Shane. As though I didn't already know that. It's been three days since they rescued me from the Wolf and during that time they have been incredibly attentive and loving, doing their best to distract me from the fact that their uncle is out there somewhere waiting to pick me off.

"I agree, which is why I think we need to find him before he finds me."

"We're trying to find him, sweetheart, believe me, but it's not that easy."

"I know that. Unfortunately, he won't be found unless he wants to be and I can't sit around waiting for that to happen," I say and the anxiety that is building in the pit of my stomach makes my voice go up at least a few octaves.

"None of us want that to happen, Angel," Conor says as he places a reassuring hand on my shoulder.

"So we only have one choice then," I swallow hard because I know they are not going to like this suggestion.

Shane narrows his eyes at me. "And what's that?"

"I reach out to him..."

"Fuck no!" Conor snarls.

"Not a fucking chance in hell," Shane agrees while Mikey and Liam scowl and me and nod their agreement.

"It's the only way."

"It's not happening, Red," Mikey snaps and my heart sinks, because I thought at least he and Liam might hear me out.

"But there's no other way to draw him out. If we don't do this now then who knows when we might get the chance again?

I can't go through my life wondering when he's going to come for me."

"He will never lay another hand on you, Jessie!" Liam frowns at me.

I only wish I could believe that. "Please just hear me out?" I plead but I am met with four serious faces.

"Anything could happen to you, Jessie," Conor snaps.

"You are not putting yourself at risk like that," Shane adds and it is clear that the subject is no longer up for discussion. I lean back in my chair and glare at the four of them. I could continue arguing with them but I know there is no point. They have made it abundantly clear that they're not interested in what I have to say, despite the fact this is my life we're talking about. I blink back the tears. I know it's coming from a place of love, but they don't understand how it feels to live a life in constant fear.

"You think he'll go to the funeral?" Liam asks.

"Not if he has an ounce of sense," Shane snaps.

"I think we should all go," Conor adds.

"All?" Mikey frowns at him.

"We're here now," Conor replies with a shrug. "We can't let Shane and Jessie go on their own and I'm happy for the opportunity to spit on his grave."

"You still want to go, Jessie?" Shane asks.

"Oh, so my opinion counts now, does it?" I snap.

Shane stands quickly and pushes his chair back, making me jump. He leans his face close to mine. "Don't," he snarls and then he walks out of the room leaving his three brothers looking at me like I just poked the bear.

I know what I have to do, whether they are on board or not.

"Sorry," I say quietly to them and Conor wraps an arm around me.

"There is no way we could let you put yourself in danger like that, Angel," he says softly.

"I know."

I LIE IN BED, sandwiched between my sleeping giants, Liam and Mikey. This is my safe place. I feel so protected and content when I am with the brothers. The deep ache in my chest almost takes my breath away, because I know this cannot last. Paul Ryan is out there. He has been watching me for who knows how long. He will always be watching. Waiting to make his move. Waiting for the perfect moment to strike. And next time, he won't make a single mistake.

I blink away a tear and it rolls down my cheek. I can't go on living the rest of my life wondering when he is going to take me. I can't continue living in my past. I will not spend another day being afraid. Paul Ryan has taken enough of my life away from me. He has my past, but he won't have my future. I know without a doubt that the brothers won't change their minds and consider my plan to lure their uncle back to me while we still have a chance. I know he's still in Ireland. I feel him. I'm as connected to him as I am to his nephews now.

I untangle myself from Mikey's arm and slip quietly out of the bed. He groans and rolls over and I freeze. "Red!" he mumbles, but then he drifts back to sleep.

I pull on my clothes and sneakers. This has to end tonight. It is the only way for me to be free. When the Wolf found me at the hotel, I was unprepared. I was paralyzed with fear. But now I know who he is. He's just a man. Paul Ryan is no longer an elusive phantom who plagues my nightmares, but a living, breathing human being.

I take the Glock from the nightstand and then with a final look at Liam and Mikey, I sneak out of the bedroom. They will wake shortly and notice I'm gone, I have no doubt. In fact, I'm kind of counting on it. I have no desire to do this alone.

I grab the keys to the Land Rover and take the red lipstick from my purse before scrawling a note on the window beside the front door. It's time to take control of my own destiny.

THE RAIN IS heavy against the window pane as I drive through the country roads of Ireland. I doubt that Paul will be at the house already, not if he has any fear of his nephews anyway. But I have no doubt he will be watching. My heart is beating in my chest like a jackhammer as I pull up outside the old stone farmhouse. There is no car outside but there is a faint light coming from the window, as though someone has a lantern or a torch. Is he in there? Waiting for me.

I take a deep breath and step out of the car. With the gun in my hand, I approach the front door.

The house is empty when I walk inside but the flashing red light in the hallway tells me there's a camera here and he'll be watching. I look up to it.

"I'm here. What are you waiting for?" I challenge him.

I sit on the staircase and wait for him. I expect he'll be here soon. This is it. One way or another, only one of us will walk out of this house alive.

CHAPTER 33
SHANE

"Shane! Conor!"

The sound of my brothers' shouting wakes me with a jolt. Instinctively, I grab for my gun and jump out of bed. I almost crash into Mikey as he comes running into the room.

"What?" I scowl at him.

"She's gone!" he says and my world stops turning.

"What do you mean? Gone?" I shout. She was in bed with him and Liam, so what the fuck is he talking about?

"I woke up and she wasn't there. Her clothes and shoes aren't there, either. She's gone," he stammers, his face full of anxiety and concern.

"She left a note," Conor pops his head inside the door and I look up at him. My insides fucking sink through my knees. *Not another fucking note.*

"What kind of note?" I snarl.

"Come see," he walks out of the room and Mikey and I follow him to the front door of the house. Sure enough, in bright red lipstick, she has scrawled us a note.

Find my iPhone

I feel a rush of relief, anger, frustration and fear all at the same time. "She's gone to find him," I snarl.

"Jessie!" Conor sighs and shakes his head while Mikey and Liam stare at the two of us, waiting for answers.

"I will tan her fucking ass when we get hold of her," I snarl. This woman is going to give me a fucking heart attack, or at least turn me gray before I hit forty.

"Someone pull up that fucking tracking app," I snap as I head back into the house. "And let's go find her."

TWENTY MINUTES LATER, we are driving as fast as the car will take us towards Paul's house in Antrim where, according to the *Find my iPhone* app, Jessie is. I am so pissed at her for taking off and putting herself in danger, but my anger is far eclipsed by my fear that he is going to hurt her or that we won't make it in time and they will disappear.

"We should have listened to her plan," Mikey says with a sigh from the back seat. "We should have known she'd pull something like this."

"How the fuck did she sneak away from you both?" Conor snaps.

"I don't know," Liam shakes his head and leans back against the seat and my heart breaks for him. Jessie Ryan is a law unto herself. She is the most stubborn woman I have ever met in my life. She is fiercely independent and way smarter than any man in this car. She might submit to us in bed, but she makes her own choices in every other aspect of her life.

"Now isn't the time for finger pointing," I say to Conor. "We all know Jessie does what Jessie wants to do. Maybe we should have listened to her."

"You for real?" Conor snaps.

"Well, we wouldn't be hurtling through Antrim at ninety miles an hour looking for her right now if we had, would we?"

He glares at the road ahead instead of answering me and I know that he is as consumed by his anger and worry as I am.

"Well, just so we're clear, are we all okay with shooting Uncle Paul in the head?" Mikey asks and I bristle at him calling him that. If I told them the truth now, would it help or hinder the situation?

"A bullet in the head is too good for the cunt!" Liam spits.

Hinder! This is not the right time to be revealing long buried secrets. Maybe we can even get through this whole thing without them discovering the truth, because I'm not sure it's something they would want to know. There's a reason they say ignorance is bliss, right?

CHAPTER 34
JESSIE

I stare at the front door waiting for Paul Ryan's arrival. This has been such a long time coming and I am ready for it. For him.

It's a sound from the back of the house that startles me. Of course he wouldn't walk through the front door like a man. Sneaking in where he won't be seen is entirely fitting for him. I walk through the hallway to the kitchen and see the basement door is ajar and the light is on. It bathes the kitchen in a soft amber glow that makes the old farmhouse look almost homely.

"Are you hiding from me?" I call. "Surely you're not afraid?"

His laugh echoes up the basement steps and it makes the hairs on the back of my neck stand on end.

"Afraid of you, little bird. Never," he hisses.

I walk closer to the steps and peer into the basement. He stands out of sight but I see his shadow on the wall. "After all these years, you're still hiding in the dark. Why don't you come up here and face me?"

"I'm standing in the light, Jessica. Come down here and see for yourself."

I take a deep breath. I know this must be a trap, but I want answers and he is the only man left to give me any. I can't go on living half a life.

I walk down the stairs, with my gun pointed straight at his head. He places his hand over his heart as though he is deeply wounded by the fact I'd love nothing more than to shoot him in the face. "Is this what we have come to, Jessica?"

"You must know I want you dead?" I arch an eyebrow at him. "This time I'll make sure to finish the job."

He rubs a hand over his throat, his fingers curling through his thick beard as he glares at me. "Hmm. That was a nasty scratch."

"How did you survive?"

He starts to laugh as he takes a step toward me. "I have survived far worse than that before. You think that you have the power to kill me? I am the Wolf!"

"You are Paul Ryan. A man who pretends to be something more is still just a man."

I point the gun as he takes another step and he looks above my head. I look up too and see the red spot on the door above me. That's when I notice the small black box in his hand. "I have them all over this room, Jessica." He holds up the box and shows me his finger over a silver button. "You'll be dead before you can squeeze off a round. As soon as your rescuers come for you, they will walk straight in here and meet their deaths. It seems everyone around you meets a similar fate, doesn't it? Perhaps you are cursed?"

"Fuck you!" I hiss.

"Hmm. We'll get to that later," he leers at me and the bile rushes up from my stomach and burns my throat.

"Why did you take me?" I ask as I walk further down the steps. I'd take my chances with dropping him before he has a chance to press that button, but I still want answers before I kill him.

"What?"

"Why? Why didn't you kill me like you were supposed to?"

He frowns at me. "I saved your life."

"No. You chose not to kill me but kidnapped and tortured me instead. Risking everything you had built. Why?"

"I risked nothing," he spits. "Money and houses and things are not everything."

"I know. But your reputation. Your livelihood. Why did you give all that up?"

"For you, Jessica."

"No," I shake my head. "You didn't even know me. Tell me why."

"I didn't have to know you to see that you were special. Alexei didn't deserve you. Your parents could not protect you. I could. I did." He beats his own chest with pride as though he actually believes that. "My nephews think they are powerful men, but they couldn't protect you either."

At the mention of his nephews my heart breaks a little inside. I wonder if they've noticed I'm gone yet.

"I wasn't yours to take," I say, my voice cracking.

"But you have always been mine. As soon as I saw you I knew that you were made for me. We are bound together. Why do you think it was my nephews who found you? So that they could bring you back to me." He looks at me with such a strange look of anguish on his face that I think he actually believes some of that bullshit.

"You're crazy. One hundred percent deluded."

"You know that we belong together. I was your first love. Your first everything. That has connected us beyond anything else ever could. I taught you how to experience true pleasure."

I feel anger bubbling beneath my skin, threatening to burst out of me at any moment. It took me a long time to deal with the shame of what he did to me. Of how he could manipulate my body into climaxing, which he used as justification for his sick and twisted torture. "You raped me, you fucking maniac!" I spit at him. "I enjoyed nothing of what we did. Nothing."

I stare at him and feel so much venom that it seeps from every pore in my body. The sound of the door breaking down and footsteps can be heard above us and my heart sinks. I can't believe I have lured the men I love to their deaths. I can't believe I thought I could beat him after all this time.

"Oh, here are my boys now," he says with a cruel smile. "Call to them, Jessica. Tell them where you are."

"Fuck you!" I spit and he laughs. I could tell them to go away, but nothing I say is going to stop them coming in here.

A moment later, Liam comes running into the room with his three brothers close behind him.

"Stop!" I shout, my voice cracking with fear. "He has the whole place rigged."

Shane grabs hold of Liam's collar to stop him walking toward me and the four of them freeze as they stare at me.

"He's got sniper rifles set up all around the room. He has the controller in his hand," I nod to Paul and he holds up the small black box in his hand.

"That's right," he says with a grin.

"He's bluffing," Mikey snaps.

"He's not," I shake my head. "They're trained on the door there where you are. He showed me."

Shane turns to his uncle. "You knew she'd come here. You set this up?"

"Yep."

"What the fuck do you want?" he snarls.

"What I've always wanted. My Jessica back," he smiles.

"She is not your Jessica!" Shane hisses.

"Oh, but she is!" Paul snarls. "You think there isn't a single inch of her body that I didn't claim long before you lot got your filthy hands on her? Who do you think it was who taught her what she really likes?" He licks his lips and I feel the bile rise in my stomach again as they have to listen to this. "I know the many ways to make her scream. In pain and pleasure!"

I press my lips together as I try to drown out his sick ramblings and think of a way out of this.

"You think telling us how you raped and tortured our girl will end well for you?" Conor growls.

"Your girl!" Paul laughs loudly. "Did she tell you that she didn't enjoy it? Did she tell you how hard I can make her come for me. She has the sweetest cream," he croons and the bile burns the back of my throat now but I swallow it down.

I keep my gun trained on him as I look between him and the brothers.

"You will never touch her again!" Conor snarls.

"Volk!" *Wolf!* I shout, using the name his ego will respond to. "Just let them go," I plead with him.

He looks at me and shakes his head. "You know I can't do that. I can't risk them telling anyone who I really am. I can't be worrying about them coming looking for us."

"They won't," I insist.

"The fuck we won't!" Mikey snaps and I suck in a breath. How the hell are we all going to get out of this alive?

Shane raises his gun and points it at his uncle too.

"Careful now," Paul chuckles. "There's a gun trained on Jessica too."

"You're lying," Shane snaps.

"Nope," he shakes his head. "If I can't have her, then I'm certainly not letting you have her."

"You're a fucking psychopath," Shane snarls at him.

"Me?" Paul shakes his head. "You're the one who's been lying to her. Manipulating her into believing that you loved her, when you were working for me all along. Isn't that right, Shane?"

Shane's frown deepens. "What the fuck?"

"Come on, now. You know it's true. Do your brothers know too?"

"You're lying!" Shane snaps.

"But we both know you're the liar in here, Shane. Do your brothers know about the other little secret you've been keeping from them?" he cackles.

Conor, Liam and Mikey look to Shane now and suddenly I see the way out. I have no idea what Paul is rambling about, but he is a deluded maniac, and I can work with that.

"I will put a bullet in your head if you speak another word," Shane hisses.

"Try it. And at least two of your brothers will die along with her if you do. Because I can push this button quicker than you can fire off a single round."

"What secret?" Liam asks and I see the color drain from Shane's face. Damn! He really does have a secret.

"He's lying," Shane repeats.

"You know that I'm not," Paul glares at him. "Tell them, Shane. Tell them what you've been hiding from them all these years. Or shall I tell them the real reason their daddy hated their guts?"

"Fuck you!" Shane spits but his brothers look between him and Paul.

I look between them too, wondering what the hell is going on here.

"Why did he hate us, Shane?" Mikey asks.

"It's not the time!"

"It fucking is," Liam barks and Shane shakes his head in annoyance.

"Go on, tell them who their real daddy is, Shane!" Paul chuckles.

"What?" Conor blinks in confusion. "What the fuck is he talking about, Shane?"

They are not going to let this go and I watch the perverse satisfaction on Paul's face as he watches the unbreakable bond of the Ryan brothers fracturing before his eyes.

"He's talking about the twins." Shane's Adam's apple bobs as he swallows hard. "Patrick wasn't their real father."

"So who is?" Mikey asks.

"He is," Shane looks up at Paul who is grinning maniacally at them.

"Surprise, boys!" he shouts. "Daddy's home!"

"Fuck, no!" Mikey shouts as Liam puts his head in his hands. "Why the fuck... Shane...?" He keeps asking half questions as the revelation ripples through them like a current of electricity that is threatening to spark and cause a fire.

"Why the fuck didn't you tell us?" Liam snarls at him.

I look back at Paul and the smile on his face makes my heart twist in agony. I turn my body slightly and point my gun at Shane. "What else have you lied about, Shane?"

He blinks at me in shock as he stares down the barrel of the gun. "Nothing, Jessie."

"Why the hell would I believe you now?"

"Jessie!" he frowns.

"You knew who the Wolf was all along! You've been planning to hand me over to him all this time."

"No," he shakes his head as Conor, Liam and Mikey look at him with suspicion now. The seed has been planted and it is growing at a dangerous speed.

"Why would we be here if we were going to do that?" he shakes his head.

"I don't think your brothers knew," I look between him and

Paul. "I think you two have been planning this all along, but now you've decided you don't want to give me up after all."

"Yes," Paul agrees while Shane stares at me.

Paul still has the remote held up in his hand, his finger hovering over the button and I realize if he is going to buy this, I am going to have to lay my heart wide open. I need to speak my truth because it is the only thing that is going to convince him.

I point my gun at Shane and I look into his eyes. My hand trembles but my voice doesn't.

"I despise you! I hate you more than I have ever hated anyone in my life." I hear his brothers' gasps at the venom in my voice, but I block them out and keep my eyes fixed on Shane. "I know that you think that I love you, but you are deluded. I could never love you. You make me sick. My skin crawls when you are anywhere near me. When I think about the times you have touched my body, I want to tear off my own skin!" The tears are running down my face now as I spit out all of the hatred and venom that I have been storing for years.

"If you ever touch me again, I would die from the agony of having to endure it. You disgust me!" I shriek and he just stares at me and takes it all.

But then I see it, from the corner of my eye, what I've been waiting for. Paul drops his hand to his side as he enjoys the show. Me turning on his nephews is what his delusional mind had been hoping for. I hate guns, but I have a perfect fucking aim.

I spin and squeeze the trigger and Paul Ryan drops to the floor before he even had time to realize that I'd moved. My only regret is that he didn't see it coming. The remote he was holding clatters to the floor and I walk over to his body. He took a bullet straight between the eyes, but I have tried to kill this ghost before. This time, there will be no doubt in my mind that he is gone. I unload the remaining five bullets into his body, which jerks as each sliver of metal tears through it. And with each shot fired, the tears fall down my face faster and harder. When the chamber is empty, I keep pulling the trigger as I stare at his lifeless body, until I feel strong arms around me.

"He's gone, sweetheart," Shane whispers in my ear.

I turn in his arms and cling to him. "I wasn't talking to you," I sob.

"I know," he soothes as he hugs me tightly to him. "I know."

After Conor checks I'm okay, reprimands me for sneaking out of bed, and then hugs me tighter than I have ever been hugged before, he and Shane tell me to go with the twins while they stay behind to take care of things, which I know is code for disposing of Paul's dead body. Seemingly unable to even look at their oldest brother after recent revelations, the twins don't argue and together the three of us walk out to the Audi they drove here in, leaving the beat up Land Rover for Shane and Conor.

Liam sits in the back with me with an arm wrapped around me as Mikey drives us back to the house. We're all quiet. There is so much to say that it seems like there is no good place to start.

"You think he always knew?" Mikey eventually breaks the silence.

"If he did, then he's not the man I thought he was," Liam replies with a sigh.

"How could he not tell us?" Mikey slams his hands down on the wheel of the car.

"I don't know. I think of all the conversations we had about how much Patrick hated us and he never once told us why."

"You think it's even true?" Mikey asks.

"I don't know. Shane said it was, didn't he?"

"But if it is, then..." Mikey doesn't finish his sentence.

"I know," Liam looks down at me with tears in his eyes. "I'm sorry, Jessie."

"Don't even!" I say as I look away and snuggle against his chest. "Let's talk about all of this when we all get back to the house. There is no use in speculating and driving yourselves crazy until then." For now, I just want to sit in this car next to Liam's warm body and cherish this feeling of being safe and loved before we deal with the fact that the man who has made my life a living hell could be the father of two of the men I love more than anything in this world.

"Hmm," Liam agrees and Mikey turns up the radio and we listen to it for the rest of the way home.

CHAPTER 35
CONOR

I wipe a bead of sweat from my forehead before it rolls into my eyes making them sting even more. It's only early morning but the July sun is already beating down on us, and chopping up a dead body with an axe isn't as easy as it sounds.

"Fuck!" Shane hisses as a splatter of congealed flesh and blood hits his t-shirt.

I grin at him. "I told you to take that off." I look down at my bare chest which is covered in blood too.

"All right, Rambo. Let's just get this over with so we can get cleaned up and back to the house."

"There are showers at this new club we got, yeah?"

"Yep," he nods as he wipes his brow and stands straight, wielding an axe in his hand like the grim reaper wields his scythe.

With a final blow, I chop through the last part of Paul's leg, detaching his foot, and he lies before us in over half a dozen pieces. Now all we have to do is feed them to Farmer Murphy's feral pigs. Jack Murphy has been offering this service for as long as I can remember. There is nothing his pigs won't eat. He charges a small fortune for the privilege, however, out of respect for our dearly departed father, who was his best customer over the years, he has given us this one for free. He asks no questions and has no idea it's our uncle his swine are about to feast on.

As soon as we got Paul's body out of his house, Shane torched the place. Nothing but bad memories there. Then we called Jack Murphy in the middle of the night and drove straight here. We have both been focused on getting the job done as quickly as possible and have barely spoken other than to discuss the task at hand. Both of us are avoiding any mention of the two huge issues that are waiting for us when we get back to the house. The fact that Jessie snuck out of the goddamn house and could have gotten herself killed, and our uncle claiming to be Liam and Mikey's father. But as we get closer to the finish line, the air becomes thicker with the tension of all the things we're not saying.

"It's a pity he wasn't alive while we were doing this," Shane snarls as he tosses our uncle's arm into the pig pen.

"Sure is. Cunt!" I snarl as I toss his foot in after. Smelling the fresh meat, the pigs squeal up a frenzy and we throw in the remainder of Paul's body parts, saving the head for the last. Shane picks it up by his hair, and then kicks it into the pen like a football.

After showering in The Peacock Club and changing into fresh clothes, we're on our way back to the house. Back to Jessie and our brothers. Shane is driving, anything to keep his mind occupied, but I can't bear the tension any longer.

"So. when did you find out about the twins?"

"About a week before Alexei took Liam."

I understand why it was hard to tell the twins, especially if he didn't even know if it was true, but it hurts that he didn't trust me. We have never kept any secrets from each other, at least that's what I'd always thought. "Why didn't you tell me?"

"How could I, Con? I hated knowing. Why the fuck would I want to put you in that position, too?"

"You should have told all of us," I say with a sigh.

"You think?" he snaps.

I turn and look out of the window.

"I know I should," he says. "I wish I had, Con. But I had no fucking idea things were going to pan out like this. If I had..."

"Yeah, well nobody could have predicted this."

"I should have," he sighs deeply.

"What? How?" I frown at him.

"It all makes perfect sense now. We knew Paul was a hired gun."

"Yeah, but there are hundreds of them all over the world. The Wolf wasn't just any hired gun."

"We didn't hear from him for years and then he resurfaces just as Jessie came into our lives?"

"Yeah, because his cunt of a brother was dying? At least that's what he said, and maybe it was because of that? You couldn't have known this was going to happen, Shane."

"So why do I feel like I've let everyone down?" he says and I hear the words sticking in his throat. He puts so much fucking pressure on himself.

"You haven't let anyone down."

He doesn't respond, he simply stares at the road ahead.

"You think it's true? Was he their dad?"

"He told Em it was true. He saw her a few days ago and he told her all about it. How he and our mom had been in love. How he wanted us all to go on the run together after the twins were born, but she wouldn't put us kids at risk and have us living on the run. Then when she died, apparently he wanted to take the twins and leave but Patrick wouldn't have it. He almost killed him and that was when Paul left and didn't look back."

"Fuck!" I breathe as I lean back in my seat. That is some information to digest. Our mom and our Uncle Paul? It doesn't make sense to me. She was terrified of our dad, she would never have risked her own life, never mind our lives, like that.

"You think his version of events is true?"

"Who knows what that sadistic prick was capable of? But that's what he told Em and that's what I'll be telling the twins," he frowns at me.

"Of course," I agree. There's an alternative version of events that I can't help thinking about because we both know our uncle doesn't particularly care about consent, but perhaps he was a different man back then? Maybe he really did love our mom? She was so excited when she found out she was having twin boys; I can't imagine that they were conceived in anything other than love.

"And what about our little runaway?" I ask.

"I feel like putting her on a leash," he snaps.

"Now that could be very interesting," I chuckle and I see the hint of a smile on his face.

"She will give me a heart attack one of these days."

"Yup. She did get the job done though."

"She could have gotten herself killed," he sighs.

"I know. But she didn't. She's safe. We're all okay and the Wolf is gone."

"If something had happened to her though..."

"But it didn't, and you'll drive yourself crazy thinking otherwise. You'll also drive yourself crazy trying to control Jessie Ryan. She's a law unto herself and the sooner we realize that I think the easier our lives will be."

"What are you saying?" he frowns at me.

"I'm saying that just because she's submissive when it

comes to fucking, it doesn't mean that goes for any other area of her life. She's one of the most stubbornly independent people I've ever met. She looked after herself for ten years. She survived things most people wouldn't."

"I know that, but that's why I want to protect her from anything like that again."

"I do too, and I'm not saying we shouldn't protect her. Of course we should, but she doesn't *need* our protection and that's the difference, Shane."

"You're losing me, Con," he frowns.

"Us thinking we know best for her ended up with her sneaking out in the middle of the night and almost getting us all killed. I think you were right earlier, we should have listened to her ideas instead of shutting her down. That's all I'm saying. If it was Liam or Mikey we would have listened, wouldn't we? Even if we thought it was completely stupid we would have heard them out and probably gone along with it too."

"Yeah," Shane admits.

"So, I'm saying is that Jessie is as strong as any of us, and we can say she's one of us, but we don't always treat her like that, is all."

Shane is quiet for a few moments, digesting what I've just said. It's hard for me to admit too. "But if I didn't have different rules for her, when would I get to punish her for breaking them?" he asks with a wicked grin on his face.

"Oh, I'm not saying she's not going to get her ass spanked for last night or that we shouldn't impose all kinds of rules for her to break," I grin back. "But the big stuff? We need to let her have a voice so she doesn't pull any stupid shit like she did last night."

"You're probably right," he admits with a sigh. "What the fuck am I gonna say to them all, Con?"

"The truth, bro. That's all they need."

CHAPTER 36
MIKEY

I can't stop looking at the clock as I wait for my two older brothers to get home. A part of me almost wants them to stay away a little longer, because then I can pretend that my world wasn't just completely ripped apart. I can imagine that Paul Ryan was lying when he said that he was our father and that, even worse, Shane knew, because otherwise how can the man who I respect more than anyone in this world, the man who raised us, have kept that from us? How could he have let us go through life thinking that our own father despised us?

Jessie is curled up on the sofa with Liam watching a movie while I pace the house looking for a better distraction. She is my perfect distraction, but I can hardly bear to look at her right now. To think that the man responsible for inflicting so much pain and misery on her – the man who did all of those awful things to her – might be my father, makes me feel sick to my stomach. Will she ever look at us the same way again? I spent most of my life wishing that I wasn't Patrick Ryan's son. How fucking ironic that now I wish for no other father but him.

The sound of the front door opening makes us all look up as

Shane and Conor walk into the room. We all stare at them as they walk over and take a seat.

"Is he definitely dead?" Jessie whispers.

"Well, his head is no longer attached to his body, Angel," Conor replies with a wink and she nods.

Shane sucks in a deep breath as he looks around the room at the four of us. "Sit down, Mikey," he says and as much as I feel like telling him to go to hell, I take a seat beside Jessie.

We all look to him. "I know that I owe all of you an explanation and an apology."

"Too right you fucking do," I can't help but snap and he scowls at me in a way that reminds me of being an unruly teenager and I sit back and shut my mouth just like I used to back then.

"Is it true, Shane?" Liam asks.

"I believe so," Shane replies with a nod and me and my twin look at each other. I don't need him to speak to know that we are both thinking the same things. Jessie takes one of each of our hands in hers and squeezes as we all stare at Shane.

"I only found out a few weeks ago before Alexei took Liam," he says.

"How?" Liam snaps.

"Aunt Em called me. When Patrick couldn't get in touch with any of us, his nurse kept contacting Em, saying he needed to speak to someone and unburden himself of something. Eventually Em agreed and he told her that our mom and Paul had an affair and that he wasn't your biological father," he looks to me and Liam.

"I don't understand," I frown. "There is no way Patrick Ryan would have stood for that."

"And he didn't. He didn't know at the time, although he suspected something. But when he did find out..."

"That was why he killed her?" Liam says what I'm thinking.

"It seems so," Shane nods.

"Because of us?" Liam adds.

"No!" Shane barks. "Because he was an evil cunt!"

"Is that why Paul left too?" Conor asks. "Did he know?"

"Yeah."

"So, he knew and he just left us with that evil fucker?" I snarl. "So, he hated us just as much as Patrick? This just gets fucking better and better." I pull my hand from Jessie's and stand up, going back to pacing the floor.

"No. Paul told Aunt Em that he wanted to take you with him, but Patrick would have none of it. His ego wouldn't let people find out that his wife cheated on him with his own brother, so he gave Paul an ultimatum. Leave or he would meet the same fate as our mom."

"So, the coward just left!" Liam spat.

"Well, I think we've all learned that Paul and Patrick Ryan were both as sick and twisted as each other."

"So you didn't know until a few weeks ago?" Liam asks.

"Of course not. You think I would have let you grow up thinking our father hated you both for no reason? I mean he hated us all, but..."

"It explains his particular cruelty to the twins," Conor finishes for him.

Liam pushes himself up off the sofa too. "You should have told us, Shane!" he barks.

"I know," Shane holds his hands up in surrender.

I look at Conor, Shane and Jessie staring at me and my twin. Are they looking at us differently now, or am I imagining it? I can't think straight. This is too much to deal with for one person. Our dad was an evil psychopath who had an affair with our mom, left us to save his own skin, and then kidnapped, raped and tortured the woman that we love. *What the actual fuck*!

"I need to get out of here," I say as I head for the door.

"Me too," Liam agrees as he follows me.

"Mikey! Liam! Where are you going?" Jessie asks.

"Let them go," Shane says to her and I scowl at him. Is he saying that because he wants rid of us now? Or because he knows that some space away from them is what we need? My head knows it's the latter, but I am pissed as hell at him, so right now, my wounded ego chooses to believe the former.

"I will never fucking forgive you for keeping this from us!" I snarl at him. "Never!"

"Mikey!" he frowns at me but I turn my back on him and head for the front door.

"I did what I thought was best," he shouts after us.

"You don't get to decide what's best for us, Shane!" Liam snarls at him. "You're not our fucking father so stop acting like you are."

CHAPTER 37
JESSIE

I sit on the sofa and watch helplessly as the twins walk out of the house. I trust that Shane knows that this is what they need so I don't try and stop them. It feels like someone has dropped a hand grenade into our happy little family. I can imagine the turmoil that they're in right now. I know what it's like to have a bombshell like that dropped on you, but I can't imagine the hurt they are feeling knowing Shane kept it from them. He's always honest with his brothers, but he's their protector, too. I don't agree with his decision not to tell them as soon as he found out, but I completely see why he did what he did. I can appreciate the untenable position he felt he was in.

"Don't think that my fuck up lets you off the hook, Jessie," he suddenly growls in my direction and I turn to look at him. He is glaring at me in that way that turns my insides to jelly.

"What?" I blink at him.

"Sneaking out of here in the middle of the night to walk into the Wolf's trap. Do you have any idea how fucking stupid and reckless that was?"

"Yes," I breathe.

"You do?" he frowns at me. "So why the fuck did you do it? Have we not had enough of you walking out on us with nothing more than a note to last a lifetime?"

"Shane!" Conor shoots him a warning look.

I swallow the ball of emotion in my throat. Hadn't we agreed we'd never bring that up again? Yet the first chance he gets, he uses it against me.

"I'm sorry. I didn't mean that," he shakes his head. "I'm just so fucking angry at you, Jessie. What if the twins hadn't noticed you were missing for hours? What if he'd taken you? What if we'd lost you?"

"I did consider all of that, Shane."

"But you went anyway?" he snaps.

I look to Conor for some support but he shakes his head at me, too. "I'm with Shane on this, Angel. I've no idea what you were thinking pulling a stunt like that."

"No, you wouldn't." I sit back and fold my arms across my chest.

"And just what the hell is that supposed to mean?" Shane frowns at me.

I lean forward. "Have you ever known what it was truly like to feel fear every second of every single day? And I don't mean when you were a kid and you were scared of your dad. I mean as an adult, when you are independent and capable and strong."

They both blink at me and I go on because they have no clue how it has felt to live my life.

"To know that no matter how strong you are, how tough you become, how good you are at firing a gun, or hacking a computer, or bench-pressing your own body weight, that it doesn't matter, because there will always be some man who is bigger and stronger than you are, no matter how hard you work. And to not know whether that man is out there, watching you, waiting for you to make one little mistake before he pounces, so that no matter what you're doing, popping to the grocery store for milk, getting your hair blown out, or just walking down the street to go home, you never ever feel completely safe? Have you ever felt that?"

"No." They answer in unison.

"I have lived that every second of every day for the past ten years. I was not prepared to let him get away and have to go through that again. So I did what I had to do." I'm shouting now and tears are rolling down my face but I can't stop. The emotions of the past few days are pouring out of me and I can't do a damn thing to stop them. "I would rather die than live the rest of my life afraid like that. So, yes I thought long and hard about what I was doing, and the only regret I have is that I put you all in danger. But if you are waiting for me to apologize for making a decision about my own goddamn life, then you will be waiting a long fucking time!" I shriek the last part before pushing myself to my feet and walking out of the room with tears streaming down my face. They didn't deserve that, but the man I am really angry at is dead, so they'll have to do.

I'M LYING on my bed when the door opens and Conor walks into the room.

"Hey," I say as I wipe the tears from my cheeks.

He arches one eyebrow at me. "You feeling better?"

"I'm sorry I unloaded on you both like that," I sniff.

He sits down on the bed beside me and places his warm hand over mine. "You've been through a lot, Angel, but you were wrong when you said we don't know how it feels to live in fear."

"I was?" I frown at him. He and his brothers are the fiercest men I know. Who could they possibly be afraid of?

"It might be a different kind of fear, but we felt the Wolf's shadow over your life as much as you did. Did you not think that we were terrified he would come for you just as much as you were?"

I open my mouth to speak but he narrows his eyes at me. "Physical pain we can endure, Jessie. All of us have had more than our fair share of it. But losing you is our single greatest fear. You don't get to be so reckless with your own life when you mean so much to other people, don't you get that?"

"I do," I nod at him. "But you wouldn't listen to me. Whenever I suggested anything that involved me, you and Shane shut me down. I felt like I had no other choice."

"We should have listened to you, Angel," he admits.

"I'm sorry I snuck out," I say, despite me being adamant that I wouldn't apologize for that just fifteen minutes earlier.

He smiles at me. "I know."

CHAPTER 38
CONOR

"Will you lie here with me?" Jessie asks as I sit and stare at her. She is so fucking beautiful and I can't believe that we almost lost her. How can I resist her? Besides, none of us got much sleep last night with her escapades. I crawl onto the bed and wrap my arms around her and she buries her head against my chest. "Is Shane going to punish me for sneaking out?" she breathes.

"No," I brush her hair back from her face. "Shane is dealing with his own demons right now. He's angrier at himself than he is at you."

"You're not angry with him, are you?" she asks as she looks up and stares into my eyes.

"No. I understand why he didn't tell anyone, but I can see why Liam and Mikey are so pissed at him."

"I'm glad he still has you in his corner," she sighs as she snuggles against me again.

"If you ever put yourself in danger like that again, you won't have to worry about Shane punishing you, because I'll do it myself," I warn her and she shivers in my arms and it's not from fear. Fuck me, this woman terrifies me. Ever since that night in

New York when I spanked her ass with Shane's belt I have been thinking about exploring that side of myself with her. It's not something I've wanted to do before because we have something much deeper than that. What's been stopping me most is the fact that she is capable of handling so much pain that I'm truly worried that I'd go too far and hurt her. I'm not sure I can wait much longer, though, because she has a dark side too and I know that going there with her would be fucking incredible.

The two of us must have fallen asleep because it's getting dark when we wake. Jessie rubs her eyes and looks at me. "You think the twins are back yet?"

"I doubt it."

"You think Shane's okay?" She bites her bottom lip and I have to stop myself from biting it too.

"Why don't you go and check on him and I'll wait up for the twins?" I plant a kiss on her forehead and then climb out of bed.

"You sure you don't want me to wait up with you?"

"No. Go get some sleep, and try and make sure Shane gets some too, okay?"

"I will." She gives me one of her beautiful smiles and I wonder how this woman just went through what she did and still radiates so much goodness.

CHAPTER 39
SHANE

I lie in bed staring at the ceiling and listening to my heartbeat pounding in my ears. I feel like every single person in this house is pissed at me. I took all of my anger out on Jessie and as much as I'm entitled to feel angry after what she did, I could've handled it a little better.

I'm worried about Liam and Mikey. I should have told them as soon as I found out but I wasn't lying when I said I didn't know how to. I didn't even know if it was the truth until Paul confirmed it himself. How the fuck was I supposed to blow their world apart on the ramblings of a dying man?

The door to my room creaks open, allowing a sliver of light from the hallway to illuminate the darkness. I see her silhouette slipping into the darkness and suck in a deep breath. If she's here to tell me what an asshole I am, I think my heart might just give out. I can't take any more anger directed at me right now. For over thirty years I have taken so much of it. My father's rage. Our mother's secrets. The guilt of not being able to protect them all. And I would do it all again for each and every one of them. Tomorrow I will stand in front of them and beg my brothers' forgiveness if I have to, but right now I am tired of it all.

"Are you awake?" she whispers as she tiptoes toward the bed.

"As if I could sleep," I reply with a sigh that vibrates through my bones.

When she reaches the bed, she lifts the duvet and slips beneath it, pressing her warm body against me. Her soft skin feels so good against mine and I wrap my arms around her, pulling her close and burying my face in her hair.

She responds in kind, wrapping her legs and arms around me like a koala and squeezing me tight. "I love you," she whispers and that is my complete fucking undoing.

I don't know what to do with the emotion that wells up in my chest and threatens to spill out of me, so I do what I know best, going to the place with her that I feel most comfortable. The place where I'm in complete control.

I roll over, flipping her onto her back and pinning her wrists above her head with one hand while I tug at her panties with the other. The fabric pulls taut against her skin as I stretch it, digging into her soft flesh. She lifts her ass off the bed, allowing me to pull them off more easily and as soon as they're down to her knees she wriggles them off herself. I settle between her thighs and my cock hardens as it presses against her pussy.

"I need you," I growl.

"I'm right here," she whispers before I lean down and crash my lips against hers, kissing her so hard she gasps into my mouth making my cock throb. She spreads her legs wider and I roll my hips against her and her sweet juices slick my cock. I shift position until I'm nudging at her opening and she groans softly into my mouth.

This is the first time we have been together like this since he took her and I'm suddenly overcome with a primal urge to reclaim her for my own, and it scares the hell out of me. I pull back from her and she blinks up at me.

"Shane, please don't," she whispers as tears form in her eyes.

Fuck! Am I hurting her? "We don't have to..."

"No," she interrupts me. "I want you to stop thinking about what he did."

I suck in a breath. How do I not think about that? And how do I tell her that it makes me want to fuck her so hard, I am the only man she'll feel inside her until the end of time? "I don't want to hurt you."

"You won't, so stop treating me like I'm fragile. Like I'm damaged." A sob catches in her throat and it slices a welt across my heart that she would think for even one second that I see her like that.

"You are neither of those things, sweetheart."

"So show me. Prove to me that nothing has changed between us."

"Jessie," I groan. "I can't hold back with you. Not tonight."

"So, don't. I need you too, Shane," she pleads.

She is so fucking sweet. I don't deserve her, but I'll take her anyway. I drive into her, forcing her a few inches up the bed and her pussy grips my cock so tightly it's a struggle to pull myself out of her again, but I do, only to drive into her even harder. I wrap my free hand around her throat and squeeze gently.

"Shane!" she gasps as she wrenches her lips from mine, blinking up at me with those incredible blue eyes and it only makes me want to fuck her harder. I rail into her, my anger and my guilt dissipating with every single thrust. She is everything I need.

"I love you, Jessie," I groan before I seal my mouth over hers again.

. . .

I PRESS my forehead against hers, our breathing fast and hard and our bodies beaded with perspiration. I brush her damp hair back from her face and she smiles up at me. Despite what I just did to her – all of the anger and guilt I just poured into her – she fucking smiles at me.

"I'm sorry I said those things to you earlier," she whispers.

"It's been a tough day for everyone, sweetheart. I could have handled it better."

"Did Shane Ryan just admit he was wrong?" She smiles at me and it makes my heart beat faster.

"No," I scowl at her. "I was completely right, but I could have dealt with it differently is all I said."

She bites on her lip, that smart mouth of hers ready for a comeback any second, so I don't let her. "When he took you, I thought I was going to lose my mind, Jessie. For real. Thinking about you out there alone and afraid and not knowing where you were almost drove me insane. That you would put us all through that again..."

"I'm sorry," she whispers as her eyes fill with tears.

"I'm not trying to make you feel bad, sweetheart." I brush her hair back from her face. "I just want you to understand how much the thought of losing you terrifies me."

"I know."

I close my eyes as the memory of feeling so helpless comes flooding back to me.

"Shane?" She reaches up and trails her fingertips over my cheek until I look at her again.

"When I realized it was Paul who'd taken you, the thought that you might think I'd known, and that I'd betrayed you..." I can't finish the sentence because the words stick in my throat.

"I didn't think that. Not even for a second."

I smile as I kiss her forehead and roll onto my back. She turns on her side and lays her head on my chest, running her fingertips over my abdomen.

"I love this tattoo," she whispers.

I look down at the one she is tracing. It is a Celtic cross with a Gaelic phrase wrapped around it. Each of my brothers have one too. "It means 'Always Remember.'"

"I know," she whispers. "I googled it. It's beautiful."

"We should get you one, too," I laugh, only half-joking.

"I don't like needles," she says with a shiver. "But you're welcome to get one of my face or something?"

"Your face?"

"Yes," she giggles.

"And where on my person would I get such a work of art?"

"Hmm?" she chews on her lip. "Your ass?"

I laugh out loud at that and she does too before she falls quiet again.

"You know what I realized in that horrible basement this morning?"

"What's that, sweetheart?"

"How much faith you have in me," she breathes.

"You did?"

"Yes. I don't know if I could have said those things I did to Conor or the twins without breaking their hearts, even if it was only for a few moments, but I knew that you would get it. Even though I was looking at you, I knew that you would understand who I was really saying those things to."

I press a kiss on her forehead. There was a second when she called me a liar that I worried she was starting to believe my uncle's bullshit, but when she spoke of hatred and disgust, I realized that wasn't for me. I have experienced the love of this incredible woman and I know that it's true as sure as I know that grass is green.

"That means so much to me after everything we've been through, Shane," she whispers.

I close my eyes and pull her tighter. "It means a lot to me too, sweetheart."

CHAPTER 40
JESSIE

I lie in Shane's arms, listening to the sound of his heartbeat. It usually soothes me, but now my mind races with questions and not enough answers. I wonder where the twins are and when they'll come home. I hope they can forgive Shane for keeping the truth from them so we can get back to our happy little unit. But mostly I think about the ghost of the Wolf. Even though he's gone, he still haunts me.

"Tell me what's going on in that beautiful head of yours, sweetheart," Shane says as he brushes the hair from my face.

I shrug. "Today has been so... I don't even know how to put it into words."

"I know it has," he presses a soft kiss on my forehead. "But there's something else going on in there. Tell me what it is."

I look up into his beautiful green eyes. "Does anything that Paul said... Does it change the way you see me?"

"No." He frowns at me. "Why would it?"

"I don't know. I just... Those things he said ... about me and him."

He cups my chin with his hand, tilting my face up towards his. "I already knew what he did to you, sweetheart. And even if

I didn't, why would that change anything between you and me?"

"Well, because it was him who taught me to enjoy pain. And that's kind of fucked up. And also, that's kind of our thing."

He narrows his eyes at me. "I think he taught you to endure pain, not enjoy it, Jessie. The fact that he provoked a reaction in your body afterwards is purely physiological and is nothing you should feel any guilt about. There is a fine line between pleasure and pain, sweetheart. Just because you endure a lot of pain, doesn't mean you enjoy it. I don't think that you do."

"But I do, don't I? With you?" I breathe.

He shakes his head. "What the Wolf did to you. What was that?"

"Pain," I whisper.

"And with me. What do you feel? Even when I make it hurt?"

"Just pleasure," I breathe.

He winks at me and the breath catches in my throat. He's quiet for a while and then he turns to me.

"You never did give me an answer to my proposal, Jessie."

"You mean your plan to marry me off to Conor and give you a whole tribe of nieces and nephews?"

"Yes."

"But then I'd have to live without you."

"I'd still be in your life, sweetheart. Just not like this."

I blink away a tear that falls from the corner of my eye. "Is that what you want?" I whisper.

"I want you to be happy."

I arch an eyebrow at him. "That's not what I asked you."

"I will never love anyone the way that I love you, Jessie Ryan," he breathes.

"Does that mean we're written in the stars?" I smile at him.

"Forever."

"You still haven't answered my question, Shane."

"Because you already know the answer, sweetheart. But I'd do anything to make you happy and you know that too. I want to make sure you don't turn around in thirty years' time and wish you'd made different choices. I want you to have options."

"I love you," I whisper.

"I know," he growls before he rolls on top of me, sealing my mouth with a kiss and I melt into him, forgetting all about the drama of our lives, if only for a little while.

CHAPTER 41
CONOR

The sound of the front door opening wakes me and I look up to see my two younger brothers falling through it. Drunken assholes.

"Shhh!" one of them giggles as they make their way into the room.

"Did you two drive in that state?" I snap at them as they stumble over to the sofa.

"No!" Liam shakes his head while Mikey giggles. "We got a caxi-tab!"

Fuck me! "Get to bed, you pair of fucking buffoons."

"Con, I don't feel well," Liam suddenly groans as he falls onto the sofa. Mikey stumbles and I catch him in my arms. The alcohol fumes almost knock me on my ass. "Have you two been drinking tequila?"

"Yesh," Mikey says with a nod.

"For fuck's sake!" I say with a sigh as I lower him onto the sofa.

They slide against each other as their eyes roll in their heads. I haven't seen them this drunk since they were teenagers. "I am not wiping up any of your puke tonight," I snap as I cover them with the huge fleece blanket from the back of the sofa.

"Conor!" Liam groans sleepily. "I feel sick!"

"Well that's what you get for drinking your body weight in tequila, numb-nuts."

"Numb-nuts," Mikey giggles before he passes out.

I sit on the armchair and run a hand over my face. I'm sorry I waited up for them now. Now I've got to sit here and make sure they don't choke on their own puke. I feel like I'm the only one keeping a lid on shit here. I've hardly had any time with my girl. I'm constantly fighting fires. I wonder if this is what Shane feels like all the time?

It's light by the time the twins wake up. Liam groans loudly as he pushes Mikey off him.

"Fuck!" Mikey hisses as he rubs his eyes and sits up. "What time is it?"

"Seven a.m.!" I say.

"What time did we get home?" Liam asks.

"About one."

"How did we get home?" Mikey blinks at me.

I arch one eyebrow at them. "In a caxi-tab, apparently."

"I'm going to bed," Liam sighs as he goes to stand up.

I frown at them. "Not just yet."

"It's too early for a deep and meaningful, Con," Mikey groans as he stands up too.

"Sit your asses down before I put you down. Now!" I snap and they both blink at me but they do as they're told.

"What?" Liam sniffs.

"I get that you two are upset. I get that yesterday was

fucked up and you've got a lot on your plate. But you do not get to walk out of here and not answer your phones and have everyone worrying about you."

"Sorry," Liam grumbles.

"Not like Shane even gives a fuck! He's not here waiting for us, is he?" Mikey snaps and the lid on my temper blows off.

"What the fuck did you just say?" I snarl.

I see his Adam's apple bob as he swallows, but that kid must still be juiced on tequila, because he glares at me. "You heard me. He's in bed with Jessie while he's so worried about us?"

I stand up and step toward them. "Yes, they are in bed after I told them I'd wait up for you. Because guess what, assholes, they've had a pretty shit couple of days too! Do you have any idea how bad Shane feels?"

Liam snorts. "He should have thought about that before he lied to us."

I suck in a deep breath as I try to stop myself from shaking them. "Yes, he fucked up. He should have told you a couple of weeks ago, but we were all kind of busy, weren't we? And I don't care how much he fucked up, he has done nothing but look after you two your whole goddamn lives. He gave up everything for us. He fucking raised you both from babies. You think he didn't have shit he wanted to do when he was younger without three kids to look after? He never wanted to leave Ireland. He had plans. You know why he built this house? So he could live here in peace. Maybe get married and have some kids. But after what happened to you both, he put all of it on hold. He took us to New York and he built us all a new life, so don't you ever let me catch you saying he doesn't give a fuck *ever* again!"

I walk away from them before I go on and say something I might regret. I get that my little brothers are angry and annoyed, but they take Shane's loyalty to them for granted. He has always looked out for all of us and never asked for anything in return.

"Con!" Liam shouts after me.

"I don't want to hear it. I'm going to bed!" I walk through to the hallway where our bedrooms are. My hand curls over the door handle to my own room, but I look across at Shane's instead. I am so fucking tired from sitting up and watching Liam and Mikey to make sure they didn't die from alcohol poisoning, but I want to fall asleep next to her.

I open the door and walk inside the dark room. She is on her side, curled up next to Shane. They both look so peaceful, I turn around to walk out again.

"You okay, Con?" Shane asks. I should have known he wouldn't be in a deep sleep.

"The twins are back," I say quietly so I don't wake Jessie.

"I heard them falling through the door a few hours ago," he says with a soft sigh.

"Oh."

"You want something else?"

"I'm tired," I reply as I walk to the bed and look at her.

"Then get in," Shane nods toward the empty space on the other side of Jessie. It's not like him to share a bed with anyone but her, but right now it feels like the whole equilibrium of our family unit is off and I imagine that he is feeling it as much as the twins. I walk around the bed and climb in beside her, pressing my body against hers. She wiggles her bare ass against me and my cock twitches in my shorts. Shane shoots me a look that reminds me I was invited in here to sleep but I can't help grinning at him. She's so fucking sexy, I know he wouldn't take much convincing if I woke her up right now and suggested we both fuck her, but I'm exhausted. I wrap my arm around her waist and kiss her shoulder instead.

"Conor," she mumbles sleepily.

"Shh. Go back to sleep, Angel."

"Okay," she sighs as she shifts her body slightly so she is nestled perfectly between Shane and me. Then I fall asleep with her perfect ass against my groin.

CHAPTER 42
LIAM

After our epic binge drinking session last night, it's late afternoon by the time Mikey and I finally roll out of bed. I got up for some water about midday and the house was quiet, so I suspect Jessie and my brothers slept most of the day away too. I think we could all sleep for a week after the drama of the last few days.

I'm still reeling from having my ass handed to me by Conor earlier. I don't want to face him. I don't want to face Shane either, but most of all I don't want to face Jessie. Learning that my real father was the man responsible for hurting her in so many ways has completely overwhelmed me. It's all I can think about. How can things ever be the same between us again?

But I can't stay in this room forever and after a quick shower, I head into the living area with Mikey following close behind me.

"Hey." Jessie looks up and smiles at us as we walk in.

"Hey, Red," Mikey replies but I avoid her gaze and sit on the armchair while Mikey hovers by the bookshelves. The tension in the room is suddenly thick and I can feel everybody's eyes on me. Standing up, I decided I'd be better off back in my room, but as I'm walking out, Jessie springs up from the sofa and stops me in my tracks.

"Liam. Where are you going?"

"Back to bed," I snap with my head down.

"You want something to eat?"

"No," I shake my head, still unable to look at her beautiful face.

"Liam?" she whispers. "Why won't you look at me?"

I hear a sob catch in her throat and it breaks my heart so much that I'm forced to look up. "How can you look at me and not see him, Jessie?" I drop my head again quickly, scared to look into her eyes in case I see something in them that I can't stand. She's too good of a person to make me feel bad about who my real father is, but she can't hide the truth from me. I can read her so well, and it's something that I've always loved about our connection, but now I wish for blissful ignorance. She places her warm hands on my cheeks and tilts my head so I can't avoid looking at her.

"I look at you and see you, Liam. The same man I saw yesterday. The same man who I'm completely in love with."

"But he's our dad, Jessie. The man who did all of that fucked up shit to you, is my fucking dad!"

"Hey! My biological father was a madman who had my whole family slaughtered, including his own twin brother. But I am who I am because of my dad – the man who raised me – and not that murderous psychopath. Just like you are who you are because of the man who raised you." She glances over at Shane and smiles. "And even though you're pissed at him right now, you know that he did a pretty good job with you and Mikey."

"I hate that he caused you so much pain," I say. I have a physical ache in my chest when I think about what that sadistic cunt did to her. It was rough enough when I thought he was our uncle, but that my own father was capable of it... Not that Patrick Ryan was much better.

"And I hate that he's causing you some now. Please, don't let this come between you and me, Liam. That would be the true pain. It would break my heart," she says as a fat tear rolls down her cheek. What the fuck I ever did to deserve her devotion, I'll never know.

"I will never let it come between us, Jessie," I say as I wipe the tear from her face.

"Good," she whispers as she leans up on her tiptoes and seals her lips over mine. I wrap my arms around her as she slips her tongue into my mouth and I melt into her, kissing so fiercely that I feel like I might run out of breath.

"Bedroom!" she breathes as she breaks our kiss for a second and what can I do but obey her as she kisses me again and I walk backwards toward our bedroom. As we pass Mikey, she reaches out and grabs hold of his hand too.

MIKEY CLOSES the door behind us and the three of us stand beside the bed. Jessie peels her top off over her head.

"Are you boys planning on keeping your clothes on?" she asks with a grin and a pop of one eyebrow.

"Fuck, no!" Mikey chuckles as he starts to unbutton his jeans. I undress too until all three of us are naked.

"What's going on in that deviant mind of yours, Red?" Mikey asks.

"I want both of you right now," she breathes as she reaches for us.

"You've always got both of us," I whisper against her ear as I step up beside her, pressing my body against her back.

"Yeah, Red," Mikey agrees as he presses against her front until she is sandwiched between us. She wraps her arms around

Mikey's neck and pulls him to her for a kiss as I press soft kisses against her neck that make her squirm. My hand slides between her and Mikey until I find her slick folds. I can't help groaning as she grinds against my hand. "You're always so wet for us, baby."

"How does she feel, bro?" Mikey breathes as he breaks their kiss.

"She's fucking soaking," I groan. "I can smell how ready you are for us, baby. You make me so fucking hard."

She gasps as I press my cock against her ass and push a finger deep inside her pussy.

"What do you want, Red?" Mikey hisses.

"I want both of you to fuck me right now!" she groans as she releases a rush of slick heat onto my finger.

I look up at my twin and he nods his head. We don't need to speak to know what the other is thinking. And I have wanted to do this with her for a long time.

"Get her onto the bed," I say and Mikey guides her to the bed before pushing her to lie down.

We both look down at her. She is the most beautiful fucking thing I have ever seen in my life. I want all of her. Her body, heart and soul. I need to know that she still trusts us, and that things are no different now that she knows who we truly are. She can tell me that things haven't changed but I need to feel it from her.

"Are you going to tell me what's going on in those devious minds of yours?" she breathes.

"You trust us, baby?" I ask.

She doesn't miss a beat. "Yes."

"You up for something a little different, Red?" Mikey grins as he crawls onto the bed beside her.

"With you two? Always!" She smiles at us both and my cock throbs in appreciation.

"We're gonna have to get her super wet," Mikey says to me with a flash of one eyebrow.

"What are you two planning?" she asks with a frown as I crawl onto the bed. I run my hands up her calves to her knees and spread her legs wide until her beautiful pink pussy is on full display.

"Oh don't worry. You're going to love it, baby," I chuckle as I bend my head low and lick her folds while Mikey kisses her. She whimpers when I nudge her clit with my tongue and it sends all of the blood rushing straight to my cock. When my tongue is joined by Mikey's fingers, she shudders and bucks so hard that I have to press on her thighs to hold her down as her orgasm reverberates through her entire body.

"Oh, God," she hisses as her juices run from her opening.

"She ready yet, bro?" Mikey chuckles as he looks down at me.

"One more should do it," I grin up at him. "Want to switch?"

"Hell, yeah," he grins back at me and we swap places.

Jessie looks up at me through hooded eyes as she recovers from her climax. "You okay, baby?"

"Yes," she pants and I assume Mikey has just done something incredible with his tongue because her eyes roll back in her head and she hisses his name. Not one to miss out on the action, I squeeze her breasts and tug on her nipples and her eyes open again and lock on mine.

"Liam," she whimpers.

"You want my fingers with Mikey's mouth?"

She nods her head as she bites on her lip and I slide my hand down her body until I find the slick, swollen bud of flesh and circle it with my fingers.

"Stop biting that lip," I order and her mouth drops open allowing me to dip my head and slide my tongue inside there instead. My cock twitches against her hipbone as I press my body against hers. I love how submissive she is when we fuck.

"You feel how hard I am for you?" I growl as I break our kiss.

"Yes," she gasps as Mikey and I bring her to the edge of another climax. I feel my twin's tongue brush my fingers as he eats her pussy as I keep toying with her clit and it makes me even harder. I love sharing her with him. I cannot fucking wait to take her together. The sooner we make her come again, the better.

I press harder on her clit and she moans. I listen to Mikey's soft groans and know that he is as eager as I am to make her come again so that we can fuck her.

CHAPTER 43
JESSIE

My head spins as I pant for breath. Liam smiles down at me while Mikey crawls up the bed, wiping his mouth with the back of his hand as he does.

"You okay, Red?" he grins at me.

I nod, unable to speak. These men do things to my body that I had never imagined possible.

"You wanna top or bottom?" Mikey looks at his twin.

"I'll top from the bottom," Liam chuckles as he lies down on the bed.

"The fuck you will," Mikey laughs and I wonder what the hell these two have in store for me. "Come here, baby." Liam takes my hand and pulls me to straddle him. He holds his cock in his hand and I lower myself onto it.

"Fuck, you feel so good," he hisses as I sink low onto him, allowing him to stretch me wide open.

"She ready, bro?" Mikey asks as he gets in position behind me.

"Yep," Liam replies as he reaches up and places his hands on my face. "Come here." He pulls me down so I'm lying on his chest and kisses me softly. "You know we'd never hurt you, right?"

"Yes," I breathe. "But we've done this before."

"Not this, baby," he shakes his head and then he winks at me. "Just relax."

Telling me to relax has the opposite affect and my entire body tenses involuntarily.

"Jessie," Liam whispers as he brushes my hair from my face before he pulls me in for another kiss. This time it is deep and full of passion and longing. His tongue dances against mine and I feel my body melting into his as Mikey's hands run over my back and ass before he grabs hold of my hip with one hand. Then his cock is nudging at me, but not at my ass where I expected. He presses it against my pussy opening and I edge forward instinctively but he and his brother hold me in place.

"I won't hurt you, Red," Mikey says as he pushes the tip inside me, along with Liam's cock.

I wrench my lips from Liam's as I suck in a breath. I suppose I did ask them both to fuck me, but I hadn't expected this. My pussy stretches wider than it ever has as he pushes deeper and the slight burning gives way to pleasure as both of their cocks throb against my pussy walls.

"You okay?" Liam asks as he cups my face in his hands.

"Yes," I grind out the word as my body gets used to the sensation of being so full.

"Breathe, Red," Mikey soothes in my ear as he leans over me. "Let me inside you."

I nod and take deep breaths to steady my breathing and my heart, which feels like it's about to burst right out of my chest.

Liam stays still while his brother pushes further inside me and I listen to the sound of their soft grunts and groans as they hold off from fucking me the way I know they are desperate to.

The knowledge that I have them in the palm of my hand makes me feel powerful beyond measure. I push back slightly, allowing Mikey to edge in a little more and both he and Liam groan loudly when I do.

"Your pussy loves this, baby," Liam hisses. "Because you are squeezing me so tight, I could come just lying here like this."

"You feel *so* good," I groan as they stretch me even further.

"Wait until we start moving," Mikey chuckles. "Tell us when you're ready."

I lie still, my pussy walls contracting as it gets used to the feeling of both of them inside me together. "I'm ready."

"Oh, fuck!" Mikey hisses as he holds onto my hips and starts to fuck me slowly. Liam remains still while his brother finds a rhythm and I moan so loudly that I know Conor and Shane must have heard me.

Waves of pleasure roll through my body as Mikey's cock goes further into me with each thrust and Liam's throbs inside my pussy. My walls clench around them, pulling them in deeper even though I'm not sure how I'll stretch to accommodate that because I know that neither of them are all the way in yet.

Liam pulls my face to his and kisses me again as he thrusts into me. He swallows my groan as his own rumbles through his chest. Then Mikey is lying on top of me, peppering kisses over my back as his hand slides between us and he begins to rub my clit while the two of them fuck me slowly. The pressure in my center feels overwhelming and I whimper as I move my hips, riding both of them as I chase the release I so desperately need.

"I'm going to come," Liam hisses as he breaks our kiss and drives into me harder. Mikey responds by pulling out of me and I groan at the loss of fullness, but he pushes his cum-drenched cock into my ass instead making me lose all control. My entire body shudders as my climax tears through my body and I release a torrent of wet heat that soaks the three of us.

"Fuck, did you just squirt for us, Red?" Mikey growls as he thrusts his cock into my ass.

"I..." I shake my head and lie down on Liam's chest. He wraps his arms around me and plants a kiss on my head as his twin goes on fucking me.

"Fuck, Red!" Mikey growls as he holds onto my hips and drives into me as Liam squeezes me tighter to him.

"Mikey," I groan as the last waves of my huge orgasm roll through me but they don't stop. They build to another crescendo and I suck in a deep breath as I bury my face in Liam's neck.

"You gonna come again, baby?" Liam chuckles.

I shake my head. "I can't."

"Let's see about that." He burrows his hand between our slick bodies and begins to rub my clit. As if I could take any more, Mikey slides two thick fingers deep into my pussy and presses on my G-spot and I cry out as stars flicker behind my eyelids and I come harder than I ever have in my life. I gasp for air as every nerve ending in my body sparks with electricity. Mikey bites down on my neck as he grinds out his own release and I continue quivering between the two of them, feeling so much pleasure that it borders on too much. These men bring me to the very edge of my limits before gently easing me back down as they rub their warm hands over my body and pepper me with kisses.

Tears roll down my face as the last tremors vibrate through me and Liam holds me tight while Mikey pulls out of me and rolls onto his back.

"Fuck, Red, that was intense," he breathes.

"Hmm," Liam agrees as he tilts my chin so he can look in my eyes. It takes me a moment to focus on him. "You okay?"

"Yes. Intense," is all I can say.

He chuckles softly and the sound vibrates through his body

and into mine as I lie on top of him, completely spent and entirely boneless.

"We are definitely gonna have to change these sheets," Mikey winks at me as he reaches out and takes my hand.

CHAPTER 44
MIKEY

After Jessie, Liam, and I took a shower, I left them in the bedroom and came to the kitchen to make a start on some late supper. I'm not sure any of us have eaten a decent meal at a regular meal time in days, and being in the kitchen is one of my favorite ways to de-stress and clear my head. The past few hours with Jessie have certainly helped. After the initial shock wore off, I wasn't as worried as Liam was about her changing toward us because of who our father was. Of all people, Jessie gets that we are not defined by our biology, but it was still a relief to know that she trusts us the same way she always has, and what we all just did proved that beyond any words she could have spoken.

I rummage in the refrigerator for some fresh tomatoes and when I hear footsteps behind me I sigh inwardly. I've not spoken to Conor since this morning when he tore Liam and me a new one, and Shane... I don't know what the fuck I'm going to say to him when I see him next. I pray this is Liam or Jessie coming in here but when I turn around it's my oldest brother standing in front of me.

Shane checks his watch. "You're cooking?"

"Yeah," I shrug. "What doesn't get eaten will keep."

"Oh," he stares at me, his hands shoved in his pockets and his jaw working.

I stare back as I close the refrigerator door, tomatoes in my hand and a dishcloth over my shoulder, but not a single word on my tongue.

Like divine intervention, someone opens the door and we both look away to see Liam sauntering in with a smile on his face. It disappears when he sees Shane and then the three of us stand there looking at each other in awkward silence, until Shane finally breaks the tension.

"Let's have this out right now, boys," he says as he walks to the kitchen table and takes a seat, indicating that we should do the same. We follow obediently, still conditioned to do whatever our big brother tells us.

I open my mouth to speak, expecting that he'll be wanting an apology from us both, but he starts talking before I can get a word out.

"I'm sorry that I kept this from you both," he says with a heavy sigh. "Em told me just a few days before you were taken." He nods to Liam. "And I'll be honest, I had no fucking idea what to say to you both."

"But..." Liam starts but Shane glares at him and he closes his mouth.

"I know that is no excuse for not telling you sooner. But every time I wanted to, something else happened. I was planning on telling you after this trip. I wanted to see if Paul knew. I didn't even know if Patrick was telling the truth or whether it was his way of trying to absolve himself of any blame for being such a shitty father to you both. Easing his conscience or something."

"I've never known you not have the right words for anything in my life, Shane," I tell him with a frown.

"Are you calling me a liar?" he glares back.

"No, but I don't buy your whole you didn't know what to say bit, is all."

"It's not that I didn't know what to say." He shakes his head. "I didn't know how to tell you and not tear your fucking worlds apart. Can't you see that?"

"That's not the only reason though," Liam adds and I turn and look at my twin.

"No," Shane swallows hard and looks at him.

"You knew I'd blame myself for him killing mum?" Liam whispers.

Shane nods in response and Liam turns to me. My twin and I are like mirror images of each other, but we are so very different. I sometimes forget how deeply Liam feels. The traumas of our childhood taught him to turn inward and look to himself for answers — and more often than not, blame — while I am more practical and deal with things head on. I use humor and my stubborn desire to prove Patrick Ryan wrong to process the shit we went through. And that was exactly what Liam did. He blamed himself. Then he questioned how everyone else would view him because Paul Ryan was our father and not Patrick, whereas for me, we simply swapped one monster for another. For me, it explained why Patrick Ryan hated our guts, and in that it has given me some peace, but for Liam it has only brought more insecurities and doubts.

"You must know that none of it was our fault, right?" I say as I place my hand on the back of Liam's neck.

"Yeah," he nods and while his head does know that, his heart will take a while to catch up.

Liam turns back to Shane. "I told you once that there was nothing you could do that would make me turn my back on you."

Shane's Adam's apple bobs as he swallows and I feel my

muscles tense as the emotion in Liam somehow spills over into me. The air in this room is so thick with tension, I could cut it with a knife.

"You are the only dad we've ever had." Liam wipes a tear from his cheek and I feel like goddamn crying myself now. "And I'm sorry I was an asshole to you. You didn't deserve that."

"Yeah. Me too," I add quietly. Liam is right. Conor has always looked out for us, too. He is the best big brother anyone could ask for, but this man right here is our father. He has protected and provided for us from the moment we were born, and how can we be pissed at him for still wanting to do that?

"I kinda deserved it," Shane says and a tear rolls down his face and I almost lose my shit. I have never seen him cry my whole life.

The sound of Jessie and Conor laughing breaks the tension as they walk through the door. They stop when they see us.

"Everything okay?" Conor asks with a frown.

Shane looks to me and Liam.

"Yeah. Perfect," Liam replies.

"Glad to hear it," Conor winks at us and I'm grateful he's no longer pissed at us because he's a scary motherfucker, and I hate him not being on my side.

"Are you cooking?" Jessie asks as she glances at the chopped onions on the side and the fresh minced beef.

"Yes," I stand up and walk over to her. "I'm making a chili."

"Oh, I love your chili," she beams at me as she takes a seat on a stool at the kitchen island.

"Nice. I'm starving," Conor agrees as he sits beside her.

"So am I after that workout," I wink at Jessie.

"It was pretty impressive," she laughs and blushes at the same time.

"What exactly were you three up to?" Conor growls at he leans down and nips her bare shoulder.

"Hmm?" She purses her lips together. Us boys have a rule that we don't talk about what we do in private with her. It kind of feels disrespectful, but Jessie is entitled to tell them anything she wants. "It was something different. New." She blushes further.

"New?" Shane walks over to her now, his interest well and truly piqued. "Now you have to tell us what the fuck you all did, sweetheart." He smiles as he sits beside her and she is sandwiched between him and Conor.

"They both..." She closes her eyes and shakes her head as her cheeks burn with heat and I can't help but laugh.

"At the same time," Liam adds for her.

"But we always do that?" Conor frowns.

Jessie opens her eyes and looks at me, silently pleading with me to put her out of her misery and tell them so she doesn't have to say the words. "Not in the same place though, bro." I wink at him and watch with a grin as he and Shane realize what we mean.

Shane turns to her. "They both fucked your pussy at the same time?" he whispers, but loud enough for us all to hear.

"Yes," she chews on her lip.

"Fuck!" Conor hisses.

"What was it like?" Shane frowns in bemusement, as though he has never considered this as an option before. And I suppose he hasn't. He's not as used to sharing as Liam and I are.

"Amazing!" she whispers.

"Fucking epic!" I add.

"Uh-huh," Liam agrees.

"It's not something I could do a lot though, if you know what I mean. I need some recovery time," she purrs and my cock twitches in my sweatpants.

"Fuck, Angel, do you have to make me constantly hard?" Conor groans.

"Like how much recovery time?" Shane frowns at her.

"To do that again? Like a week or two, maybe?"

"And how about for just regular stuff?"

"I'd say nothing involving this whole region," she waves a hand over her groin, "for at least four days."

"Four days?" Conor snaps. "Fuck that!"

"You put our girl out of action for *four days*?" Shane glares at me and Liam and I see Jessie's shoulders shaking as she laughs silently.

"She's fucking with you." I grin at him and he turns to her.

"Are you?"

"Of course I am," she chuckles. "I'll be fine tomorrow. Just nothing more tonight, okay?"

"Fine," Shane says before kissing her temple, but Conor sighs deeply and shakes his head. Jessie wraps her arms around his neck and whispers something in his ear that I don't hear, but it makes him laugh out loud. Then he kisses her too and she sits at the kitchen island with a huge goofy grin on her face and my older brothers looking at her like they might eat her if I don't get this chili made soon.

CHAPTER 45
SHANE

We all sit around the dining table having devoured second helpings of Mikey's chili, which I had almost forgotten tasted so good.

"It's a good thing Jessie is already out of action for the night," Mikey laughs as he pats his flat stomach. "Because I don't know about you all, but I am fit to bursting and I can barely breathe, let alone do anything more fun."

Liam nods and groans his agreement.

Conor is sitting beside her and he wraps an arm around her shoulder. "Well, neither of you are getting your filthy little mitts anywhere near our girl tonight anyway, because she is spending the night in my room."

"Yes I am," she smiles and rests her head on his shoulder. "I need some TLC."

Conor kisses her forehead softly.

My cell is on the table and it starts to vibrate as Erin's name and number flashes on the screen and I frown. Why the hell is she calling me after ten at night?

"Hello," I answer, feeling Jessie's eyes burning into me.

"Shane," she purrs. "I have the final papers for your father's estate here. We should really get them signed as soon as possible so that everything can be tied up before the funeral on Wednesday, and then we can head back to New York immediately after."

"Fine. I'll call round to your firm's offices tomorrow."

"Actually, I have to fly to London tomorrow and I won't be back until the morning of the funeral. It would be best if we could get these signed now."

I sigh and run a hand over my jaw. "Where shall I meet you?"

"I'm still at the hotel."

"The hotel? I'll meet you there in an hour."

"Good. I'll see you soon."

I end the call and put my cell on the table as four pairs of eyes stare at me. "You're meeting Erin in a hotel?" Mikey arches an eyebrow at me.

I look at Jessie when I answer him. "I need to sign some papers for her."

"Can't it wait until morning?" Conor asks.

My eyes stay fixed on Jessie's and hers on mine. "No. She has to fly to London first thing apparently. I'd better get going so I can do this and get back here."

"Drive safely," she says and for once, I can't read her at all. She is either completely okay with this or being sarcastic.

I push my chair back and stand up. "Come here." I hold out my hand to her and she takes it. I pull her up from her chair and wrap my arms around her waist. "It's just business. I'll be back soon."

"I know," she says before pushing up onto her tiptoes and kissing me softly. I kiss her back, wrapping her hair around my fist and tilting her head to the perfect angle so I can tongue-fuck her mouth. Her soft moans make my cock hard and I have to pull back from her and look down at her beautiful face. I dust my knuckles over her cheek.

"I'll be back in two hours."

"I know," she says and I think she has finally learned to trust me where Erin is concerned.

"Good girl," I whisper in her ear and then with a final squeeze of her ass, I walk out of the kitchen.

AN HOUR LATER, I am standing at the door to Erin's hotel room waiting for her to answer. I'm almost expecting her to come to the door in a negligee or some lace underwear complete with stockings and suspenders, but she wouldn't do that. She's never been that obvious.

A few seconds later, she opens the door and confirms that I no longer know her at all. She is wearing a barely there piece of pale pink silk fabric that skims her ass. Her hard nipples are clearly visible and I could kick myself for even giving them a cursory glance.

"Shane," she breathes. "Thank you for coming over so late."

"Seemed like I didn't have much choice," I say as she opens the door and I step inside. Does she really think this is going to work? One last desperate ploy to win me over?

"I have the papers here." She glides over to the small table near the window and indicates the small manila folder.

I sit at the chair and open the folder, scanning the contract before I sign it. It relates to the sale of our family home and also the house in Carrickfergus where we are currently staying. It is the last home we have in Ireland and it's time to let it go.

"Would you like a drink?" Erin asks as she holds up the bottle of Jameson Black label. It's half empty and I wonder how much of it she has drank already this evening.

"No thanks," I shake my head.

"Not even one to commiserate?" she pouts.

"Commiserate?"

"That was going to be our house, Shane. Remember?" She sniffs and a tear rolls down her cheek.

I do remember. "That was a long time ago, Erin. Things have changed."

"If we hadn't gone to New York, if we hadn't had to get away because of your brothers, do you think we would have made it?"

I look at her. I did love her once although it felt like a different kind of love to what I feel with Jessie. It was safe and familiar. The love I have for Jessie is fire and fury, but she is home to me in a way that Erin never was. I held onto a piece of Ireland because in my heart it still felt like my home, but now my home is wherever Jessie Ryan is.

"We might have stayed together," I tell her honestly, "but we wouldn't have been happy."

"What?"

"We never really made each other happy, Erin."

"We did," she insists. "Don't try and rewrite our history, Shane. Just because you've found a whore who'll let all your brothers fuck her..."

I push my chair back and stand so quickly that she flinches, but she has nothing to fear from me; I would never lay a hand on her ever again. I lean down and sign the papers. "Done."

"I'll get them filed tomorrow and then I can start looking at the contracts for the clubs you bought."

"No," I shake my head. "You misunderstand me. When I said done, I meant done. For good."

"But I've worked for you and your family for years, Shane," she snaps.

"You just called one of my family a whore," I snarl at her. "Consider our working relationship terminated."

"You're just going to throw away everything we have built together for her?" she shrieks. "I can give you everything, Shane. Everything!" She walks over to me, pushing her tits out so that her nipples are almost touching my chest.

She breathes heavily. I smell the whiskey on her breath and the sweet perfume she has dabbed on her neck. Her pupils are dilated and her cheeks are flushed pink.

I lean my face close to hers and she gasps at the closeness. "You have nothing that I want," I say and then I walk out of her hotel room.

CHAPTER 46
JESSIE

I'm pulling my hair into a ponytail as I walk into the living area and blink in shock as I see Shane, Liam and Mikey wearing dress pants and dress shirts and looking good enough to eat. As I get nearer, I can smell their cologne too. I just finished a bath and I'm in one of Conor's t-shirts. It's Patrick's funeral tomorrow and I'd thought we were all going to have a few beers and watch a movie together.

"I didn't realize we were going out?" I say with a frown as I look down at my under-dressed state.

Mikey pulls me into his arms and runs his nose along my throat. "We're going out, Red, but not you."

I step back and stare at him in surprise while Shane and Liam grin at me. "What? Why?" I can't help feeling a little hurt that they're all going out without me.

"You're staying with me, Angel," Conor growls in my ear as he walks up behind me and slides his arm around my waist too, until I'm pressed between him and Mikey. "The boys are giving us the place to ourselves."

The tone of his voice sends shivers skittering up my spine. God, I have missed him. "Why?" I breathe.

"You'll see," he chuckles.

Shane leans forward and kisses my cheek before he looks over my shoulder at Conor. "Be good," he warns.

"Of course," Conor replies.

"See you in the morning, baby." Liam gives me a kiss on the cheek too before Mikey seals his lips over mine and slips his tongue into my mouth while Conor holds onto me.

"Come on," Shane says, pulling him away. "I thought you two were going to drink me under the table."

"Oh yeah," Mikey chuckles and the three of them head for the door.

"We won't be on clean up duty when you get home, so don't come anywhere near either of us if you're going to puke. You got me?" Conor says to their backs and they all nod and mumble their agreement.

A few seconds later, they have left and closed the door behind them, leaving Conor and me alone. I turn in his arms and wrap mine around his neck. "Not that this isn't a lovely surprise, but why do we need the house to ourselves?"

"Oh," he flashes his eyebrows at me, "with everything that's happened, I forgot to give you your punishment."

"What punishment?" I breathe, feigning my innocence even as a wet heat rushes between my thighs.

He frowns at me. "For flirting with Sean O'Connor!"

"I did not flirt!" I insist.

"You smiled at him," he reminds me.

"Smiling is not flirting!"

"Hmm." He leans down and kisses me softly. "I think I'm going to have to torture a confession out of you, Jessie Ryan."

I chew on my lip as I look up at him. This is the side of Conor I only see glimpses of. It's terrifying and exciting all at the same time.

I take a deep breath. "You think we're ready?"

"Yes," he nods his head. "But we don't have to do anything you don't want to. I'm just as happy to fuck you all night, Angel if that's what you need?"

"No." I shake my head. "I trust you completely."

"Hmm." He rubs a hand over his jaw and we start to walk toward his bedroom. "You say that now, but wait until you see what I have in store for you." He chuckles darkly and I shiver.

"Have you got some of those jiggle balls, or something?" I grin at him, remembering the fun Shane and I had with them.

"Oh, Angel, they're for amateurs," he winks at me and I wonder what the hell I've gotten myself into.

When I walk into Conor's room a moment later, my heart skips a beat when I see the things he has laid out on the bed.

"I wanted you to see everything," he says softly as he guides me over to the bed.

I look at the array of equipment, floggers, a paddle, a butt plug with a beautiful green jewel on the base, leather cuffs and a blindfold. But the thing that intrigues me most are the lengths of chain. What the hell? "Where did you get all of this?" I ask as I reach down and stroke my fingertips over the soft leather of the flogger.

"Didn't Shane tell you?"

"Tell me what?"

"We just bought a chain of clubs. We have one here, London, Chicago, LA, Paris, and one in New York."

"And what do sex toys have to do with your new clubs?"

"What do you think?" He grins at me.

"They're sex clubs?" I gasp. "How did you not tell me about this?"

"I'm pretty sure they're not called 'sex clubs,'" he laughs. "Shane was going to tell you. I suppose he forgot with everything else going on."

"Wait! That's not where they've gone tonight, is it?" I frown at him.

"You honestly think they would go there without you?" He frowns back.

"No," I shake my head.

"You're okay with it then? I mean it's just business for us, but ... it has its perks too," he says as he picks up some nipple clamps that I hadn't even noticed.

"Of course. And I'd love to go sometime," I smile at him.

"Hmm." He narrows his eyes at me and I don't know if that's a yes or a no. "You ever used these before?" He holds up the clamps.

"I've had them used on me," I whisper. It wasn't a particularly pleasurable experience, but I imagine there is nothing Conor Ryan could do to my body that I wouldn't enjoy.

Thankfully, he doesn't press me for details. "You okay with them?"

"Yes. I'm okay with anything you have in mind," I breathe as my heart races in my chest and he pulls me into his arms.

"That's a pretty dangerous thing to admit, Angel," he growls.

"It's true though. So, what have you got planned first?" My eyes are drawn back to the toys on the bed.

"First off," he slides his hands down my back and starts to peel off my t-shirt, "I want you naked. And wet."

The second part is already taken care of as he discovers a few seconds later when his hand slips into my panties. "Fuck, Jessie," he growls as his fingers slide through my folds and the next thing I know he is lifting me up and throwing me into the middle of the bed. He towers over me as he tugs off his sweatpants and tosses them onto the floor.

"Turn over," he commands and I do it without hesitation. Then he crawls over me, nudging my thighs apart with his knee before he nestles himself between them. The tip of his cock nudges at my opening and I suck in a breath right before he drives into me.

"Conor!" I groan loudly as the endorphins floods my body and my walls squeeze around him. What the hell happened to all the toys he had lined up?

As if reading my mind, he growls in my ear as he nails me into the mattress. "I just need to fuck you first, Angel."

He pins my wrists above my head as he drives into me over and over again, and the wet sound of my arousal fills the room. As soon as he senses I'm on the edge he increases his pace until my orgasm comes hard and fast. As I squeeze him in deeper, he groans loudly before pulling out of me and finishing on my ass.

"Conor!" I say and he chuckles as he starts to rub his cum down the seam before pushing a finger inside.

"On your knees, Angel," he says as he taps my ass.

I push up onto my knees and look behind me to see him reaching for the metallic plug. He rubs his hand over it and that's when I realize he's using his own cum as lube and it's so hot it makes my insides tremble.

A few seconds later, I feel the metal, warmed by the heat of Conor's hands, pressing against the seam of my ass. I lay my face against the bed and push my hips back against him, groaning as he slides the plug all the way inside.

"And I thought your ass couldn't look any more beautiful," he groans as he pushes two fingers deep into my pussy, making me groan too. "So wet, Angel."

I feel him climb off the bed. Taking hold of my hips he pulls me toward him and smacks my ass hard with his hand. The sound echoes around the room, masking my sharp intake of breath.

"You'll tell me to stop if it starts to hurt, right?" he growls.

"Umm," I mumble, earning myself another hard slap.

"Right?"

"Yes!" I gasp, willing him to do more. This is a side of him I rarely get to see, but that I adore. My calm, controlled Conor, unrestrained and almost feral with desire.

"Up on your knees," he barks and I push myself, allowing him to blindfold me before he pushes me back down. Taking hold of my ankles, he pulls my legs wide apart until I am lying spread open with my ass in the air. I breathe heavily as I wait for whatever is next.

The thwack of the paddle stings my ass as it cracks loudly, sending a rush of wet heat searing between my thighs.

"Conor!" I moan as he brings it down again and I feel my juices dripping out of me and running down my thighs.

He brings it down again, and this time the tip of it lands on the plug, pushing it deeper and sending shivers of pleasure tinged with pain skittering up my spine. My knees almost buckle but he holds me upright.

"Talk to me, Angel," he growls, "or we stop this now."

"I need more," I groan.

"Fuck!" he hisses as he goes on spanking me with the paddle until my ass is on fire. When I think I'm almost done, I hear the paddle dropping to the floor as Conor pants for breath behind me. His rough hand rubs over the flaming skin of my ass cheeks before he slips two fingers inside my pussy again and I push back against him. I want more of him.

"You're soaking, Angel," he pants. "Why do you love having your ass spanked so much?"

"I don't know," I gasp.

"Yes you do." He pumps his fingers in and out of me. "Because you know how fucking hard it makes me, and you know you're going to be fucked good when I'm done, don't you?"

"Yes," I breathe as he pulls his fingers out of me and grabs hold of my hips. I brace myself for what's about to happen. My legs tremble with need as I wait for what I really want from him. When he finally sinks his cock deep inside me I cry out in pleasure and relief. His hands are so huge they almost wrap around my waist, and as he holds on to me while he rails into me, he pushes his thumb against the head of the jeweled plug and ripples of pleasure roll through my body.

"Please, Conor?" I beg him as he leisurely fucks me.

"Soon, Angel," he chuckles as he pulls his cock out of me, making me groan in frustration. "Now, on your back."

I roll over onto my back and as soon as I do, Conor's hands are sliding over my legs. He wraps one of the leather cuffs around each ankle and spreads my thighs wide apart before he chains my legs to the bed. I swallow hard as my heart races in my ears.

"You okay?" he asks as he straddles me.

"Yes," I breathe.

"Good." He leans down and sucks one of my nipples into his mouth, making me whimper with need. He nibbles and sucks as one of his hands slides between my thighs and toys with my pussy at the same time until I am trembling with an impending orgasm.

Then he stops.

His tongue disappears to be replaced by one of the clamps. The bite stings for a second, before it draws the blood to my breasts and my entire nipple pulses with a gentle throbbing heat. He does the same to my other one and all I can do is moan and whimper while he plays my body expertly. A few moments later he pushes himself up and disappears again. I swallow hard as I listen to him moving around the room. The clinking of chains as I wait for him makes tremors skitter along my spine. It is pleasure, laced with fear.

"It's only me and you here, Angel," he soothes as he takes

my wrist and wraps a leather cuff around it before he chains both of my hands to the bed so I'm completely bound and spread open for him. I pull at my restraints but there is so little give I can barely move. They are tight and expertly fitted.

"I know," I whisper.

"We leave our ghosts at the door, okay?"

"Yes."

This is the best way I know how to exorcise those ghosts of my past and he knows it better than anyone. I'm not sure anyone else would know that this is what I need. His uncle used to chain me up. He did it a few days earlier in the basement of his farmhouse. This is different. This is about trust. And love.

CHAPTER 47
CONOR

I look down at Jessie lying on the bed and have never seen anything so beautiful in my entire life. She is chained to the bed, her ankles and wrists bound to either side so she's spread wide open for me. Her beautiful pink pussy is on display as it drips with her cum. I pick up the leather flogger and trail it over her abdomen and she shivers in anticipation as I drag it between her thighs. I used to think I couldn't do this stuff with her. I used to think that I couldn't bear to cause her any pain, but now I know her better, and she understands herself more, we both know this is only about pleasure. Hers and mine.

"Conor," she moans softly as the tails of the flogger slide through her slick folds.

"I'm right here, Angel," I tell her and she chews on her lip.

I give her a short flick to her pussy and she yelps. "Stop biting that damn lip," I growl.

"Sorry," she breathes.

Trailing the flogger back up over her body, I bring it down sharply over her torso. It grazes the clamps, making them bite into her flesh slightly harder. She sucks in a deep breath and her thighs tremble.

I step closer to the bed and slide a finger into her pussy and she raises her hips to meet me. When I pull it out again, a rush of her cum comes with it and I have to stop myself from burying my face in her. I continue with the flogger, trailing it over her gorgeous curves and flicking my wrist every so often so that she feels its sting. Her pussy clenches every time as her breathing gets faster and harder. I'm pretty sure with practice I could make her come like this, but my patience will only stretch so far tonight. My cock is busting to be inside her.

Tossing the flogger onto the floor, I crawl onto the bed and she whimpers when my hands brush over the skin of her thighs. When I press a soft kiss on her pussy lips, her hips grind against my face, but I pull back.

"Not yet, Angel," I whisper as I move up her body. Trailing kisses over her stomach. I tug on the delicate chain that holds the nipple clamps together and she groans loudly. "Conor! Please!"

I slide a finger inside her again and her walls squeeze me. I add another and finger fuck her slowly while I go back to her breasts, sucking on her nipples through the clamps and making her squirm. When I finally pull one off, her nipple springs out so I can suck into my hot mouth and she rewards me with a rush of slick heat. I do the same to the other and the sound of her whimpers and moans as she creams all over my fingers makes me desperate to drive my cock into her. But I know that when I do, this is all over, because I won't be able to stop until I have blown my load in her and she can barely stand. Instead I move back down the bed and lick her pussy lips, lapping at her juices as they run out of her.

"I need you inside me, Conor," she breathes. "Please?"

"I'm inside you, Angel," I chuckle as I curl my fingers against her G-Spot and she bucks her hips.

"No... I need..." she pants as her breathing gets faster and louder.

"You need what?" I tease her because she rarely says the word cock. It makes her blush.

"Your cock!" she moans as her orgasm suddenly tears through her body and she pulls at her restraints as every part of her shakes and trembles.

Tears rolls down her cheeks as she shudders.

"Damn, even I wasn't expecting that, Angel. Where the hell did that come from?"

"I... don't..." she shakes her head, unable to form a sentence.

I crawl off the bed and start to unchain her hands and feet. "What...?" she breathes.

"I love having you tied up and spread out for me, Angel, but I want to bend you over and fuck you from behind."

I pull her blindfold off too and she smiles up at me. "Flip over and stick that ass in the air," I snap and she obeys without question while I make sure the chains won't be in our way. Her ass and pussy on full display is a sight to see and I cannot wait to fuck her now. I love taking her from behind. I crawl onto the bed behind her. Her juices are dripping down her thighs and I dip my head and lick them from her before I straighten up again and line my cock up at her entrance.

"Is this what you really want, Angel?"

"Yes," she moans softly as she pushes her ass back so I slip in an inch. I run my finger over the jeweled plug in her ass and she shivers. Then I drive into her, pressing down on the plug so that her ass and her pussy are filled at the same time and she shouts my name. I grab onto her ass cheek with my other hand and fuck her harder than I have ever fucked anyone in my life, and when she's come for a third time and soaked my cock in her cum, I pull the plug out of her ass and fuck her there instead.

"*Conor*!" She moans my name over and over again and it is the sweetest thing I have ever heard. A few seconds later, I swear I almost fucking pass out from how hard my body comes for her.

When we're done, I fall down onto the bed beside her and pull her quivering frame on top of mine. We both lie here gasping for breath, our bodies stuck together with perspiration as we recover from whatever the fuck that was. It's Jessie who speaks first.

"God, Conor. That was..." She gasps for air again. "Freaking incredible. Can you please punish me like that all the time."

"Yes," I breathe. "Whatever you want, Angel."

"I love you," she purrs as she nestles her head against my chest.

I wrap my arms around her and kiss her head. "I love you more."

CHAPTER 48
SHANE

The house is quiet when we get back home. There is no blood on the walls, so I suppose that's a good thing. Not that I would have left Jessie alone with my brother if I had thought for a second that there would be. It was time for him to show her his darker side. They were both ready for it.

"Why are there four of you?" Mikey looks through me as his eyes roll in his head and Liam giggles like a naughty teenager. I shake my head at the pair of them. "I thought you two were supposed to be drinking me under the table?"

"We did," Liam slurs. "We drank waaay more than you."

"No." I shake my head. "But you idiots were drinking tequila and you know that you can't handle it. What is it with you two and tequila?"

"It's being here. In Ireland," Mikey whispers behind his hand as though he's divulging a huge secret. "It makes us crazy."

"Yeah. It makes us all crazy, kid." I smile at him. "The pair of you should get to bed."

"Yes, Sir," Liam salutes me and then the two of them

stumble off in the direction of their bedroom, laughing to themselves. I smile as I watch them. The three of us needed tonight. I needed to make sure they were okay. That the three of us were okay. And now I know that we will be, even if we're not quite there yet.

I walk to Conor's room. There's no reason I shouldn't check in on them both. As I reach his room, the faint light from the television beneath the crack in the door gives me all the permission I need to go inside. He is lying with his arms behind his head watching the TV and Jessie is curled up on his chest asleep.

"Hey, bro," he whispers.

"Hey," I say as I walk over and sit on the bed. "How was your night?"

He looks down at her as she sleeps and smiles. "Epic," he finally replies.

"Good."

"How was yours?"

"Good. It was fun. I think we cleared the air. They're going to be okay."

"Where are they now?"

"I sent them to bed."

He arches an eyebrow at me. "Hammered?"

"Yep," I laugh. I look down at her and my heart beats faster in my chest.

"You want to get in here with us?" Conor offers.

"Yeah." I take off my clothes before he can reconsider because I want nothing more than to sleep with her beautiful soft body pressed up against me.

"You going full-on commando?" Conor says as I pull off my boxers too.

"Yep. You got a problem with that?"

"No." He laughs and shakes his head. "I've seen more of

your cock these past few months than I've seen in a lifetime."

"Well, you'd better get used to it, because I'm pretty sure our girl loves being fucked by the two of us together."

"She sure does." He flashes his eyebrows at me as I pull back the duvet and climb into bed beside them. I run my hand over her back and she moans softly. I don't want to wake her, but she's lying on Conor and I want her lying beside me.

"Shane's here, Angel," Conor says softly as he gently lifts her off his chest.

"Shane?" she says sleepily.

"Yeah," I reply as I help Conor move her, pulling her into the middle of us so that I can wrap my arm around her and feel her ass pressed against my groin.

"Hmm," she purrs as she wiggles her ass and I bite my lip, willing my cock to not get any harder because I want to sleep, but if she wakes him up then none of us will be sleeping for a few hours.

"Go back to sleep, sweetheart," I whisper and she sighs softly.

"You ready for tomorrow?" Conor asks.

"Yeah. You?"

"Yep."

"Good. Then as soon as this funeral is done, we can go home."

Conor nods. "I can't wait."

I rest my head next to Jessie's and close my eyes, breathing in the scent of her hair. Conor continues watching the TV and I hear it faintly in the background as I drift off to sleep. As I lie there somewhere between sleeping and waking I realize that I need to talk to Jessie and tell her that my proposal no longer stands. I want her to be happy, but I am also a selfish bastard and I never want to live without her. Besides, we make her happy. All four of us. Why would that ever need to change?

CHAPTER 49
JESSIE

I don't think I've ever been to a funeral before when it hasn't rained. It's fitting, isn't it? Almost like the sky is crying too. But there is no rain today. On the day of Patrick Ryan's funeral, the sun is shining brightly and the weather is hot and sticky. I stand between my four boys, who are all dressed beautifully in suits and ties. They keep their heads bowed respectfully and anyone watching would think they were dutiful sons paying their respects. As the coffin is lowered into the ground a woman nearby wails loudly and I glance sideways at Mikey just in time to see him roll his eyes. I reach for his hand and squeeze and he winks at me.

Soon this will be over and we can go home.

Home. It's funny to be thinking of a place as my true home after spending such a long time feeling like I didn't belong anywhere. We have a flight booked for tomorrow morning. I was pleased to hear that Erin won't be joining us and even more pleased to hear she has decided to stay behind in Ireland. After the funeral today there will be a huge party, as is the tradition in Ireland, but we won't be there. The boys and I, along with their Aunt Em and cousin Aoife, will go back to the house and have a barbecue and some drinks. Not to celebrate Patrick Ryan's life, or even his death, but because this is our last night and Em and Aoife don't want us to go. They have promised to visit though and I hope they do. I have loved getting to know them.

I will raise a silent toast to Patrick and Paul Ryan later though. They might have been sadistic psychopaths, but these four incredible men beside me wouldn't be here without them.

I SIT on one of the lounge chairs with my face tilted toward the sun as I listen to the Ryan family chatting happily in the background, mostly about Aoife and Noel's upcoming wedding.

"I wish you could stay for the wedding," Aoife says with a sigh. "It's only two weeks away."

"I wish we could but we have to get back home," Shane replies.

"You promised to visit after you've had the baby," Mikey reminds her. "We'll show you the best New York has to offer."

"I'm looking forward to visiting the States," Em adds with a contented sigh.

I open my eyes and look at them all. "Don't forget to send me lots of pictures of the day, Aoife. Especially your dress."

She waddles over and sits beside me, groaning softly as she rubs her baby bump. "I will." She takes my hand and squeezes it. "I'm going to miss you."

"I'll miss you too," I say. "And I definitely want tons of pictures of the baby when they arrive too, okay?"

"Oh I'm going to bombard you with them," she laughs. "You'll be fed up of baby pictures."

"You want a top up?" I ask as I see her empty glass of lemonade.

"Yes please." She holds out her glass to me.

I walk back to the house, passing Shane as I do. "Can you help me with the drinks?"

"Of course," he replies with a frown because everyone except Aoife has a full glass.

"Everything okay?" he asks once we're inside the house.

I swallow hard. I don't know how to tell him this, but I have been thinking a lot about my future and what I want in my life and for the first time in forever, I am certain about what that is. "I need to talk to you," I whisper.

He narrows his eyes at me. "Okay."

"With all this talk of Aoife and Noel's wedding, I remembered that I finally have an answer for you."

"An answer?"

"Your proposal, remember? In Em's garden. Me marrying Conor?"

"Oh? Yeah." His Adam's apple bobs as he swallows hard.

I take a deep breath. I need to just tell him quickly and get it over with. It's just like ripping off a Band-Aid, right?

CHAPTER 50
JESSIE
SIX MONTHS LATER

Smoothing my beautiful silk dress over my thighs, I smile at Aoife as she hands me my bouquet. It is a stunning mix of red, white and olive green roses, with blue tulips.

"You look fabulous, Jessie." She gives me a soft kiss on my cheek. "I have never seen a smile so wide," she adds with a chuckle.

"Thank you, Aoife," I say. I feel so nervous my legs and hands are shaking, but my smile is real. I am excited and happy beyond belief. Today is my wedding day and I cannot wait to start this new chapter of my life.

"I'll see you out there." Aoife flashes her eyebrows at me before she leaves me standing in the room alone. I look out of the huge double doors of the beautiful log cabin that Shane has had built in the last six months, at that spot on the lake where he took me a little over a year ago. It seems like a lifetime ago now.

I look out at the beautiful gardens as I prepare to make my way towards the small arch of roses and ivy near the lake where the ceremony is about to take place. I have no one to walk me down the aisle today, but that doesn't matter to me. I feel my family by my side, and of course I'm now starting a new one too.

I step out onto the deck and onto the small stone path. My head is down; I'm almost frightened to look up in case this is all a dream, but then I take a deep breath and do it. It is Conor's eyes I see first. He stands there in his tux looking finer than I have ever seen him look before, and that really is a feat. He smiles when he sees me and it's a smile that almost takes my breath away. He nudges Mikey who stands beside him, deep in conversation with his twin brother. Mikey and Liam look up too and I bite my lip as they stare at me. Tears prick at my eyes as Liam puts a hand over his heart and Mikey blows me a kiss. They look just as handsome as their older brother.

But where is Shane? My heart skips a beat as I scan the small alcove and he's not there. I know this day is not going to be easy for him. But then he steps out from behind the trees and my heart almost stops beating in my chest as he looks up at me and our eyes lock. I am close enough now that I see the deep green of his irises and it takes my breath away when I see the tears in them.

Is this too hard for him? As Conor puts a hand on his older brother's shoulder, it breaks the spell between us and Shane takes his place next to Conor.

When I reach them, I suck in a deep breath. I can't believe we're really doing this.

"You look..." Conor shakes his head, unable to finish his sentence.

"Beautiful." Shane finishes for him.

"Yeah. You look hot, Red," Mikey grins while Liam winks at me.

"Thank you," I whisper and then the five of us stand there staring at each other.

"Are we ready?" Aunt Em clears her throat, making us all

turn toward her. She is officiating today. Not that she's licensed to, but this wedding isn't exactly traditional.

"Yes," Conor says with a firm nod of his head.

"Yes," I breathe.

"Then let's begin," Aunt Em says. "I know we're doing this your own unique way, so do you boys have the rings?"

"Yup," Mikey says as he pulls one from his pocket.

I bite on my lip as Mikey takes hold of my hand and slides the beautiful thin platinum band onto my finger. It is set with a small, but exquisite ruby. "Red, because you'll always be our Red, and because it's the color of love," he says.

I swallow the lump in my throat as Liam steps up next. "Blue for those incredible baby blues of yours," he says as he slides the second band onto my finger which has a small sapphire stone. It slides against the first one perfectly, the two stones sitting slightly adjacent and the platinum shaped to fit together like a jigsaw.

Conor steps up next. He takes my hand in his and brushes his fingertips over my knuckles before he slips the third band onto my hand which is set with an emerald. "And green for all the Irish in you," he smiles at me and I giggle.

He bends and kisses my hand before he steps back into line.

"We're not at the kissing part yet," Aunt Em chides him good naturedly.

Finally Shane steps forward. He takes my hand and slides the fourth ring onto my finger. His hand is covering it and I don't see it until he has it secured in place, fitting perfectly against the first three. The final piece in the puzzle. It is a beautiful pink diamond. The three other stones are set slightly off center, allowing them to fit together seamlessly. But this one is larger, and in the center of the ring. Like the star on top of the Christmas tree. "And a diamond for forever," he says, his voice thick with emotion and I want to pull him into my arms and kiss him right now. I want to kiss all of them. To spend the rest of my life with any one of these men would make me happier than I had ever dreamed, but to share it with all four of them is beyond my wildest imaginings.

Of course this isn't a legal ceremony and our wedding won't be recognized by the state of New York, but we don't care. As Em told us, we are expressing our commitment to each other to the universe, and to Mother Nature herself.

"Do you have your rings, Jessie?" Em asks as I stand there staring at the stunning jewelry these men have just placed on my finger. They are cut so that they seem like four pieces of the same ring, and that's so fitting, because these men are four pieces of the same heart. And they have captured mine completely.

"Yes," I stammer as I take the small velvet pouch from inside my dress. I open it and shake out the four platinum bands onto my hand. They are simple thick bands of precious metal, but each bear the same inscription.

We were written in the stars.

CHAPTER 51
JESSIE

It has been an incredible day, not that I had expected any less. I've heard plenty of people talk about their wedding day and how special it was, but I never thought I would experience one myself. I certainly didn't think I'd be sharing it with the four hottest and most amazing men to ever walk this earth. Our honeymoon for now is a long weekend in our beautiful house on the lake, but we didn't want to be away from the city any longer because Aunt Em, Aoife and Noel, along with their four month old son, Archie, are visiting from Ireland and we don't want to be away from them for too long. We have two weeks in a villa in the Caribbean booked for a month from now, and I cannot wait for that, but in the meantime I'm happy here with my boys.

We waved Em, Aoife and the boys off a few moments earlier. Shane did offer them the use of a couple of bedrooms for the night, seeing as we are only likely to be using one of them, but thankfully they politely declined.

Now it's just me and my four husbands. They chat amongst themselves and I busy myself clearing some of the glasses and plates we have used. Suddenly the room is quiet and when I look up I see the four of them staring at me, their eyes roaming over my body with such desire that I feel like my panties are about to melt off me.

"What is it?" I whisper.

Mikey chews on his lip while the other three continue to stare at me.

"I think we're all thinking the same thing, Jessie," Shane growls.

"And what's that?" I breathe.

"Which one of us gets to be the first to fuck Mrs. Ryan," he replies with a wicked glint in his eye.

Dear God!

"We could let Jessie decide?" Liam suggests.

"No," I shake my head. "I can't choose between the four of you."

"How about we settle this like we used to when we were younger?" Shane offers with a grin.

Conor frowns. "With an arm wrestle?"

"You got any better ideas?" Shane shrugs as he starts to remove his suit jacket.

"Fine by me," Mikey grins as he does the same and the next minute Conor and Liam are taking theirs off too.

"You're seriously going to arm wrestle to decide this?" I fold my arms across my chest and glare at them.

Mikey winks at me. "Yes. And we know you think it's hot really, Red, having the four of us competing for you."

The heat flooding my core confirms he's right. "Well, yeah. But I'm worried this is going to get a little competitive."

Conor sidles up to me, running his hand over my ass and planting a soft kiss on my shoulder. "Oh, it's about to get *very* fucking competitive, Angel," he chuckles before he walks into the middle of the room and starts arranging the furniture with Mikey and Liam for their impromptu tournament.

"How about Liam and Mikey go first?" Shane suggests.

"Fine by me," Liam nods. "I'll get rid of my toughest competition first round before I deal with you two old timers."

"You're pretty cocky for a kid who was taught everything you know by these two 'old timers,'" Conor says with an arch of his eyebrows before he throws a sofa cushion at Liam's head.

"Let's just get down to business, eh?" Mikey says as he takes a seat. Liam laughs as he takes a seat opposite him. Conor hovers beside them, making sure they are going to fight fair. I watch in twisted fascination as the two of them prepare to arm wrestle and I'm so distracted that I hardly notice Shane isn't anywhere near his brothers but is now standing beside me. As Liam and Mikey grip each other's hands, he hoists me over his shoulder, making me yelp in surprise and then he runs out of the room and towards the stairway.

"Shane!" I half shriek, half laugh as he starts to take the stairs two at a time.

He slaps my ass and laughs to himself as his brothers start shouting after us. "Shane! You cheating asshole!" I can hear the sound of furniture being pushed over and their feet on the wooden floor as they run after us. Shane runs into our bedroom and sets me down on my feet before he locks the door behind us. Then he turns to me with pure fire and lust in his eyes. "Take the dress off, sweetheart. Right now," he growls as he steps towards me, backing me towards the bed.

I reach behind and undo the zipper as he starts to undress too. "You cheated." I arch an eyebrow at him.

"I play to win, sweetheart. By any means necessary."

The sound of his brothers banging on the door distracts me and I look over his shoulder.

"Open the fucking door, Shane!" Conor shouts.

"You fucking cheat!" Mikey adds while the three of them try

and punch and kick their way through. The doors in this house are solid oak, but they are no match for three angry Ryans.

"You know that door won't hold out much longer?" I say.

"I know." Shane laughs and the sound makes my heart flutter. His genuine, playful laugh is a sound not often heard and it is a beautiful thing. "But I plan on being buried inside your hot cunt by the time they make it in here."

He removes the rest of his clothes quickly. Just as I'm stepping out of my dress and before I can even straighten up, he pushes me onto the bed and crawls over me, trailing kisses down my stomach as he pulls my panties down and over my legs. When he's taken them off completely, he rubs his nose along the folds of my pussy, inhaling deeply before he presses a soft kiss directly on my clit that makes me shudder. The low growl that rumbles in his throat vibrates through my body.

"Shane!" I pant as he moves up the bed and holds himself over me before pressing his hard cock against my entrance as his brothers go on trying to break the door down. "You ready to be fucked, Mrs. Ryan?" he breathes.

"God, yes!" I groan just before he drives his cock into me. He takes my hands, entwining his fingers with mine as he pins them either side of my head. Then he seals his lips over mine, pushing his tongue inside my mouth as he nails me to the bed, and claiming me completely.

The sound of the door bursting open a few seconds later, distracts me temporarily and I glance up to see his brothers tumbling through it. They grumble and shout incoherently as they pull off their clothes. Knowing that my eyes are on his brothers, Shane drives even deeper and harder, making me groan into his mouth and give him my full attention.

I hear stumbling and some laughing and then someone is beside us on the bed. In one swift movement, Shane slides a hand to my ass and rolls us both onto our sides, hooking my thigh over his as he continues kissing and fucking me. A hard chest is pressed against my back as soft kisses are peppered along my shoulders and I recognize Liam's mouth and then his hands as one slides up my back and onto my throat. Shane lets me up for air and Liam takes the opportunity to cup my chin and turn my head to him.

He smiles down at me, his deep brown eyes twinkling. "Hey, baby."

"Hey," I purr before he kisses me softly.

As Liam kisses me, Shane's hand slides to my hip and his fingers press into my tender flesh. Then he pulls his cock out of me and Liam pulls his lips from mine before looking at his brother. "Fucking cheat!" he says, narrowing his eyes at him, but there is no malice in his words.

"I did what I had to do, son," Shane chuckles.

"Hmm," Liam murmurs as he begins to kiss my neck and Shane turns my face back to his and slides his tongue inside my mouth again. Liam's hand slides down my back and between my thighs before he pushes a finger inside me and I moan.

"Damn, Jessie. I love how soaking wet you get for us," he growls as he slips his finger out and pushes his cock inside me instead and I groan into Shane's mouth, wondering why he has stopped fucking me to allow Liam to. He's usually not so accommodating. But then Liam pulls out of me again and pushes his cock against the seam of my ass instead and I realize that Shane has only allowed him temporary access to my pussy. It amazes me how these four men always seem to know what the other is thinking.

"So fucking wet, baby," Liam whispers against my ear as he pushes the tip of his cock into my ass and I roll my hips forward against Shane, who rewards me by pushing himself back inside me. The moan rumbles through my body and Liam seizes the opportunity to drive his cock all the way into me and the two of them find a perfect rhythm as they fuck me relentlessly. My orgasm builds quickly, the warmth pulsing through my entire body as Shane and Liam rub their hands over my hot skin and Liam kisses my neck while Shane swirls his tongue against mine. I feel like I'm about to pass out as stars flicker behind my eyelids.

"Fuck, Jessie!" Liam growls as he squeezes my breast tightly and I come with a rush of wet heat, wrenching my lips from Shane's as I gasp in a lungful of air.

"Damn, Hacker," Shane hisses. "Your cunt feels so good on my cock."

I groan as Liam slides deeper into my ass and wraps an arm around my waist, pulling me close against his chest while him and his oldest brother continue railing me.

"You're such a good girl, the way you take our cocks, baby," Liam growls in my ear. "Conor and Mikey are going to fuck you as soon as me and Shane are done, and I'm going to enjoy watching you come apart for them. And then I'm going to fuck you again."

"Liam," I moan and Shane responds by biting into the tender skin of my neck until I moan his name too. I run my fingers through his hair, pulling his head back so he can kiss me again, but he brushes his lips over my cheek instead. "She's close to the edge, and I want to feel her come on my cock again," he says to Liam who laughs softly and slides his hand between my thighs before rubbing my clit.

"You going to come for us again, baby?" Liam whispers.

"Yes," I pant as Shane increases his pace. "God. Shane. Liam!" I moan so loudly that Conor and Mikey start urging them to hurry up and a few seconds later Shane roars my name as he comes inside me, tipping me over the edge as he does.

Liam stills but he kisses my neck softly as his cock twitches in my ass. Conor crawls onto the bed behind Shane and holds his cock in his hand. It glistens with precum and I look up at him to see him glaring at me with such ferocity that it makes me squirm. After Shane pulls out of me, he rolls over and sits up before jumping off the bed and Conor seamlessly slides into his spot. Lifting my thigh into the air, he drives his cock into me and I'm pushed back further onto Liam who hisses in my ear.

"Fuck, Angel. This pussy is so good," Conor growls as he rolls his hips, releasing another rush of wet heat from me.

My body trembles as they hold me between them. "You ready, Liam?" Conor asks.

"Uh-huh," Liam moans against my neck before he begins to suck on the sensitive spot beneath my ear. Then the two of them start moving together. Not one in and one out like they usually do, but both thrusting inside me at the same time. It is a delicious feeling of fullness, teetering on the verge of pain and it has me on the edge of oblivion again. I reach behind me, wrapping my arm around Liam's neck and pulling him closer as he and Conor move in perfect sync with each other. Conor bends his head and sucks my nipple into his mouth and I swear I pass out for a few seconds. I can't tell where one of us ends and one begins.

"Jessie, don't come," Conor groans as I squeeze around him, pulling him in deeper.

"I can't help it," I pant as my orgasm tears through my body.

"Fuck!" Conor shouts as he comes with me. "This pussy!" He thrusts harder into me as he spills every last drop of his seed.

Liam groans behind me as he stills his movements again.

"How the fuck are you still going, kid?" Conor frowns at him over my shoulder.

"Stamina, old man," Liam chuckles.

I smile at Conor through my orgasm induced haze and he leans down and kisses me softly. He narrows his eyes at me. "You just made me look bad in front of my little brother, Angel."

"Sorry!" I whisper and he winks at me before pulling out of me. To my shame, a rush of cum follows and drips onto my thighs and down the seam of my ass. Liam's cock throbs inside me and he mutters under his breath. As soon as Conor rolls over, Mikey is crawling into his space. He lies on his back though and I look at him as he rubs a hand up and down his shaft.

"Come ride me, Red," he arches an eyebrow at me. "Liam can get behind you. Let's see how long he lasts like that," Mikey grins at his twin, challenging him.

"Okay," Liam says as he slides out of me. He taps my ass and I move over to straddle Mikey and as I do another rush of cum falls out of me. Liam catches some in his fingers and works it up the seam of my ass before pushing two fingers inside me.

Mikey holds his cock as I slide myself onto it. "Damn, Con, no wonder you couldn't hold on much longer, because my wife's pussy is fucking hot!" he groans as I slide all the way onto him. "And so damn wet."

I bite my lip as I stare down at him and heat flushes my chest and neck. "I like it when you call me your wife," I purr.

"I like it too, Red," he growls as he holds onto my hips and thrusts into me, causing me to whimper.

Liam lines up behind me, his hands just above Mikey's as he slides his cock into my ass again. "Fuck. You're tighter this way, baby," he growls in my ear. "And I can get in deeper too." As if to prove his point, he drives into me, all the way to the hilt and I cry out in pleasure. I plant my hands on Mikey's chest as the two of them fuck me together. It's not long before Shane and Conor crawl onto the bed beside us. Both of them are hard again and I know what's about to happen. I have thought about this for a very long time. Shane moves first, squeezing my breast with one hand as he squeezes his cock with the other. When he kisses me, I whimper into his mouth as Conor takes my other hand and slides it onto his cock, working it up and down the shaft. Then his lips are on my throat, kissing and suckling. Or is that Mikey? Because now there are more lips on my neck and hands all over my body as Mikey and Liam go on fucking me to the same relentless rhythm. I have to close my eyes to deal with the overwhelming sensations.

Suddenly, Shane pulls back. "Look at me!"

I open my eyes and focus on his face. His eyes burn into mine and I know what he's thinking. I lick my lips and he doesn't hesitate. He pushes himself up onto his knees until his cock is level with my mouth.

"Suck it, sweetheart," he orders and my pussy walls contract in response, causing Mikey and Liam to groan loudly. I suck him into my mouth, as far as I can go, while the other three continue their delicious torture. Kissing my neck and my nipples. Their hot hands all over my skin as Conor keeps me working his cock. I flick my tongue over the tip of Shane's cock and a moan vibrates through his body before I take him to the back of my throat. But the maddening teasing of my body means I lose focus and my eyes roll into the back of my head as an unexpected orgasm tears through me like a wildfire. I moan loudly but the sound is muffled by Shane filling my mouth. Sensing that I need him to take control, he weaves one hand through my hair, grabbing it with just the right amount of pressure as he holds my head still and starts to fuck my mouth. My eyes water as he hits the back of my throat and I suck harder as my hand moves faster on Conor's cock.

"Where the fuck did you learn to suck cock this good, Jessie?" Shane moans as he drives his hips into my mouth and I suck him harder until he spurts hot and heavy against the back of my throat.

Once I have licked him clean, a second hand is on my head,

fisting in my hair. Shane pulls back and Conor turns my head. "My turn, Angel."

WITH SHANE and Conor's hands and mouths on me, Mikey rubbing my clit, Liam's fingers digging into my hips and their cocks filling me, I feel my climax threatening. They keep me teetering on the edge.

"You think we're going to make our wife squirt?" Liam growls.

"I don't think we can call this a successful wedding night if we don't," Mikey chuckles.

I shake my head. "Please?" I beg. If they don't give me some release soon, I think I might pass out.

Shane and Conor each suck a nipple into their hot mouths while the twins increase their pace and pressure and my orgasm goes off like an atomic bomb, drenching Liam beneath me as well as the sheets. I have no doubt that everybody got a little of it because I have never experienced a rush like it, but I have no shame. These boys caused it after all.

I have no idea if the twins came too, but realize they must have because they both groan and pant and stop moving. Liam finally slides his cock out of my ass before Mikey pulls me down to lie on his chest.

"Wow, Red!" Mikey pants, his breath ruffling my hair as our bodies stick together with perspiration.

"I can't..." I breathe. "I have no bones." I melt into him, completely unable to move.

Someone chuckles softly beside us and I can't even lift my head to see who it is. But I feel warm hands on my back and hear the steady breathing of all four brothers as we lie there catching our breath and enjoying the post-orgasmic haze of whatever the hell they just did to me.

. . .

When I wake later in the night, I'm facing Liam with Conor at my back.

"You okay, baby?" Liam says softly as I shuffle beside him.

"Yes. Are you?"

"Not really," he whispers.

"Why? What's wrong?"

"Well, I just realized that I'm the only man in this bed who didn't get to fuck your pussy tonight," he chuckles softly and I swat him in the chest.

"No. But you're the only one who fucked my ass," I remind him.

"Not the same as your pussy though," he breathes. "I mean, your ass is hot, baby, but your pussy is like next level fire."

I giggle as he slides his hand onto my ass and presses my body against his hard cock. "I suppose you're planning on rectifying this situation now then?"

"Hmm. Are you sore?" he whispers.

"A little."

All three of his brothers are in the bed with us, so there is no room for him to roll on top of me. Instead, he pushes himself up and pulls me beneath him, nestling himself between my thighs. "I promise to be gentle, baby," he says as he peppers soft kisses on my throat and slides his hand between my folds. "You're already wet for me," he hisses.

"I know."

He draws his hand back and wraps my legs around his waist before he sinks his cock deep inside me. "Fuck, Jessie! You feel so good."

"Liam!" I groan softly.

"Can you two keep it down?" Conor mumbles sleepily beside us.

"I'm fucking my wife, Con," Liam chuckles. "I can't help it if I do it so well she can't control herself."

"We'll *all* be fucking your wife if she keeps moaning like that, so keep her quiet," he chuckles back.

"Sorry," I giggle as I clamp a hand over my mouth.

"No you're not," Conor replies as he turns on his side and slides his hand between Liam and me until he finds my clit and starts to circle softly as Liam fucks me slowly. Liam takes my hand from my mouth and pins it above my head and then the two of them take turns kissing me, swallowing my moans and whimpers as they coax a long rolling orgasm from me.

CHAPTER 52
JESSIE

I stare down at Archie's beautiful rosy cheeks as he lies snuggled in my arms. His long dark lashes flutter occasionally and he makes the cutest little grunts that turn my insides to melted chocolate. I'm going to be sad to see him go home with Aoife and Noel. It has been over a week since our wedding and I have had the absolute best time, not only on my weekend honeymoon with my four hot husbands, but with the extended Ryan family afterward too.

"We really need to go," Noel laughs as he walks toward me. "He's kind of hard to stop staring at though, isn't he?" He looks down at his son with such love and pride on his face that it brings a tear to my eye.

"He is," I say as I hand Archie over to his father who takes him to his car seat and straps him in. "You'll come back and visit us soon, won't you?" I look to Aoife and Em now, who I am also going to miss dearly.

"What?" Aoife flashes her eyebrows at me. "Now that Shane has bought that incredible plane, you try and stop me. You'll be fed up of us dropping by."

I wrap my arms around her as she reaches me and we hug

tightly. "I'm going to miss you," she whispers in my ear. "It's been so much fun."

Em comes up behind her and wraps her arms around us both. "Me too."

"We really need to go if we're going to catch our flight. I know it's their plane, but they still have to take off on time," Noel reminds them.

"We know," Aoife says as she breaks our hug and wipes the tears from her eyes.

The brothers hug their aunt and cousin too, and Noel shakes their hands before giving me a brief kiss on the cheek and we wave them into the elevator.

"You okay, Red?" Mikey says as he wraps an arm around me as we walk back to the kitchen.

"Yeah," I say with a sigh, "but it was nice having them here, wasn't it?"

"They'll visit," Conor says as he walks beside me, placing his arm around me too and kissing the top of my head.

We all walk to the kitchen and Conor and Mikey make a start on dinner. I'm about to help when Shane pulls me to one side. "I feel like someone else stole your heart this week," he says with a smile.

"Archie?" I smile back.

"Yeah."

"Hmm. Kind of. I mean he's super cute. And such a good baby."

"Yeah," Shane says with a nod as he stuffs his hands into his trouser pockets. "Is that what you want, Jessie?" His face is suddenly serious as he narrows his eyes at me.

"What?" I say, aware that all of the brothers' eyes are on me now. "No. We talked about that. No kids. Remember?"

"Hmm." Shane rubs a hand over his jaw. "I swore I'd never have kids."

"Exactly."

"Because I'm worried I'd be a terrible father. Just like mine was."

"I know," I say softly as I place my hand on his arm. "You don't have to explain."

"But mostly, I was worried that I might hate the kid. Like our dad did us."

"I know."

He stares at me. "But I looked at my cousin's kid, and fuck I would protect that chubby little fucker with my life, and he's not even mine."

I swallow hard as I stare at him. Glancing around the room, I see that Conor and the twins are staring, too.

"Imagine how much I'd love a kid that was part of you, Jessie? Or any of us?" he goes on.

"What are you saying, Shane?" I stammer, because my heart can't take this if he doesn't mean what I think he does.

"I'm saying that if that's what you want, then I'm happy to give you it, is all." His Adam's apple bobs in his throat as he swallows.

"You'd have children?"

"With you? Yes."

"We're making babies?" Mikey shouts as his face breaks into a grin.

I look up at him and Conor and Liam and the three of them stand there smiling.

"I already spoke to them about it," Shane says and I look back at him. "But we're all okay with not having kids if that's what you want too, sweetheart."

"What?" I stammer, opening and closing my mouth like a goldfish, because of all the things I ever expected Shane Ryan to say to me, that he would be willing to have a child was the absolute bottom of the list.

"You don't have to decide right now."

"If we did do this, how would it work? How would we know...?"

"We wouldn't," Conor answers as he walks toward me. "That's the only way we could see this working. We're all the baby's father."

"I love that idea," I smile. "You know that twins run in both of our families though, right?"

"Yeah, but you got four dads to share the nightly feedings and diaper changes with," Liam says as he walks over to join us too.

"I know Shane just said you don't have to decide right now, but I kinda need to know, Red," Mikey says with a shrug. "Am I gonna be a baby daddy, or what?"

I can't help but laugh as he stands there with his 'Kiss the Chef' apron on and his hand on his hip.

"Yes!" I say with a smile and suddenly I am in the middle of a giant group hug, being smothered in kisses.

EPILOGUE

JESSIE

Two weeks later

I walk into the den to see all four of my boys in there. Liam and Mikey are playing pool while Shane sips coffee and scrolls through his cell phone and Conor is reading a book.

"Hey guys," I say as I walk into the room.

They all look up and smile at me and my heart might burst with how much I love them all. Mikey puts his pool cue onto the table and walks over to me, picking up a small paper bag from the coffee table as he does.

"We got you something, Red," he says with a grin as he hands it to me.

"For me?" I arch an eyebrow. "What is it?"

"Well, open it and see," he replies.

I look around the room and the four of them are watching me. I open up the bag and pull out the small white box inside.

Turning it over in my hand, I laugh out loud. "Ovulation tests. Really?" I arch an eyebrow at him.

"Yep."

"So, we're really serious about this baby thing then? I only had my implant taken out a few days ago," I protest, although the fact they are so into this gives me butterflies in my stomach.

"Well you didn't think we were about to start wearing condoms, did you, Angel?" Conor growls as he puts his book down and stands up.

"Well, no. But..."

"But what, Red?" Mikey frowns at me.

The color flushes over my cheeks. "I'm not sure we need these," I whisper as I hold up the box of tests.

"But they'll tell us when you're ovulating."

"I know that..." I stand there with my mouth open. These men know my body inside out, so why am I so embarrassed to say what I'm thinking.

"I think what Jessie is trying to say," Liam winks at me, "is that there isn't a single day that goes by when she doesn't have someone's cum in her. Isn't that right, baby?"

"Yes," I whisper as I blush to the roots of my hair.

"Ah," Mikey chuckles. "But these will let us know exactly when the time is right to make a baby. And, I mean, we kinda wanna know when that is, Red."

"We sure do," Conor agrees.

"I thought we agreed we were happy not to know who, you know...?"

"Who scored the home run? Whose little guys were the strongest swimmers?" Mikey kindly offers.

"Yes," I whisper.

"And we don't, but we still want to know when the time is right," Conor says as he stalks toward me.

"Yep. If we're making babies, I want to bring my A game," Mikey winks at me.

"Why do I feel like this is going to get really competitive?" I fold my arms across my chest and try to glare at them with all of the indignation I can muster, but I can barely keep the smile from my face.

"Oh it is!" Conor replies.

"Super fucking competitive," Mikey agrees with a flash of his eyebrows.

"So, go do the test," Liam says.

I shake my head and that's when Shane stands up and walks over to me. Mikey steps aside and Shane stands directly in front of me. "There's only two to three days a month you can get pregnant, right?"

"Yes," I bite on my lip.

"So for two to three days a month, my brothers and I are going to be lining up to fuck you. Fighting over who gets to fuck you. Fucking you harder and for longer, because believe me, sweetheart, we will *all* be bringing our A game." He leans his head close to my face until his breath skitters over my cheek and I shiver in anticipation. "Are you really telling me that even thinking about it hasn't already got you wet and wanting to be fucked?"

I suck in a breath as the heat floods my core, because damn, that might just be the hottest thing I can imagine. "Okay," I whisper.

"Thought so. So go pee on the goddamn stick, sweetheart," he growls.

"I'm going," I breathe.

I STARE at the small white piece of plastic in my hands. Two lines. I'm ovulating! Damn!

They're all waiting for me in the den. When I tell them the result... Holy fuck! The rush of wet heat almost knocks me off my feet.

I walk down the hallway and when I reach the den, I lean against the wall, watching them for a few seconds before they notice I'm back. They are chatting and laughing amongst themselves, and I am overwhelmed with love for them.

It's Conor who spots me first. "Everything okay, Angel?"

I hold up the plastic stick. "I'm ovulating," I say with a smile.

I have never seen four men move so fast in all of my life. Liam pushes Mikey out of the way as he runs toward me. Conor vaults the sofa while Shane drops his cup of coffee where he stands and sprints toward me. The four of them hurtle to me and my entire body sizzles with excitement and anticipation. I turn around and run down the hallway, hardly able to breathe I'm laughing so hard.

It's Conor who catches me first, and he hoists me over his shoulder and carries me into the nearest bedroom which happens to be my own. He throws me down onto the bed and starts stripping off his clothes as his brothers run into the room on our heels and begin doing the same.

I stare up at them watching them undress, their broad chests and thick arms all covered in tattoos, including the matching one they now all have of my name which winds around the base of their necks. "You ready to make some beautiful Ryan babies, Angel?" Conor growls.

"Yes," I whisper.

Now that this part of the series is concluded, are you ready to see what happens next for Jessie and The Ryan Brothers?

Ryan Renewed is available now

ALSO BY SADIE KINCAID

Sadie's latest series, Chicago Ruthless is available for preorder now. Following the lives of the notoriously ruthless Moretti siblings - this series will take you on a rollercoaster of emotions. Packed with angst, action and plenty of steam — preorder yours today

Dante

Joey

Lorenzo

If you haven't read full New York the series yet, you can find them on Amazon and Kindle Unlimited

Ryan Rule

Ryan Redemption

Ryan Retribution

Ryan Reign

Ryan Renewed

New York Ruthless short stories can be found here

A Ryan Reckoning

A Ryan Rewind

A Ryan Restraint

A Ryan Halloween

A Ryan Christmas

A Ryan New Year

Want to know more about The Ryan Brothers' buddies, Alejandro and Alana, and Jackson and Lucia? Find out all about them in Sadie's internationally bestselling LA Ruthless series. Available on Amazon and FREE in Kindle Unlimited.

Fierce King

Fierce Queen

Fierce Betrayal

Fierce Obsession

If you'd like to read about London's hottest couple. Gabriel and Samantha, then check out Sadie's London Ruthless series on Amazon. FREE in Kindle Unlimited.

Dark Angel

Fallen Angel

Dark/ Fallen Angel Duet

If you enjoy super spicy short stories, Sadie also writes the Bound series feat Mack and Jenna, Books 1, 2, 3 and 4 are available now.

Bound and Tamed

Bound and Shared

Bound and Dominated

Bound and Deceived

ACKNOWLEDGMENTS

I'd love to thank all of the wonderful women who have supported me to write this book - my beta readers, Anna, and Rita, ARC reviewers and the wonderful writing community. With a particular mention to TL Swan, Vicki Nicolson and the rest of the Cygnets who are an amazing and inspiring group of women.

I will always give a special mention to Sue and Michelle who have championed my writing from the outset, and to Kate, who listened to my ramblings and helped to make Shane Ryan the man he is today - because, in my head at least, the others were already perfect ;)

And the most special of mentions to my dear friend, Mary, not only for her eagle eye, but because she always believed in me, even when I didn't believe in myself.

To my incredible boys who inspire me to be better every single day. And last, but no means least, a huge thank you to my husband, who is my rock and my biggest supporter.

I couldn't do this without you!

ABOUT THE AUTHOR

Sadie Kincaid is a dark romance author who loves to read and write about hot alpha males and strong, feisty females.

Sadie loves to connect with readers so why not get in touch via social media?

Join Sadie's reader group for the latest news, book recommendations and plenty of fun. Sadie's ladies and Sizzling Alphas

Sign up to Sadie's mailing list for exclusive news about future releases, giveaways and content here